Los Angeles

Also by Peter Moore Smith

Raveling

Los Angeles

A NOVEL

Peter Moore Smith

Little, Brown and Company
New York Boston

Little, Brown and Company
Time Warner Book Group
1271 Avenue of the Americas, New York, NY 10020
Visit our Web site at www.twbookmark.com

First Edition

Library of Congress Cataloging-in-Publication Data

Smith, Peter Moore.
    Los Angeles : a novel / Peter Moore Smith. — 1st ed.
        p. cm.
    ISBN 0-316-80392-8
    1. Los Angeles (Calif.) — Fiction. 2. Missing persons — Fiction. I. Title.

PS3569.M5379126L67   2005
813'.54 — dc22   2004003003

10 9 8 7 6 5 4 3 2 1

Q-Mart

Designed by Meryl Sussman Levavi

Printed in the United States of America

For my mother

Los Angeles

I LOOK BACK AND FEEL TERROR — COMPREHENSIVE, ABSOLUTE — like I was living through one of those familiar bytes of live violence on the news. But at the time, at that instant, I stood on the cool of the kitchen tiles in my charcoal-colored bathrobe, sipping my usual fusion of coffee and psychopharmaceuticals. I had pulled the miniblinds up, uncharacteristically, because I was searching for that cat. She had been mewling out there all night, crying like a human baby, and now, of course, the moment I decided to look for her, she was gone. It was probably the medication, but I found myself mesmerized by the unfamiliar six-in-the-morning brilliance, entranced by the sunlight glinting off the crappy sedans and SUVs in the parking lot below. The whole scene seemed so oddly calculated. Soft beams weaving over the blue and white hyacinths of the old man's overgrown garden next door, hard gleams shimmering off the waxy leaves of his laurel tree — it was all almost too thought-out, as though devised by some cinematographic genius. In the quiet rustle of overhanging branches, I even thought I heard a director whisper, *"Action!"*

Then, shattering my reverie, the phone rang.

I had been expecting a call, actually, from my father's lawyer's office because there had been a problem with one of my credit cards at the Vons the other day, and I had left a message with one of the assistants to sort it out. My only thought when I picked up was, why would they call so early?

"Hello?" I answered.

She said my name.

Then, *click*.

It was her, it was Angela, there was no doubt about it.

Unlike that cat, Angela had been absent all night. I had stayed awake long past the hour she usually came over, then grown bored of waiting and had used the free time to rewrite a few pages of my screenplay before taking a couple of Restorils and crawling off to bed.

Right now I replaced the phone in its cradle, thinking she would call back any second. She probably wanted to explain where she had been last night, I told myself, and had been cut off, that's all.

I looked out the window again. A man I had never seen before walked from my building to his car. He removed his gray suit jacket and laid it neatly over the passenger seat before starting his old Honda and driving away. I tried to imagine the office he worked in — a desk, a computer, a coffee mug filled with pencils, maybe even a potted plant, its tendrils curling.

Then too much time passed, too many blue minutes on the blue digital clock of the coffeemaker. This wasn't right, I kept thinking. She should have called back by now. I picked up again, punched star-69 and listened to the smooth electronic voice of the computerized operator tell me the number of the last call that had come through. I was instructing myself not to freak out. The whole time I was thinking, Stay calm, stay focused. I wrote Angela's cell number down on an old unfilled prescription slip and dialed it immediately, listening to those five impersonal rings before her own recorded message said, "Hi, it's me." She was too cheerful, too sincere. It was an answering-machine answer and didn't capture her personality at all. "Leave a message, I'll call you back."

This made no sense. If Angela had just called from her cell, why wasn't she answering it now?

I replaced the cordless in its cradle once again and picked up my coffee mug, taking that final, gritty sip.

I lowered the miniblinds.

I pressed my ear to the wall between our apartments.

I walked out into the hallway and knocked on her door, even though I knew there would be no answer.

I considered the way she had said my name, that tone in her voice, and waited a fraction less calmly.

With every passing second I became a fraction less calm.

I dialed her number again, this time leaving my own message. "It's me," I said, trying to make my voice sound unconcerned. "What did you want, anyway?" But since I hadn't spoken to anyone all morning, it came out broken.

I let ten more minutes pass, then called again.

"Is everything all right?" I asked the telephone, much more clearly this time. "Angela, what the fuck is going on?"

I hung up.

"A woman," I said less than a minute later, "my neighbor." This time I had dialed 911. I knew it was alarmist, but I was starting to panic.

"What about her, sir?"

"Something's happened. She's afraid."

"Can you be more specific?"

I gave the emergency operator Angela's address; except for her apartment number, it was the same as mine.

"What is she afraid of?"

"I don't know," I blurted. "She called . . . she called from the dark. It was in the tone of her voice. It was unmistakably the voice of a person calling from the dark."

"From the dark?"

I stepped out of the kitchen. "From the dark." I had an image of Angela. She was inside a closet, under a bed, deep inside a thicket of bushes. She was hiding, terrified, in danger.

I was agitated, I admit, becoming increasingly irrational.

"Did she say something was wrong?"

"Not in so many words."

There was a pause, then the sound of hard fingernails typing on a computer keyboard.

I thought I detected the sound of disbelief, too, that telltale sigh of skepticism.

"Can you send someone over?"

The light, if you've ever noticed, does things to the human

voice. In bright light, people tend to speak through their teeth, unless their eyes are closed, which causes them to speak softly. In midafternoon light, people speak normally, their voices originating from inside their throats. As the light fades into evening, the human voice fades with it. Alcohol, I've noticed, can keep a voice bright and strong as the light disappears. In evening darkness, as the eyes become accustomed to moonlight or artificial incandescence, the voice grows quieter, steadier, more intimate; in total darkness, in complete black, the voice is often just a whisper.

Try it. Close your eyes and speak:

A loud voice in the dark is as unnatural as a scream.

When Angela called and said my name, her voice was barely a voice at all, but it contained everything — confusion, panic, fear. Inside it was everything I needed to hear.

———

Weeks before, a couple of months before, I'm still not clear on what day this was, obviously, but at some uncertain point in time, there was a soft, uncertain knock. It was early evening, dinnertime for most people, morning for me. I looked through the peephole and saw a blurred, convex image of a pretty young woman holding a bright orange casserole dish, her hands inside two floral pot holders. I had the idea that she was on some sort of evangelical mission, so when I opened the door, I gave her my iciest smile.

I expected a reaction. I expected, at least, a look of mild apprehension.

But she just stood there, paralyzed.

The light in the hallway was blue fluorescent, a grim, impoverished glow containing only the cold end of the spectrum, and far too bright for these pale irises. I squinted automatically, raising a hand to my forehead, and waited impatiently for her to say something.

A black girl in her late twenties, relatively tall, with long straightened hair colored an unnatural reddish blond, she wore jeans, a Guns N' Roses T-shirt. Her feet were bare, her toenails painted a glittery green metallic. Oddly, her eyes were cobalt, azure, robin's egg — a shade of blue I didn't know human eyes came in.

A good five seconds passed.

"I'm so sorry," she said finally. And something peculiar was developing in those eyes, too, something I didn't expect. "I didn't mean . . ."

My own eyes, I should mention, are the color of Caucasian infant flesh. My skin is marble-veined, ivory, translucent. My hair is snowy white, aluminum, a shock of fiber optics. I am white, white, all white, even my eyelashes are white, and what isn't white is stark pink. I am, if you haven't guessed already, an albino. "It's all right," I said. "I know you didn't mean anything." I had to clear my throat because I hadn't spoken to anyone in days. "It surprises people sometimes, that's all." I forced what I hoped was a warmer smile onto my lips. "My appearance."

There was something else about this woman, something genuinely . . . not contrite, exactly, or even apologetic — her expression had gone from stunned to understanding almost instantly, like water pouring into a glass — *kind,* I guess is the word.

"I'm Angela?" she said as if it were a question. "I just moved in down the hall?"

A scent of spices rose from the casserole dish, something mouthwatering I didn't recognize.

Covertly I inhaled, straining to identify it.

"I heard you," I said. "I mean, yesterday I heard the truck outside." There had been the wheezing of air brakes, a couple of moving men shouting to one another in the stairwell.

"I hope the noise didn't bother you."

I shrugged. "I sleep during the day."

"Me, too!" she exclaimed. "I sleep during the day, too!" It was as though we had something so incredibly uncommon in common, as though we were the only two human beings in West Hollywood who stay awake all night. Then her face filled with realization, with that look of kindness again. "I'm really sorry." Her voice was slightly raspy, permanently damaged. As if a low volume now would prevent her from disturbing me then, she let it drop to just above a whisper. "Did I wake you?"

I suddenly became aware of my frayed bathrobe, the chalky skin beneath it. I pulled it closer across my chest, tightening the belt. "It doesn't matter. I'm not going anywhere." I wasn't adequately medicated at the moment, having just gotten out of bed, and was becoming more and more self-conscious, wary of a strange emotion I hadn't experienced in a long time.

She inched forward, those intense blue eyes growing wider, and somehow bluer. "I always think it's nice, you know, when I move somewhere new, to make something special for my neighbors, especially my next-door neighbor." She laughed, maybe a little too cheerfully. "You know what I mean? It's sort of like an apology in advance. But maybe, maybe I already owe you one for the noise. Anyway," she added, "I made lamb stew. If you're —"

I didn't bother to hide my amazement. "Holy shit."

"— a vegetarian, I can always —"

"No," I said. "No, no."

"Well . . ." She held out the casserole, eyebrows lifted. "I hope you like it."

I took the bright dish and floral mitts into my hands, an awkward exchange because we had to do it — because we were strangers — without touching.

"My mother used to make lamb stew," I confessed.

"Really?"

There was another lull in the action, as though a piece of dialogue had been cut from the script. We stood there silently, regarding one another, waiting, awkwardly smiling. Finally, I offered her one of those I-have-to-go-now head jerks, as if something desperately important awaited me inside my apartment.

"Um . . ." She bit her lip. "Aren't you going to tell me *your* name?"

Now it was my turn to hesitate.

My name.

This is always embarrassing, but around the time I was born, my father worked on various films as a kind of associate producer, procuring actors, securing locations, setting up meetings. It was, it continues to be, his greatest talent. In the movie *Barbarella,* on which he worked for Dino De Laurentiis in this capacity, there is an absurd character with white hair and white-feathered wings whose name is Pygar the Angel. And my parents, under the psychedelic influence of the era, so the story goes, named me after him.

I should be thankful; I could be named Pygar.

I had to force myself to tell her, but when I did, her whole body seemed to brighten. "What are the chances?" she asked.

"The chances of what?"

"I'm *Angela,* and you're *Angel.*"

I hadn't noticed the similarity at all, to tell the truth. Besides, I imagined the chances were relatively high — they're just names.

But it didn't matter anymore, because at that moment, the woman who had told me her name was Angela turned around and vanished into her own apartment, her swiftly closing door forcing an artificial breeze down the corridor.

———

Back in my living room, *Blade Runner,* Ridley Scott's great noir science fiction thriller, played on my large-screen TV. In those days, I just let the disk rotate endlessly in the DVD player, the volume set to inaudible, as a kind of low-level light source and most of the time the only well of illumination in my whole apartment. I didn't need to hear it because I had memorized all the scenes anyway. The one that was on at the moment was from early in the movie, where Tyrell, the scientist who created the replicants, clasps his hands behind his back and says, "Commerce is our goal here at Tyrell. More human than human is our motto."

"More human than human," I murmured in unison.

In case you don't know, it's a movie about a bunch of renegade androids, or replicants, who are searching for their creator. Harrison Ford plays Rick Deckard, the police detective whose job is to hunt the replicants down and kill them. Mostly, I liked the way the film looked, the futuristic brights and shadows, the glossy blacks and vivid neons.

Right now, I stepped into my minuscule kitchen and pushed the array of psychiatric medication bottles out of the way — the Valium, Librium, and Centrax, the Ativan and Xanax, the Inderol, Prolixin, and Navane, the Adapin, Vivactil, and Ludiomil, as well as the Ambien and Restoril — all the drugs I had been prescribed for anxiety, depression, and social phobia, as well as the other meds designed to counteract the side effects of the first set. Standing a little higher than the rest of the bottles was the container of the drug I simply called Reality. This was the maintenance drug, the one that never seemed to have an effect, except to make my mouth dry and my imagination disappear.

I set the casserole on the counter and removed the lid with one of Angela's flowery pot holders, inhaling the scents of rosemary, sage, and pepper. I noticed the chunks of brown, flaky meat in there, the white potatoes, and orange carrots. There were bright green peas, too, which meant she had probably cooked them separately and placed them in at the last minute, since otherwise they would have gone mushy and gray. I closed my eyes and lived an entire lifetime inside that aroma, and when I took the first bite straight out of the dish, standing there on the cool kitchen tiles, I imagined my vibrantly blue-eyed, glittery-green-toed neighbor driving over to the Vons market on Sunset to buy these ingredients — rosemary, thyme, pepper, carrots, peas, potatoes, lamb. I pictured her gorgeous face in the severe commercial lighting, illuminated like a portrait of a medieval saint, and wondered achingly when I would see her again.

Simultaneously, the weirdest noise was emanating from the parking lot below my kitchen window, an indefinable high-pitched shriek that for the past several minutes I had been forcing myself to ignore.

What the hell was it? Whining, moaning, crying.

I lifted the miniblinds to see.

It was that fucking cat, a female in heat, by the way she was screaming. Somewhere between brown and gray, between calico and tiger-stripe, she stretched on her forepaws and stood on the rusted hood of a battered white Celica, her tail curving like a question mark.

———

My full name, just to get it all out of the way right now, is Angel Jean-Pierre Veronchek. My father is Milos Veronchek, and unless you've been living on the dark side of the moon for the past twenty-five years, you've seen at least ten of his films. Big, splashy productions crowded with flamboyant explosions, spectacular car chases, preposterous love scenes, they usually generate the longest lines at the multiplex, not to mention the greatest profits for Universal. Dad was a director himself until the late seventies, when he gave up any remaining pretense of artistry and began focusing entirely on the business end of moviemaking. My earliest memories, therefore, are of on-set trailers, of sleeping on cots next to makeup tables, of countless assistants, hairstylists, and actresses taking me into their warm, perfumed laps. They always commented on my skin, my hair, my eyes, these girls, saying, "He's so white," saying, "I never knew a person could be so white." And so I believed, no, I was *told*, that I was special, that my oddness, my very pink-and-whiteness, was somehow exceptional.

At some point, however, when Dad started sleeping with other women — he was screwing those very same assistants, hairstylists, and actresses, not coincidentally — my mother and I didn't visit him on set anymore. For a long time we lived in luxury hotels. I remember gray marble lobbies, white-carpeted suites, underlit blue pools where I was allowed to swim at night by special permission of the management, places where even the most insignificant meal was a production. Imagine macaroni and cheese wheeled in by a white-jacketed waiter and presented on a silver tray. Picture Kool-Aid in a wine decanter.

Later, as Dad rose through the studio ranks, Mom and I settled into our house in Beverly Hills, a colonnaded villa on North Rexford Drive with adobe walls and terra-cotta-tiled floors. My mother took up a life of shopping and cosmetic self-destruction, visiting her plastic surgeon every couple of years until she was a bizarre impersonation of Hollywood youth. I spent semesters in freezing Montreal, at the inappropriately named Vancouver School, and summers in the cool darkness of my parents' basement. Still believing I was special, still regarding myself as oddly, even preternaturally exceptional, I was a junior scientist, an adolescent microscope visionary, a chemistry set prodigy. Those summer mornings, after consuming an anemic breakfast of grapefruit and black coffee prepared by my anemic French-Swiss mom, I allowed myself to become psychologically consumed, enraptured by a kind of ersatz intellectual reverie; I had developed a full-scale preoccupation with the costume of science, if not the character.

Anyway, when my parents divorced, as all Hollywood couples are scripted to do, I was almost finished with high school. My cosmetically altered mom kept the house and a generous, ongoing settlement. My ever more successful father continued screwing those assistants, hairstylists, and actresses. Eventually, though I'm getting ahead of my story by about five years, Dad married Melanie, a doe-eyed young producer belonging more to my generation than to his. A year or so after that, they adopted a baby, an African American boy they named Gabriel, and built a Deconstructivist abortion of glass and steel overlooking the glassy, steely Pacific. I graduated from the Vancouver School and enrolled at UCLA. I had wanted to go to college back east but because of Mom had felt obligated to stay here. My intention was to study physics and, ultimately, if things went well, to specialize in the science of light.

My physical condition, as you can probably guess, has been the cause of a greater-than-average sensitivity to brightness, and has for this very same reason inspired a kind of perverse fascination. Believe me, there is no one with a greater instinct for the behavior and properties of light than Angel Jean-Pierre Veronchek. It is written into my genetic code; it is inextricably braided into the threads of my DNA and lasered across my overly sensitive, blood-red retinas. I have become obsessed over the years with the poetry of Los Angeles light, how it glimmers off the morning traffic and glows through the smog, how it ignites the fires that periodically burn entire sections of our city to their asphalt foundations. And in those days, I also yearned to understand its scientific underpinnings, to comprehend polarization, reflection, refraction, diffraction, electromagnetic radiation, and, deeper still, to grasp its theoretical roots, Einstein's universal constant, Schrödinger's thought experiments, the fundamental basis of Heisenberg's uncertainty principle, the very building blocks of our universe, of reality itself. I was intellectually impassioned, as consumed as ever by the ambitious dream of science, if not entirely prepared to face its philosophical implications.

But things didn't go so well at UCLA. It turned out, not surprisingly, that I am not exceptional, preternaturally or otherwise. Even though I studied the concepts I was expected to study, even though I read the textbooks I was supposed to read, I failed my exams, I choked on essays, I couldn't speak up in class. I was fascinated by the material, even obsessed with it, yet when it came time to express myself, I froze, paralyzed, rigid with fear. I had always been timid, but in college, my pathological shyness developed into a full-scale social phobia.

I was no longer oddly special, it turned out —

I was just odd.

Then, one afternoon during the second semester of my sophomore year, I found myself squinting up into the fluorescent ceiling fixtures of the UCLA hospital psychiatric ward, where it was concluded that things might go better for all concerned if I left the university, at least for a while, that perhaps this was all a hair too stressful for someone so delicate, so physically unusual, as me. I was remanded to the care of my lifelong psychiatrist, the distinguished Dr. Nathan Silowicz, then brought to a precarious mental balance with the assistance of his strict regimen of Freudian analysis and psychoactive meds.

I have never been cured; it goes without saying that a person is never cured of these things, but after a subsequent period of readjustment, Dr. Silowicz and I decided I might be better off living on my own, that my mother's influence was psychologically . . . what's the word he used?

Stultifying.

Which is when I relocated to my lightless cave on San Raphael Crescent, a one-bedroom in a small building on an unpopular cul-de-sac off Hollywood Boulevard — a building peopled with the castoffs of the movie industry, the might-have-beens and the almost-weres, screenwriters who work in bookstores, actors who tend bar, directors who manage all-night pharmacies. I moved in thinking I would use my newfound independence to do something important, something artistic. I've always had a gift for description, so I planned to write the ultimate screenplay of Los Angeles, the definitive insider's story of glitter-town disillusionment. If I had to be alone, I imagined romantically, I'd become a reclusive writer, an enigmatic genius, a seeker of ten-foot-tall, all-caps, neon-lit TRUTH.

But as anyone who has tried it knows, writing is hard, and the truth is elusive.

———

Was it that look on her face, the flash of kindness? Or that low, slurry voice that always seemed to imply she was sharing some breathtaking secret? Could it have been those eyes, so blue when I first met her, that later on changed colors? It's hard to say what caused my initial fascination, and I think it's safe to conclude that, in large part, and in view of the fact that the simplest explanation is usually the right one, it was because she was beautiful, friendly, available . . .

And it was because I was lonely.

Whatever caused it, from the moment I saw that first transformation in her face, that fluid expression of apprehension-to-understanding — she had looked past the colorlessness of my skin instantly, I had seen it happen, had watched it in the clear water of her emotionally transparent face — I was obsessed, distracted with thoughts of her, and could think of nothing, of no one, else.

Therefore, three days after the lamb stew introduction, I followed two tabs of Inderol antisocial phobia medication with an even more courage-enhancing mug full of Jack Daniel's, slipped out of the old charcoal robe and into some normal clothes, grabbed Angela's now empty and well-scrubbed casserole dish, and stepped into the fluorescent hallway. I had heard her coming home every night around three-thirty, the *clack-clack-clack* of her strappy heels on the polished concrete steps outside my door.

I let a few minutes pass, plenty of time for her to settle in, I thought, then approached her door and knocked, using three carefully rehearsed taps.

"Angel?" After a few moments, Angela peered around the threshold, the door open just a crack.

I tried a warm smile, always an awkward expression for me, always an aberration on my face. "It was just the way I remember it," I said.

There was a note of surprise in her whispery voice. "The way you remember what?"

"The way my mother used to make it." This was only partially true: Monique's attempts at cooking were almost always failures, and her lamb stew, as I recalled, lacked a certain . . . well, it was terrible.

But Angela didn't react. It occurred to me that she was on something. Those eyes, which in this bright hallway light I couldn't quite get the color of, were deeply dilated, a pair of empty holes. She just stood there, reluctant, for some reason, to take the dish out of my hands.

"Do you want me to bring it back later?" I asked after a moment.

"Bring what?"

I held it forward. "The dish?"

"No, no," she said, coming to. "Thank you, Angel. Thank you." She looked away now, suddenly bashful. "You really liked it? The stew?"

I nodded. "It was fantastic."

Her face filled with generosity again, that look of understanding. "Sorry, I —," she started. Even from here I could smell the combination of too-sweet perfume and the night of sweat beneath it. "I'm just tired, you know, and kind of —" She had something sparkly on her skin. She was flushed, luminous, a source of light herself.

"You don't have to explain," I said.

She took the casserole dish, finally, and when Angela and I exchanged the pot holders this time, our fingers touched.

My heart was crashing around inside my chest like a predator in its cage.

She moved away from the door to place the dish somewhere inside her apartment.

"I'm sorry to be bothering you so late, and I'd make you some-thing in return," I offered, speaking up, "but all I really know how to make are Stouffer's microwave dinner entrées. I mean, I'm not much of a —"

"I'd *love* one." She came back to the threshold, eyes wide.

"Are you serious?"

"I don't have anything in the kitchen," she answered, "and I haven't eaten in forever."

"Spaghetti and meatballs," I blurted, "or chicken with mush-room gravy and wild rice?" These were the meals that I ate in those days, mostly, although I had been known to get on a French bread pizza kick that could last weeks.

She followed me down the hall. "Chicken" — she inhaled dra-matically — "with mushroom gravy and wild rice."

I hurried into my kitchen, opened the freezer, and grabbed a box of Stouffer's. "You're seven minutes from heaven," I said, acti-vating the microwave.

She was looking around the living room, and despite the meds I had taken, I became instantly self-conscious.

My apartment was not exactly designed for company. The walls were lined with paperbacks; and since I didn't have any shelves, I had stacked them in precarious columns, some of which had fallen over and lay in broken piles on the floor. In the middle of the space, I had an old, creaking swivel chair and a gray metal conference table on which my computers nestled amid piles of junk mail and scraps of note paper. There was nowhere for anyone else to sit, really, other than the floor, which was covered by a soft, black, fuzzy rug called a flokati — something my mother had bought me as a housewarming gift years before, when I moved in. Even more embarrassing were the stacks of colored paper all around my desk, each color representing a draft of the movie I had supposedly been writing and arranged according to the hues of the electromagnetic spectrum.

"This is so . . . weird," Angela said finally.

"Yeah, well," I said from the kitchen, "I don't really have people over very often."

"You're a writer?"

"I edit technical manuals, professionally." This was a lie, of course. I only said that because I was embarrassed to explain that I accepted money from my father and that I had never had an actual job. "But I'm writing a screenplay, you know, which is my real work."

I heard the sound of her fingernails tapping on a stack of paper. "Is that what this is?"

"Yeah." I stepped back into the living room. "An early draft."

"What's it called?"

I told her the truth because I didn't have time to think of a better answer. "*Los Angeles*. But that's just a working title. I have a number of other —"

"Wow, I like that."

"Really?"

"Sounds important."

No one had ever expressed any interest in my writing before, not even my psychiatrist, and I have to admit, I didn't know how to react. "Important?" I said. "Do you really —"

"Why is this on?"

Angela had turned around to stare at my television, the colors muted, the sound impossibly faint. At the moment, it was the scene where Deckard is attacked by Pris, the most beautiful of the replicants. A pleasure model, Pris leaps up and wraps her legs around Deckard's neck, then pulls his head around by his nostrils, then punches him.

"Are you watching this?" Angela asked, touching a finger to the screen.

I experienced a wave of panic. *"Don't touch that."*

———

Frozen dinner entrées followed, chicken with wild rice on the flokati, a shared exchange that gravitated imperceptibly toward talking and drinking, me sipping Jack Daniel's and coffee, Angela bringing over her bottle of Stoli and a carton of orange juice. Then, over the course of the next few weeks, there developed between us an even more indistinct transition from talking and drinking to kissing and sampling the prescriptions that cluttered my kitchen countertop. I fell into a delirium, a waking dream fueled by all those meds but also by a fathomless infatuation. Amazingly, Angela's eyes, which I had first thought were so blue, changed mysteriously — from blue to brown to green, even violet, virtually every color of the spectrum. Some people's eyes appear to change slightly depending on what they're wearing or the ambient light, but Angela's morphed completely, dependent, it seemed, on her state of mind, like a pair of mood rings. Her heels would clack noisily on the steps outside my door, and minutes later she would appear, smiling, eyes transformed.

We would lie on the flokati and listen to the messages on the answering machine: Dr. Silowicz calling to reschedule sessions, so deeply concerned about my psychological well-being; Melanie, my father's young wife, inviting me, no, *begging* me, to visit little Gabriel and my dad; my father's lawyer calling, too, the satanic Frank Heile, Esquire, ostensibly to relay some practical detail, to question a cash advance on one of my credit cards, but really to remind me I was a drain on the system, a character who was dragging the whole production down and was better off cut from the story line. Angela and I — we ate, drank, fed each other's appetites. We slept, we kissed, we stared — there's no better word for it than *longingly,* I swear — into one another's eyes. It was every night like this, and I have to admit I was starting to think of her as more than just a neighbor. I was still too reticent to use the word *girlfriend* in a sentence, but I was envisioning scenarios, projecting more than one day into the future, for the first time in recollection.

And throughout — and this is not insignificant — there was that cat. That fucking cat. Mewling, crying, caterwauling, shrieking like a disturbed inhuman spirit from a gothic novel, she leapt from car to car, crying insanely up at my kitchen window, baying pathetically at the Hollywood moon.

———

"I want you to come see me," Angela said. This was a week, maybe two, after the lamb stew introduction. She sat up and stabbed out a burning Ultra Light in a dish. "I want you to see me at work."

I wasn't sure what she meant. I looked into her eyes and saw that they were brown tonight, flecked with miniature spots of yellow. "Come where?"

"I want you to see what it's like," she whispered. "I'll give you a free lap dance."

I had known it, actually, had guessed from her clothes, the glitter she wore on her skin, the ridiculously high heels, the strange hours.

"I appreciate the offer." I shook my head.

Angela hit me, a bejeweled fist on my upper arm that was a little too hard to be playful. "What's wrong with you? *Everyone* wants a free lap dance."

What was wrong with me was that I was terrified. A public place was frightening enough, and over the past several years, I had developed the courage, with psychotropic help, of course, to visit the supermarket, the pharmacy, Supercuts, and even the Gap. But a topless club . . .

"I have a problem with new places."

"Then let's go somewhere familiar." Angela dragged me into my bedroom and pushed me down on the mattress. She pulled my shirt over my head. She undid my pants, pulling the zipper, sliding them off my legs, slipping them off my feet. She reached for my boxers.

"What are you doing?" I grabbed her hands.

"Shhhh." She tugged on the elastic waistband.

"Angela, please." I had an erection. My penis was ready for this, all too conspicuously, but I wasn't.

"Okay." She shrugged. "So leave them on."

I tried to keep my eyelids open but couldn't. An hour or so earlier, I had taken several tabs of Ambien. I felt the warmth of her body, skin as smooth as cotton sheets. I felt her warm breath in my ear. "What are you doing to me?" I was too self-conscious to have sex, and it had been too long.

And I was so tired. So incredibly tired.

And afraid.

She reached over to the side table and turned on my electronic wave machine, then nestled in next to me, wiggling her hips. "What do you like?"

We had slept together, kissed, held one another, nuzzled, spooned, sighed into one another's eyes, done everything, anything but sex. "I like orange sherbet," I answered childishly. "I like green Jell-O."

"I mean sexually." Then she laughed. "Or is that what you mean?"

An electronic surf washed over the room, a placid ocean of synthetic noise enshrouding the too-loud televisions blaring in the upstairs apartments, the car engines igniting in the parking lot outside. The wave machine was something Dr. Silowicz had recommended, years ago, to help me sleep, and right now it was working all too well.

Angela reached over to the side table for another cigarette. "I'm serious, Angel. Don't you like sex?" She lit it and exhaled.

I felt the warm smoke against my face. "I don't really —," I began. "I don't really think about that kind of thing very much."

This was a lie, of course. I thought about it constantly. Sex was all I ever thought about.

She brushed her lips against my cheek. "Don't you trust me?"

"I trust you."

"Then tell me."

"Tell you what?"

"Something perverted."

"You *want* me to be a pervert?"

"I wouldn't mind."

I turned onto my side, facing her.

She dropped her cigarette into a glass by the bed and slid down, pressing her entire self against me. Angela crushed her face into my neck and squeezed her legs around mine, her surprisingly strong arms tight around my torso.

"You're not really white, Angel, do you know that?"

"I'm not?"

"Your aura, your true colors."

"My aura?" This erection would not go away. "What color am I, then?"

"Red. Orange. Bright yellow." She laughed. "Burning."

I thought for a moment about what this could mean. "What color are you?" I asked.

"Blue," she whispered. "Blue, blue, electric blue."

"Like your eyes?"

She reached inside my boxers and placed her hand over my penis. Her fingers were cool. It must have been around six in the morning because a blade of incandescence appeared on my bedroom wall, a thin band of yellow-white that was growing exponentially brighter.

Red. Orange. Bright yellow. Burning.

It was cast there by a fissure in the miniblinds, like a crack in the shell of the universe itself.

"Sure," she answered, "like my eyes."

"Your eyes are brown," I said, as though exposing a terrible secret.

"Tell me something," Angela insisted another night. "Tell me anything." Her lips touched the back of my neck, and I could feel the dampness of her mouth, and I thought I could hear the liquid insides of her body.

"There isn't anything."

"Do you like this?" She touched her tongue to my skin, just below my ear. She tucked her knees under my knees, burrowing into me.

I didn't answer.

"This?" She bit the edge of my earlobe. Her teeth felt huge.

I was quiet.

"This?" She nuzzled into my neck, pushing her wet lips over my skin.

Mornings, after she left, I would slip downstairs and look around the parking lot for that cat. She was so desperate for contact, it seemed, screaming for attention, and I wanted to find out if I could quiet her, soothe her screaming even for a moment, by scratching that patch of sensitive skin behind her ears. But as soon as I stepped into the lot, she would vanish, hiding under a car or running into the old man's garden next door. It had become a kind of game, actually, though I didn't know why I was playing. I wasn't sure what I was planning to do if I found her, either. I certainly wasn't prepared to take an alley cat into my apartment. Can you imagine the fleas? I just wanted to touch her, I guess, to see if she would stop wailing, if only for a few moments.

And sometimes I would get stuck, caught by the impossible gorgeousness of the Los Angeles morning, catatonic in the apprehension of a phenomenon too beautiful, too cinematic to be real.

It was because her eyes kept changing colors. It was because her breasts were fake. It was because she came home at half past three in the morning but acted like it was three in the afternoon. It was because she said she was a vegetarian and made me lamb stew. It was because she was older than me but wouldn't admit it. It was because she constantly contradicted herself, denying entire conversations. It was because she was a liar and so was I. It was because she wore way too much perfume and way too much makeup and way too high high heels. It was because when she slept, she rested the back of her hand on her forehead like Scarlett O'Hara. It was because of her laugh, soft and low and wicked. It was because sometimes she bit me. It was because of the way she pressed herself into me, as though she were literally trying to crawl

29

under my skin. It was because she had those tiny cracks at the corners of her eyes. It was because she never asked me why I lived alone, staying awake through the Hollywood night, writing my senseless, pointless scenes. It was because she understood every crazy thing I said, or pretended to, anyway.

It was because when I saw her, when she came into my apartment, she would smile, smiling at me, only me, because of me.

It was because of all these things that a few days later, I parked the Cadillac in the rear lot of the strip mall strip club, walked around to the front through the yellow illumination of the Sunset Boulevard street lamps, and approached the door. The bouncer who guarded it wore prison denim and sunglasses even darker than mine. I gave him my ten-dollar entrance fee and flinched as he tried to stamp my hand.

"I won't be needing that," I said. I shook my head, backing away. I didn't like the idea of that infrared ink touching my skin.

The bouncer shrugged. "You'll need it when you want to get back in."

"If I leave," I told him, "I won't want to get back in."

He didn't bother to look at me, just hunched over like Rodin's *Thinker* on a bar stool and said, "*Everybody* wants to get back in."

The Velvet Mask was a strip club I'd been driving by for years. Only tourists went in there, I'd always thought, or Japanese businessmen, or ad guys from New York. Only assholes.

I walked down a narrow corridor, the snarling music inside the club growing exponentially louder, and emerged through a pair of swinging saloon-style shutters into the main room.

Which was exactly as I had pictured it, exactly as Angela had described it: the flashing laser lights, tubes of red, yellow, and blue neon curling around the edges of the stage in wildly oscillating stripes. The music couldn't have been worse. You'd think they would have played something upbeat, something lighthearted and sexy, but instead, it was industrial dirge music, disco for psychos. There were girls dancing on two separate platforms, each in her own metamorphosing pool of luminescence, and around each of the dancers sat a ring of gawking imbeciles. In one, Japanese businessmen in dark suits and bright ties, wearing their crisp white shirts and precise, salaryman haircuts, smiled serenely up into the hairless genitalia of a blonde so thin she could have blended in at Buchenwald. In the other was a bunch of drugstore clerks on their night off. They had overly gelled hair and underdeveloped mustaches; they wore heavy gold chains and T-shirts emblazoned with indecipherable, but still somehow profane, slogans. The girl in their circle of light was darkly beautiful, with undulating hips, small, high breasts, and eyes like Egyptian hieroglyphs. Her hair was so shiny that it flashed, reflecting shades and hues of light in the laser beams like sheets of glistening rain.

In the back, under the exit sign, I noticed a colossal man in a formal suit, an even larger example of homo erectus than the gorilla who guarded the door. He had one of those wide ties, silvery gray, the kind butlers wear in old movies. A *cravat,* I think it's called. His shoulders were much narrower than his belly, and he was completely bald, which made him look like a Buddha on his way to a funeral. He dangled his arms, eyes narrowed to inscrutable slits, and sat on his stool, criminally huge, menacingly inert.

I took a seat on the banquette along the wall and looked

around, hoping to see Angela right away, to get this the hell over with.

"There's a two-drink minimum," a voice said, "and we don't serve alcohol." Its owner was a waitress, probably a former dancer. She was a few years out-of-date but still sexy enough to command the leers of the nearby table of conventioneers.

I took a chance. "Do you have water?"

She had dark Bettie Page hair and a soft, round face. She wore a purple minidress and a small black velvet mask, the kind a person would have worn to a costume ball decades ago. Looking around, I noticed that all the waitresses here wore black masks. She pushed hers up onto her forehead so she could flutter her heavily eye-shadowed lids. "Pellegrino," she recited, "Evian, Mountain Spring, Vittel, or tap. But if you get tap, we still have to charge you eight bucks. So I'd get the Pellegrino." The waitress winked. "It's the best value."

"Pellegrino," I said, adding, "I'm all about value." I had taken so many Inderols before I left the apartment that I had enough confidence to make small talk with a stranger. This had a two-sided effect, unfortunately — I had acquired the confidence to kid around but had sacrificed the clarity to be funny.

"Two Pellegrino's coming right up."

"Oh —" I reached out a hand and almost touched her hip, but a glance over at the angry Buddha under the exit sign made me think better of it. "Sorry," I said, "but do you know . . . do you know Angela? I was supposed to meet her here."

"You mean Cassandra? She's in the back, probably changing." The waitress gave me a discreet smirk. "And that makes you Angel."

Funny. She hadn't mentioned this other name. "Cassandra?"

"We all have different names in here, sweetie." The waitress winked. "Are you really an angel?"

I think I may have blushed. "It's just my name."

"That's not what Cassandra says."

It felt weird to hear Angela referred to by another name; weirder to imagine her telling people about me. "What did she say?"

"Just that you were coming." The waitress wrinkled her nose. "And to be nice."

"Really?"

"I should have guessed when I saw you." She raised an eyebrow so it disappeared beneath her mask. "We get all kinds, you know, but not many"— she paused here, considering what in the world to call me —"angels."

———

"Don't move," I said. This was another morning, whether before or after the night at the Mask, I'm still not sure.

"*Why?*" Angela froze. "Is there a bug on me?"

"It's the light." A hard beam of sunlight had ruptured through the miniblinds of my living room window, and Angela's face had become starkly illuminated, chiaroscuro, like a Rembrandt. I ran into the bedroom to get my camera. I'd had it for years, since college, a high-end Leica my father bought me in a futile hope that I would develop an interest in something he understood. Recently, I had found it in an old shoe box, deep in the back of my closet, with a roll of film still inside it, amazingly enough.

I took it back into the living room. "Ready?"

Angela turned toward me, shadowed, romantic, as I adjusted the focus. "Ready." Then, just as I depressed the shutter release and the automatic flash went off, she sneered and flipped me the bird.

"What did you do that for?"

She shrugged. "So take another one."

I looked at the little read-out that displayed how many pictures remained. "That was the only one left."

She lit another cigarette. She was smoking Salem's today, the menthol vapors polluting the air. "So maybe sometimes I don't like to have my picture taken." Sometimes Angela smoked constantly, crushing her cigarettes into little dishes all over the apartment. When she was gone, I had to go around cleaning, vacuuming, dusting. Sometimes she didn't smoke at all.

I sighed and sank down next to her on the rug. I had gotten into the habit of slipping out at night to gather more supplies, another bottle of Stoli for Angela, Jack for me, to refill my prescriptions, and to load up on Stouffer's entrées. I would drop the roll of film off at the one-hour photo booth, I told myself, and pick the pictures up in a few days.

"Do you trust me?" Angela asked out of nowhere. Her arms, I remember, snaked around my waist.

But this was weeks later, weeks during which we had graduated from acquaintances to friends to something else entirely, though I was still trying to work out exactly what that something else was. "Trust you?" I let a sigh leave my body. It contained suspicion, doubt, misgivings. I looked into her eyes and saw that they were blue again. So recently they had been green. "What are you going to do?" I asked her blue eyes.

"Where are your car keys?"

The keys were on a stack of books by the door. I indicated their direction with a slight nod of my head.

Angela turned and saw them, then got up, jumping quickly. "Get your clothes on," she said, "and do it fast, before this passes."

"Before what passes?" I got up, too, though less athletically, and stepped into the bedroom. I pulled on a pair of cargo pants and buttoned a shirt.

When I turned around, I saw her holding my robe and slipping the belt out of its loops.

"What are you doing?"

"You said you trusted me."

I didn't sigh this time; this time, I lowered my eyes. "Are you planning to tie me up?"

She laughed, pulling my hand. She took the belt with her and led me through the living room, into the hallway, down the stairs, through the lobby door of the apartment building, past the twin midget palms that guarded the entrance, around the side to the parking lot. It had been a couple of days since I had taken out the Cadillac, and it was covered with waxy brown leaves that had fallen from the old man's laurel tree next door.

I seized the opportunity to look around for that cat. I still wanted to find her.

"She's not out here, Angel," Angela said now. "Leave it alone."

"But I just heard her, just this morning."

"We scared her away."

Dark out, the air was angry and stale. The Santa Anas had been blowing all day, a vicious wind from the desert hills, and the asphalt heat still radiated from the long day's sun. Angela opened the passenger side door for me and I got in. She pulled the seat belt across my chest.

"What is it?" I said finally.

"She's in heat, that's all."

"No, what is it —" I was about to ask what it was Angela was doing, what it was she had planned, but in midsentence I changed course. "What is it that you're doing with me? What is it you see in me?"

She pulled out of the parking lot, taking the short, twisty street of San Raphael Crescent to Hollywood Boulevard, then onto Sunset, where, a few minutes later, we passed the strip. The trendy bars and restaurants had filled with the shapes of people, the crispy-haired young men holding their long-necked beers, the overly worked-out girls in their cleavage-revealing dresses and bright red lipstick, and I could hear their peals of laughter, the throbbing bass beat of vapid pop polluting the already lush night air. "I see all kinds of angelic things in you," Angela answered eventually, "authenticity, truthfulness, purity, but right now"— she handed me the belt from my robe, which had been curled serpentine on her lap —"right now, I need for you not to see anything."

At first I was confused by her twisted logic, but then I guessed at what she meant: "You want me to wear a blindfold?"

"You said you trusted me."

"I know, but . . ." This time when I inhaled, I smelled the inside of what had once been my mother's burgundy-colored Cadillac, the accumulated years of dust, the nauseating odor of milk that I had spilled in the backseat at some point in the distant past and that had never come out, as well as the perfume Angela wore, and I inhaled faith, conviction, belief.

I gave in, tying the belt around my eyes.

"Make sure you can't see anything," she said.

"How much longer is this going to be?" I was searching for some sort of clue, looking for anything, however vague.

Angela hesitated, then said, "It's hard to say."

I lowered the window and felt the warm air on my skin. I inhaled my way through the city, breathing the exhaust fumes of cars and the scent of flowers and fresh-cut grass.

I stuck my head out the window like a dog.

"We're on the freeway," I yelled eventually. The wind was strong in my face. It smelled like gasoline and gardenias.

"You're a regular detective." I could hear the smirk on her face. I could hear the very arch of her eyebrow. "But do you know which direction we're heading, Lieutenant Columbo?"

I admitted I didn't.

We sped along the night streets, me in my blindfold, the windows open, until I could feel the traffic slowing.

Angela was turning, sitting at corners, waiting at lights.

"Can anyone see me?" I asked.

"People are staring," she taunted. "They're all looking at you, Angel, pointing and laughing."

"Really?"

"Jesus," she said. "You're so fucking paranoid."

"Are we almost there?"

"Almost."

We drove for a while longer, and I listened to the sounds of other engines, wheels on pavement, music blaring from the stereos of other cars. We had been on the road for roughly forty-five minutes, which in L.A. meant we could have been anywhere.

"Okay," she said, finally bringing the car to a stop.

I started to take off the blindfold, but Angela prevented me, clutching my hands.

"Not yet," she said.

"This is starting to get . . ." I searched for the right word. *"Vertiginous."*

"Soon," she promised.

"Can I at least get out?"

"Just be careful."

I opened the door and stepped onto concrete, my hands extended searchingly to make sure there wasn't anything in front of me. My sightlessness had become disquieting. I believed that one step away was a precipitous cliff, a drop-off into pure space, or maybe something worse, something pointy, a cactus or a wall of nails. Also, I had tied the blindfold too tightly, and I was beginning to see a dizzying galaxy of stars, neon whorls, and patterns that flashed across my mind's movie screen.

I felt Angela's hand on my wrist, a slight pressure. "This way," she said. She guided me across what I took to be a parking lot, then made me wait while she opened a door. It sounded like metal against metal, and something closed behind us with a hard *clang*. "Here," she said, leading me farther.

We stepped into what sounded like a large room, a marble floor. Our footsteps echoed.

"What are we waiting for?" I asked.

"No questions," she told me. "Just trust. Remember?"

"Do you have any idea how hard that is for me?"

"I know, little prince," she said, "I know."

"My mother used to call me that." That was her nickname for me, in fact. She always said I looked like him.

"All alone on your little planet, all by yourself in your crazy apartment, surrounded by your books and your stacks of colored papers. . . . I can see why."

"You're pulling me out of my shell," I said. "Is that it? I'm a reclamation project?"

"Absolutely. This is an after-school special."

I heard the hissing of elevator doors and I was ushered inside. There was a brief discontinuation of contact as Angela pressed a button, then a pause, an infinitesimal dip, and I felt the elevator ascending, rising higher.

How tall was this building? I wondered. Were we going up three floors or three dozen?

It stopped then, and the doors opened with an electric sigh.

She led me into a hallway, then around a corner. "Careful," she said, leading me by the waist. "There are stairs right in front of you."

Tentatively, I lifted my foot and felt the first step.

"Not too quickly."

I lifted my foot again, one step after another.

"A landing," she said. "Turn here."

I turned, going up three short flights this way, and heard the squealing sound of a door opening.

"Ready?"

I felt a breeze, cool air mixed with warm. I smelled something vaguely familiar, something keen, acrid, ambiguously chemical.

I said, "You have no idea how terrified I am."

"Don't take it off yet, whatever you do . . ." I felt her unbuttoning my shirt.

I backed away, uncertain. "Christ, what are you doing now?"

"Trust me, Angel. You said you trusted me. Remember?"

I resigned and let Angela remove my shirt. Then she started tugging at my pants.

"Are there people here?" I hissed. "Can anyone see this?"

"Do you hear anyone?"

I listened for a moment. There was nothing but a high-pitched wind and the distant sounds of traffic, and something . . . something weird, like glass breaking far away.

"There's no one," she said. "Just us."

"You promise?"

"I *promise*. Now take off your sandals."

I reached down and reluctantly slipped them off.

She unfastened the button of my pants, then unzipped the fly, pulling at the waist.

I stepped out of them, aware that I wore nothing now but a pair of gray boxers and I had no idea where I was or who might be watching.

"Now?" I asked.

"Hold on." I heard the sound of her shoes being dropped, of her jeans slipping off, of her T-shirt being pulled roughly over her head. "I want you to take one step forward." She was somewhere behind me. "Step forward one small step at a time, Angel. Can you do that?"

I did as she asked, hands reaching tentatively in front of me.

"One more step," Angela said. "One more tiny . . . step." I felt her nude body coming up directly behind mine. I felt her lips against my ear, saying, "Keep your eyes closed until I tell you to open them, okay?"

I nodded, and she removed the belt from my eyes.

I had to fight the urge to open my lids, to see where I was.

Her lips were against my earlobe, and I could feel the wetness of her mouth. *"Ready?"*

"Ready," I said back. But I almost didn't want to. The darkness had suddenly become comforting.

"Open your eyes."

———

There is a greater moment of adjustment for a person with eyes as pale as mine. The transition from dark to light takes several seconds longer than it might for most people. In a normal human eye, the iris acts like a camera shutter, regulating the amount of light passing through to the retina. As the amount of light diminishes, the iris dilator muscle pulls away from the center, causing the pupil to dilate and allowing more light to reach the retina. When too much light enters the eye, the iris muscle pulls toward the center, causing the pupil to constrict and allowing less light in. A person with albinism, however, has no pigmentation in the iris. Normal pigmentation results in opacity, which blocks light; lack of pigmentation causes light to scatter throughout the eye, which is called *transillumination*.

That's why I'm always blinking. I'm trying to regulate the amount of light blasting across my unprotected retinas.

At this moment, I imagine, my iris dilated dramatically, allowing as much light in as possible.

Melanin is also important in the functioning and development of the retina. Because I am an ocularcutaneous albino, my retinas did not develop properly in early infancy, which means they don't process light as efficiently as they should. I'm lucky in that my eyesight is relatively normal. A lot of albinos are practically blind.

Anyway, light causes a chemical reaction in the photoreceptors, or rods and cones inside the retina. Activated photoreceptors stimulate bipolar cells, which consequently stimulate the ganglion cells. These impulses continue along the axons of the ganglions, moving through the optic nerve to the visual center at the back of the occipital lobe.

Amazingly, the brain can detect *a single photon of light* being absorbed by a photoreceptor.

At first I only comprehended a dull, flashing glow.

I saw a blur of blue, then a silvery ripple.

Gold.

The reflection of a luminous, liquid moon.

Saffron-colored lamps burned beneath a vitreous surface, a plane that oscillated, streaks of spiny light creating momentary, ephemeral shapes . . . shapes that divided, then recombined, fracturing like glass.

I had never before in my life felt the impulse to catch my breath.

I caught my breath.

Angela was still just a voice in my ear, soft lips against my skin, saying, *"Look."*

I lifted my eyes.

Windows glimmered like fireflies. Dark silhouettes rose against an orange-blue ashen sky that was spotted with radiant windows of blue and white and red and green corporate logos and twinkling air traffic lights. "What is this place?"

"Step forward."

"How did you —"

There was no one here. No one but us.

"Step forward," she said. "One more step. One more tiny little step, little prince."

I was standing on the very edge. I closed my eyes again and stepped forward.

A white rush. Blinding. A surge of cold.

I let myself sink, allowing my whole body to submerge, letting my skin adjust to this new temperature. From underneath, I opened my eyes and looked up at the black sky and the water's moon-silvered surface. Angela had splashed in after me, and I saw her face fast approaching now, teeth flashing, eyes smiling. She was naked, so I slipped out of my boxers and, rising, threw them onto the pool's edge.

Now I was naked, too.

She came up, splashing, pushing that fake blond hair, stringy and wet, out of her face.

"I know the manager," she told me breathlessly. "It's a health club. But it's not open this late. It's all ours, all night."

I found the middle of the pool, where I could stand shoulder deep, and Angela thrashed ungracefully toward me. "I'm not a very good swimmer," she said, laughing. "You have to rescue me if I drown." She paddled toward me and placed her hands on my shoulders.

"What is it?" I asked again. "What do you see in me?"

She looked up, down, and sideways all at once. Suddenly she was like a bashful kid. "You want to know the truth, Angel?"

"The truth," I said. "Please."

Then she pushed herself away, laughing weirdly.

"You really want to know?"

"I really want to know."

"You're all the same, you know that?"

"Who are all the same?"

"Men."

"What men?"

She rolled her eyes.

"What men?" I repeated.

Suddenly she sank, disappearing beneath the surface.

I waited for her to come up, watching the shape of her body quiver like a flickering television set beneath the water.

But she didn't.

I waited another five seconds . . . another ten . . .

What the hell was she doing?

I couldn't wait anymore and swam down after her, diving in, curling my arms beneath hers. I had to fight her twisting, slippery limbs. She thrashed against me, bubbles rising, trying to get away. I had to scoop her up and drag her to the surface.

She gasped, coughed, choked.

"What the hell was that?"

"See?" she said, still coughing. "You rescued me. I was drowning, and you rescued me."

I held her buoyant in the water, making sure she could breathe. "Are we speaking metaphorically?"

"Metaphorically." She shook her head, still coughing. "Sure, Angel . . . metaphorically."

"That can't be all there is," I said, releasing her. "That I rescued you, that I was there when you —"

"Why not?"

"Because then I could be anyone."

"You are *so* not just anyone." Angela pushed away from me again, moving toward the shallow end.

"But you would fall in love with whoever rescued you? A fireman, a policeman —"

"What is it people see in each other?" she asked. "Why does anyone ever love anyone?" She splashed water at my face. "If you look at it too closely," she said playfully, "it disappears."

"You really think so?"

"Angel, don't you realize," she went on, "that you did this, that you came here wearing a blindfold, and you didn't need to take any of those pills?"

"Maybe I've taken so many," I suggested, "that the residue in my system is holding me psychologically aloft. Maybe the blindfold somehow tricked my psyche."

She only laughed.

I let it go. I had something else I wanted to talk about. "I want to tell you something."

"What is it?"

"When you're gone," I confessed, "I fall apart, I just lie there thinking of you, I don't eat, I don't sleep, I don't take my medication, I smile all the time, I laugh out loud and there's no one there . . . I stare into space."

Angela laughed. "Me, too." She swam toward me. "Me, too, you."

I looked around. "How did you know?"

"Know what?"

"When I was a kid, this was my favorite thing. My mother would take me, in all those different hotels. She would speak to the manager. 'My son,' she would say, 'his skin.' And they would open the pool at night and let me swim. How did you know? Did I tell you?"

Angela closed her eyes, then reached across the surface of the water to place her autumn-colored hand on my winter-colored shoulder.

———

When I was seven years old, I told her one night, I had the idea that if I just gave myself a severe enough sunburn, my skin would develop some color, some melanin, anything but this pallor of pink and white. I would actually say the word *tan,* raising my arms in the California brightness, eyes closed against it as if in prayer, as if saying the word aloud could magically bring some pigmentation into being. I remember lying on a lounge chair by my parents' blue-and-gold mosaic-tiled pool in our old house on Rexford Drive, letting my body marinate in my mother's tanning oil. Naked except for a pair of underpants, I turned myself like a chicken on a spit. I closed my eyes, facing the mid-July, Beverly Hills sky, light so harsh that beneath the protection of my lids, it flared and morphed, the colors oscillating from ultraviolet to infrared.

Red. Orange. Bright yellow. Burning.

Our housekeeper discovered me. She pulled me from the chair and brought me into the kitchen, the whole time muttering to herself in Portuguese. Poor Annabelle covered me in butter, greasing her hands on a stick from the refrigerator and slathering it across my skin. The butter felt cool, at first, and then gradually melted and warmed. All over, it bubbled, dissolved. Within minutes, the outer layers of my epidermal tissue rose away in a thin, blistery film. Tiny bumps formed, hard at first, like Braille, then ran in nodules across my back, down my chest, over my forehead, cheek-bones, and nose, a line of blisters covering my legs down to my knees. My legs and arms began to swell, and then my eyelids and lips flared up, too, my entire face bloating in thick blistery welts.

My mother stepped into the kitchen at that moment with her shopping bags, pastel tissue paper rustling inside them. She put the bags down and placed a bony hand over her mouth. "What did you do?" she said. "Angel, Angel, Angel . . . *what did you do?*"

"I got a tan."

"Never, never, never." She turned to Annabelle. "What did you put on him?"

"Butter," she explained.

"*Butter?* Get towels." My mother was tall and blond, with clear, intelligent, ash-colored eyes. She was still beautiful then, still human. "Get towels and soak them in cold water," she said. *"Hurry!"*

Annabelle ran to the linen closet while my mother's spidery fingers hovered over my blistered, buttered seven-year-old body.

I opened my mouth, I remember, and screamed.

———

"Hello?"

Angela said my name.

Then, *click.*

———

I wanted to scream like that right now.

Still holding the phone, I stepped into the living room.

In the scene that was on television at the moment, Deckard sits across from Rachael and aims a futuristic empathy-testing instrument into her eyes. He recites one scenario after another.

"You've got a little boy," says Deckard. "He shows you his butterfly collection, plus the killing jar."

Rachael holds a cigarette nervously to her pouting red lips, and her eyes are so liquid they seem about to pour out of her face.

"I'll notify the police," the 911 operator said. "I'll tell them everything you told me."

I paced back and forth over the flokati the whole rest of that day, waiting for the phone to ring, anticipating the usual sound of Angela's stiff heels in the tiled hallway outside. I must have called her cell phone a hundred times, my messages becoming more and more frantic. Why wasn't she answering? I had been unable to sit, unable to think about anything except the tone of her voice and the terror I'd heard inside it, that whispery, nearly voiceless formation of my name.

I pictured her: She was curled up, lips trembling, arms around her knees, eyes wet, the only source of light the luminous liquid crystal display of her cell phone.

Had she punched in my name? Did it say *Angel?*

"Mask," a man answered.

The day had passed. The night darkness had arrived.

There was music in the background, or what you might call senseless screaming over a toxic rhythm. This was disco made monstrous, dance music transformed into a quick-step funeral march.

And why hadn't she called back? What was she waiting for? It only confirmed that I was right.

Something had happened. Something was wrong.

"I was just wondering if Angela was working tonight," I said, trying to sound detached.

I thought it might be a good idea to check. Maybe I was wrong about the dark. Maybe she had called from the club and her phone had died. Maybe she had thought of something she had to do and changed her mind the minute she heard my voice.

"Who?"

"Angela," I said. "A dancer. She's kind of tall, brown skin — ah, shit." I remembered. "I mean *Cassandra*. I think she dances under the name Cassandra."

"Dancers use their own phones."

"She's not answering her own phone," I said. "Besides, I don't need to talk to her, I just need to know if she's there."

"Lots of ladies here," he said. "Can you hold on?"

I waited.

I stood by the front door of my apartment in the hopes that I would hear her coming up the stairs.

"Hey!" the guy on the phone was shouting to someone. "Some guy wants to know is Cassandra here!" I held a section of the kitchen miniblinds open with my fingers and scanned the parking lot. The blue numbers on the coffeemaker said it was nine-thirteen. There was an answer, presumably, because the guy got back on the line and said, "Cassandra's off tonight. Maybe another time, all right, boss?"

The tiles of the kitchen floor suddenly felt like ice on my feet. One of my arches started to cramp, as though someone were making a fist inside it. I hung up the phone and hopped into the living room, onto the flokati, then reached down to massage my sole. On television, the replicant named Roy was breaking Deckard's fingers. "This is for Zhora," he was saying, snapping one digit after another. "This is for Pris."

I sat down at my desk, turned in the old, creaking swivel chair, and massaged my foot.

From here I could look into the kitchen, at the countertop populated with bottles of alcohol and pharmaceuticals. I could see the half-empty bottle of Jack Daniel's on the counter, the almost completely empty bottle of Stoli. They sat next to the plastic bottles of antidepressants, antipsychotics, and anti-anxieties. It was an account, I understood, of my own decline, an archeological site revealing the artifacts of my own undoing.

"Angel?" Angela had said.

For some reason I thought of my aura again:

Red. Orange. Bright yellow. Burning.

The phone rang.

"Angela?"

"Angel, it's me," a soft voice said. "It's Melanie."

Shit. Fuck. Crap. It was my father's wife. I released a heavy breath. "How are you, Melanie?"

"I'm so glad I caught you." She gave me a nervous laugh. "Usually it's just the machine. Who's Angela?"

"She's just, um —" I wasn't sure what to tell her. "She's someone . . . she's a friend."

"Oh," Melanie said. "Well, I just wanted to invite you for dinner this weekend. Your father isn't shooting right now, so he's home for a while, and I thought it would be great if you could see Gabriel." Gabriel, their son, had something wrong with him. His eyes were vacant, uncomprehending. He rocked back and forth and spoke gibberish into his knees. "He's really starting to come out of his shell, you know, and —"

"Melanie," I said, "I'm expecting a call right now, actually. Can I get back to you?"

"Sure, Angel, it's just that —"

———

The night Angela took me to the pool, she had stared into my eyes for one of those long moments that merge romance with unease. I had been fighting the impulse to press her about her past, to ask where she came from, what her last name was, who her parents were, anything that would reveal the life she had lived before the moment she came to my door, orange casserole dish in her hands, sympathy written across her face. I had fought against it because I was afraid if I scratched too hard at the surface of reality, I'd fall through the tear.

But I want you to see her. I want you to see Angela the way I saw her, to experience the way she appeared at my door, holding that ridiculous dish, the scent of stew like perfume in the air of the stairwell, the way she approached me in the club that night, happiness radiating from her entire body. I want you to feel her wrists, how they were all bone and so little flesh, her thighs all flesh and no bone. I want you to know what it was like to feel her dry feet on my feet, the coolness of her skin against my skin, the warmth of her breath mixed with mine, her limbs tangled with my limbs. Picture the way her real hair, dark at the root, veered away in two directions from the nape of her neck, the way the fine black down in the small of her back whirled like a miniature galaxy. I want you to visualize the tiny lines at the corners of her eyes like creases in wax paper and the gelled implants inside her breasts, the light bands of stress pulling against the skin.

She was a universe.

The mascara smudged around her eyelids, the lipstick smeared after so much kissing, sometimes for hours, all night. The feel of her tongue, of her lips pulling, tasting, of her cool hands on my body, my skin, the narrow, tapered fingers. I want you to see her the way I saw her, feel her the way I feel her still, I will always feel her.

If I could, I would let everyone experience these memories, these images of Angela, I would let the world inside me just to meet her, if only so you could understand what it felt like when she disappeared.

IT WAS GIVEN LOW PRIORITY, THE LOWEST, OBVIOUSLY, BECAUSE the police didn't even arrive until quarter past two in the morning, and by that time, my anxiety, despite my ingesting an inordinate amount of Ativan and one or two calming shots of Jack Daniel's, had developed into a full-scale hysteria. I had been pacing for hours, unable to sit, and when I heard the buzzer, I rushed to the door and looked at the little black-and-white screen of the surveillance camera.

There they were, two policemen, one thin, one fat, standing between the twin midget palms like Laurel and Hardy. I buzzed them in and listened to their heavy footsteps on the polished concrete stairs.

"I was the one who called," I told the cops when they knocked on Angela's door, squinting against the cruel fluorescence. "Angela isn't home."

One of them, the skinny one, said, "What seems to be the problem, sir?"

The other one sighed and held a hand over his weapon, giving me a look of total disinterest.

"My girlfriend," I said. "Something's happened."

"Did you hear something?"

"She called me."

"She called you."

"She called and said my name."

The skinny one removed his hat and pushed his hair back. "Okay . . ." Then he replaced it.

"And then she hung up."

"What's her name again?"

"Angela."

"The last name?"

I remembered then I didn't know.

There was a pause while the cops looked at me. "She's your girl-friend and you don't know her last name?"

I didn't have an answer.

"You an albino?"

I sighed.

One of the policemen tried the door, and it opened easily.

I cursed at myself for not trying that. I must have knocked on that door at least fifty times. Why hadn't I just turned the stupid handle?

"How long have you known her, sir?" He appeared intelligent, the fat one, his left eye permanently squinting. The other cop, the skinny one, seemed tired, with sharp features and blinking, red-rimmed eyes. He removed his hat and combed his hair with his fingers again, then replaced it again. He just kept doing this over and over.

"She just moved in a few weeks ago." I tried to remember how many times I had canceled my psychotherapy appointment. I hadn't seen Dr. Silowicz once since Angela and I had met. "Maybe it was more than that," I said. "I don't know, a month, six weeks?"

"I wonder why she didn't lock the door."

"She's trusting."

"Yeah?"

"Forgetful, too," I corrected myself.

"That's more like it."

This from the skinny one. "You said she called you?" He took his hat off again, ran his fingers through his hair again.

"And I could tell by the tone of her voice that she was calling from an enclosed, dark place, so I think —"

"Wait, wait, wait. You could tell that by the tone of her voice?"

I nodded.

He paused, giving me a long look. "I'm trying to understand what you mean by that, sir."

I let a half second pass before I answered. "She called from somewhere," I said, "somewhere inside something . . . I could hear it. I could hear it in the way she said my name."

"She was speaking low, whispering?"

"Exactly. So it must've been dark. It must've been —"

"You're saying you could tell it was dark where she was calling from?" This was the skinny one again, incredulous.

"She said my name."

The two cops stepped across the threshold of Angela's front door, and the fat one flicked on the overhead. As usual, I let a hand fly up to my eyes, shielding myself against the brightness.

"Your name?"

"What?"

"You say she said your name?"

"That's what I'm telling you."

"What is it?"

"Angel."

"Angel what?"

"Veronchek," I offered reluctantly.

"Hello?" the fat one said to the room. "Hello? Hello?"

I stood on the threshold and looked in, which is when I realized I had never been inside Angela's apartment before.

It was nothing special, anyway. There was a blue love seat. There was a white rattan rocking chair. There was a matching kitchen table with a glass top, also made of white rattan, and two aluminum folding chairs. Everything was brand-new, everything appeared to have been bought yesterday. The walls were white, entirely absent of pictures.

"Look in the bedroom, Trip."

I followed the cop named Trip, the fat one, into the bedroom, which smelled like citrus, spices, and musk, like Angela, as a matter of fact — it must have been the perfume she wore. The overhead light was already on. A few empty cardboard boxes had been stacked under the window facing the parking lot. The bed, which I could tell was also new because its plastic wrapping had been tossed into the corner, was covered with a pale blue comforter and matching pillows, the DO NOT REMOVE tags still attached. On the floor rested a digital clock, its enormous numbers glowing crimson, and there were two hard-shell Samsonites, both the same size, one blue, one red, with jeans, T-shirts, and underwear spilling out.

Trip turned around and looked at me. "Ah, shit," he said, "you're not supposed to be in here."

"Why not?"

"What if this is a crime scene? You didn't touch anything, did you?"

I looked at my hands. "A crime scene?"

He sighed.

"The closet," I said. "Try the closet."

He opened the door.

"There's nothing here, either. Some shoes . . . nada."

I stepped behind him and peered over his shoulder. All I saw were a few pairs of heels and three dresses on wire hangers.

"What does she do?" the cop asked.

"What do you mean?" I asked.

"Her job, what is —"

"She's a dancer. But only until she finds something else."

"Well" — Trip turned to face me — "maybe she found that something else, because she's not here."

"Here's what happened." The other one, the one I had been thinking of as the dumb, skinny one with the red-rimmed eyes, came out of the bathroom. "Here's what *transpired*." He said that word like a person who had just purchased it. "She called from her wireless phone, dialed you up, you know, and you answered. She said your name, and just like that, she lost the connection. Happens all the time. Drove out of range, went through a tunnel."

"She was calling from the dark." I had heard it in her voice. Darkness. And fear. "And why didn't she call back?"

"So she was in the dark somewhere," he conceded. "Maybe you're right. A bar or somewhere, probably where she works."

"There would have been loud music if she'd called from where she works." I shook my head. "I've been there. Besides, I spoke to them already, and she's not working tonight. This was a small, enclosed place, like a closet." A new thought occurred to me. "Or the trunk of a car." I pictured a stifling obscurity, heavy air, a pair of hands around Angela's neck, fingers tightening.

"Where is it?"

"What?"

"Where she works."

"The Velvet Mask. It's on —"

He rolled his eyes. "We know where *that* is."

"Sir," Trip announced, shaking his head, "you can't tell if a person is in the dark just from the sound of their voice." He was losing his patience, I was beginning to understand, with this white mutant in his tattered bathrobe in the middle of the West Hollywood night.

"Can you describe her?"

"Describe her?"

We had moved back into my apartment so I could give them a complete statement.

"Her appearance." This was the dumb cop asking. He ran his fingers through his hair, replaced his hat.

"She's black," I said. "At least I think she is. Part black, at least. Maybe Spanish."

"Dark skin, light skin?"

"Medium skin," I answered. "Medium to light. Cinnamon," I said. "Reflective."

This got a smirk from Trip. "Cinnamon skin."

"Anything in particular about her appearance that stands out?" the skinny one asked. "I mean, besides the reflectivity?"

"Her eyes change colors."

They both stared at me.

"Sometimes they're blue," I clarified, "sometimes they're brown."

Trip muttered as he took down notes. "Might be wearing colored contacts."

"Nice body?"

"Fake breasts," I said, making a gesture. I had felt the implants beneath her skin.

"How tall?"

"Tall, I guess." I thought for a moment, remembering how high she came up on me. I am just over six feet. "Five nine, maybe. Five ten?" I became sarcastic. "But I'm fairly sure her height is real."

We stood on the flokati, the three of us, and I worried about what might be on the soles of their shoes.

On television was the scene where Leon reaches into a container of freezing liquid and pulls out a pair of android eyeballs.

"Is that on TV?" Trip asked.

"It's a DVD."

"Oh." He nodded.

"There's nothing else you can do?"

"Nothing happened," said the skinny one.

"There's no sign of foul play," said Trip, taking a hard look around, as if Angela might be hiding in my apartment for some reason.

A few seconds later, they were heading toward the door. "There's nothing to do even if we wanted to do something," Trip said.

"All you've got is a missing woman," I said sarcastically.

"All *you've* got is a missing woman. All we've got is someone who says he received a phone call. You have to understand," the skinny cop said, "we get these crazy calls all night." He was still taking his hat off and pushing his hair back, over and over and over. "There's no evidence that anything happened. There's nothing to even lead us to that conclusion. Anyway," he added, "it looks to me like she may have hit the highway."

"She would have told me."

"How well do you know her?"

"What do you mean?" I rubbed my hands over my face.

"You said she's your girlfriend, I mean —"

Trip laughed. "He doesn't even know her last name."

"Anyone around here you could ask?"

"Why don't you wait until morning," the skinny one said, "ask your neighbors. Maybe someone knows something."

We stood by the door for a long, awkward moment. "You know there's a show on TV about a guy named Angel who lives in Los Angeles?" Trip said finally.

I shook my head. "I don't watch much television."

"He's a vampire."

As they walked down the stairwell, I heard him, Trip, the cop I had been thinking of as the intelligent one, say, "Jesus, Mike, we meet some weirdos out here, but *that* guy —"

————

I sat down heavily at my desk, the chair squeaking against my weight. I wanted to piece together what remained, what was left of Angela in memory, but there were only fragments, scraps of dialogue, out-of-focus images. I had confessed so much, traveled over so much emotional terrain and in such a short amount of time, and now when I considered what I really knew about her, I realized that she had told me almost nothing. It was all contradictions, prevarications, meaningless chatter. She had no past, not even a last name. We had been lying on the floor of my apartment, talking, kissing, drinking, eating pills. Her mouth had been moving, and words had been spilling out of it like rainwater from the mouth of a gargoyle, but what those words meant was slipping away. I tried to sort out what was true, what was untrue, what had been simple exaggeration, what were lies. I tried to pin down in memory what practical clues I had to go on, what she really had given me that might be meaningful, and found myself at a loss.

"Angel?" Angela had said.

It was the voice of a person calling from inside the deepest ventricle of the blackest heart of an infinitely terrifying universe, and it was all I had left of her.

From here I could see into the kitchen, all the way to the blue numbers on the coffeemaker. It had become five-thirty-five in the morning somehow.

I automatically got up to take one of my twice-daily doses of

Reality but paused to read the warning label. I had read it a million times before, of course, but right now, I was trying to notice things, trying desperately to stay alert. This was the drug I was expected to take every day, once in the morning, once in the evening, the crystal-shaped green pills that came with no immediate sensation other than a benign loss of imagination. This was the maintenance drug, with side effects that included "dry mouth, irritability, problems urinating, memory loss." Lately, I had been missing days. Since Angela had begun coming over, I had been skipping it because when I took it, nothing ever happened, there was no sensory effect, nothing seemed to change except that it banished me to a colorless present tense. To be perfectly honest, I've always preferred the kind of drugs that bring a little something extra to the party.

Besides, right now I needed a clear mind. I needed my thoughts. My memory, weakened though it was by years of chemical abuse, was all I had to go on.

I put the bottle back down and swallowed a half cup of bourbon instead, then went back to sit at the computer again.

At a certain point, I felt the light of the sun curving around the horizon. All the blinds were drawn, yet the apartment was growing brighter.

That's because even in the darkest of circumstances, the light finds its way in. Photons force their way one particle at a time, if they have to. In a closet, for instance, or a dark room, a sliver of light will appear around the door, a gray line that, over time, will become to the person hiding there like a razor of illumination.

Try it. Turn out the lights.

A room that was formerly black will gradually become gray, and shapes will appear, eventually shadows will form.

The *picture,* I thought.

Of course. I had taken a photograph.

Surrounding my computers were stacks of junk mail, illegible notes on my screenplay, and old unfilled prescription slips. Frantically, I searched through the clutter until I found the thick envelope I had picked up a week ago at the one-hour photo place.

My hands were shaking as I sifted through them.

The first photo was of a house, an ordinary one-story dwelling in the Valley with a red-tiled roof, a lavender bougainvillea half in bloom. The next one was of the same house at night, the windows glowing like bug lamps over a darkened lawn. I stared at it but did not remember taking this photograph. Here was a brown-haired woman inserting a key into the door of a gray-morning-mist Ford Taurus. She was thin, with limp hair that hung halfway down her back, wearing a canvas tote bag over her shoulder. Behind her, sunlight perforated the trees of a parking lot like a thousand prismatic needles piercing a veil. There were other pictures, too, photos of the same woman walking through a long, linoleum corridor. Here she emerged from a Hallmark store. In this one, she entered a gray institutional building.

I had no recollection of taking any of these pictures. Maybe there had been a mistake at the processing place, I thought, and these photos belonged to someone else.

But then I came to the last one.

It was Angela all right, sneering into the lens, her face completely out of focus, offering that petulant middle finger.

Okay, I thought. That's a start.

In the bedroom, I slipped out of my robe and into a pair of black cargo pants and a black shirt, the same uniform I had worn to the Velvet Mask a couple of weeks ago. It was morning now, and I noticed through the kitchen window that the sky outside had turned the color of that scary Buddha's tie, silvery gray, with an argentine glow originating from the east. A heavy smog had lowered, too, and it seemed like the city itself wore that old charcoal-colored robe of mine.

I stepped next door into Angela's apartment and found that the cops, thankfully, had left the door unlocked. I was thinking there must be *something* with her full name on it somewhere . . . an envelope, an old credit-card receipt, a magazine. I took a look around the living room. There was the blue love seat, the cheap rattan table and aluminum folding chairs, the matching rocker. Nothing. I went into the bathroom. The medicine cabinet contained a single bottle of Motrin, nothing else. The sink featured a red toothbrush and a tube of Crest. In a kitchen drawer, I found a set of cheap utensils, newly bought, but nothing useful. On the counter was Julia Child's *The Way to Cook.* I flipped it open, and it automatically settled on the recipe for lamb stew. There was a gravy stain on the list of ingredients, a splash of savory brown obscuring the words. I looked in the trash and found an empty carton of orange juice, a few paper napkins, and finally — yes, *this* was what I was looking for — way at the bottom, a couple of envelopes.

One was just an offer for a credit card and was addressed to someone named *Jessica Teagarden,* indicating a street in Santa Monica called Orange Blossom Boulevard. The other envelope, turquoise blue, greeting card–size, bore the same Santa Monica address and said *Jessica* in blocky handwriting. It had been torn open, and whatever it had contained, like Angela herself, was gone.

Jessica Teagarden — was that her name? So why would she tell me it was Angela?

I couldn't be completely sure if this Jessica person was really Angela, or if someone named Jessica had simply been over and used Angela's trash can, but it was the only thing I had to go on. She had gone by the name Cassandra at the Mask, I reasoned, so maybe Angela was just another alias. Or perhaps Jessica was just someone Angela knew, a friend who had been over to visit, another girl who danced at the club, and maybe *she* knew where Angela was.

I went back into my own apartment and grabbed an amber cylinder containing pink, oval-shaped anti–social phobia meds from the kitchen counter. I'd need a whole handful of these, I thought. Christ knew what I might encounter out there in the light.

————

Minutes later, I was squinting directly into it, the harsh sun flashing off the gleaming metallic paint and glittery chrome automotive accents on the 10. I was feeling that rush, the surge of medication kicking in, chemicals being rerouted, synapses suppressed, that smooth adjustment to my jagged psyche. I was thinking about what had happened to Angela. I had imagined an enclosed, dark space, her body sealed inside it, and then I remembered the way her hands felt on my chest, those sharp, glittery nails scratching the outlines of imaginary figures over my skin. I wondered irrationally if she had been spelling out a message of some kind, if she had been trying to tell me something.

I was looking straight into the bumper-to-bumper traffic, the brutal glare resonating off the metallic cars, when the girl in the Honda in front of me adjusted her rearview mirror and flashed a vicious reflection. And there it was. I rubbed my eyes for a few seconds, hoping it would go away, but it was still there, just a dot at this point, a minuscule speck of shine in my field of vision.

The aura.

It wasn't composed of glowing colors like the brilliant red, yellow, and orange Angela had described, and there was nothing karmic or spiritual about it, believe me. This was a migraine aura, an amoeba-like shimmering thing that appears directly in my field of vision and heralds an oncoming migraine. It usually appears after I've inadvertently looked straight into a bright light — the brighter the light, the bigger the amoeba, the bigger the amoeba, the more painful the migraine.

I knew that within a half hour, it would grow and the pain would ascend, bringing with it a dull throb behind my left eye that eventually would become a cutting blade of luminous torture, that eventually ripples of nausea would undulate through me, gathering strength until they became tidal cascades. I would taste that gush of warm saliva at the back of my mouth and then experience the unquiet, queasy feeling of needing to get it out, a Stouffer's frozen dinner entrée, generally, or microwavable French bread pizza, whatever it was, to get it the flying fuck out of my body. I could look forward to spastic convulsions, puking until there was no longer any food in my stomach and all that was left was acidic, green bile, some of it squirting out of my nose.

I didn't know if I should turn around and try to make it back to my apartment or pull over and try to ride it out. I'd spent more than one afternoon lying in the back of Mom's old Cadillac, stretched on its smelly rear seat, parked in the shade, a T-shirt covering my face to keep out the invading light. Right now, I took the first exit and pulled over behind a strip mall. It was almost noon, and the sun, having burned away the smog that blanketed the city, blazed angrily through a hazy sky like the eye of an Old Testament God.

Why hadn't I brought my sunglasses? It was unlike me, jumping into the car without thinking. Usually I was so careful when I went outside. Usually I wore long sleeves, a baseball cap, and the darkest shades possible, with glare-resistant, polarized, ultraviolet filtering lenses. I checked in the glove compartment to see if I had left a pair in there but found nothing. I picked through the empty soda cups and fast-food wrappers on the floor of the passenger side. Nothing there, either. I explored under the front seat with my hand and felt something complex.

Aha.

A pair of Mom's old enormous, octagonal, pink-tinted, tortoise shells. How long had they been down there? Years, probably, since the car had been hers, which also demonstrated how long it had been since the floor had been vacuumed. They were prescription, unfortunately. My own eyes, despite their photophobic sensitivity to brightness, were spared most of the usual problems associated with albinism and are close enough to twenty-twenty that they don't require prescription lenses. My mother, on the other hand, was practically blind.

I slipped them on, seeing the world, ridiculously enough, through rose-colored lenses.

My mother's migraines have always been worse than mine, too, if you can believe it, and hers can happen almost anytime, regardless of whether she is looking into the light. She closes her eyes and a vibration ripples across her forehead as though someone dipped an imaginary finger into the surface of her skin. I can see it instantly, the pain building there. She affects a weak smile, lights a Benson & Hedges 100, and starts massaging her temples, stroking her eyelids with her French-manicured nails. Sometimes the pain strikes her instantaneously, like an invisible knife has soared down from the heavens and stabbed her in the back of the head. By the look on her face and the way she moves, a hand flying to her face, a violent jerk away to the right, it seems like she has been hit by a bullet. Every now and then she actually faints.

When I was old enough, I'd say, "Mom, why don't you lie down?"

She'd sigh, telling me it was nothing, that it would "go away in a sec."

"Mom," I'd say, "they never go away."

Sometimes she'd yield, but mostly she'd try to stay in the light until the nausea overtook her and I had to escort her to the bathroom. At least twice a month for my entire childhood, I'd spend half an hour outside her bathroom door, wherever we happened to be staying at the time, listening to my mother's breakfast of grapefruit and black coffee gush into the toilet. She went to doctors about it for years, had taken every conceivable medication, including ergotamine, ephedrine, beta blockers, and Imitrex, not to mention phenobarbital, Percocet, and Fiorinal, plus acupressure and biofeedback therapy. But nothing ever worked. When she came out of the bathroom, she would be as pale as me, saying, invariably, "Angel, I have to lie down." She required absolute silence at that point, and if we were staying in a hotel, I would call the front desk and ask if the maids could please be quiet in the hallways.

My mother had been so glamorous once, an ice blonde with a French accent. Tall, thin, a runway model in Zurich and Paris in the late sixties, a fixture in the society pages, the kind of girl who belonged in the passenger seat of a Fiat Spider, a scarf around her neck, long legs, a gamine. She'd made one movie, met my father, then retired. Originally she had straight hair, frosty blond, but at some point in the seventies, she'd had it styled in a Farrah Fawcett cascade, which became the way she wore it all the way through the eighties, even into the nineties. At the first sign of wrinkles, she started visiting Dr. Jerome Phelps, a famous plastic surgeon and a plastic surgeon to the famous, and the skin on her face kept getting tighter and tighter, weirder and weirder. She'd had her cheekbones redone, her lips injected with collagen, the bags removed from under her eyes, her ass tightened, her breasts lifted, her hair dyed, her thighs lipoed . . . I couldn't stand her anymore, was the truth. In all honesty, I hated what my mother had become. As far as I was concerned, Monique Veronchek had ceased to be a person a very long time ago.

———

Things were blurry now, but a little darker at least.

Pink, in any event.

I sat in the strip mall parking lot, wearing my mother's prescription lenses, and waited futilely for the aura to fade. It shimmered, flickered, sparkled, flashed. Sometimes, very rarely, the headache didn't arrive, or the aura turned out to be a trick of the eye. It was hard to tell right now which way it would go. I was still blind, but fuck it, I thought.

I turned the ignition and drove defiantly toward my destination, this time off the freeway, to Orange Blossom Boulevard, nearly sightless from the aura and my mother's ridiculous rose-colored glasses, to the address of someone named Jessica Teagarden.

As soon as I pulled onto that street, however, I stopped the Cadillac at the curb, swung the door open, and puked into the clean concrete gutter. The vomit was gelatinous, formerly Stouffer's spaghetti with meatballs, which I didn't remember eating, for some reason, and which didn't contain enough liquid because I had been overly medicating and drinking too much and was as dehydrated as a spoonful of Tang.

I was lucky not to be coughing up orange dust.

The nausea phase had come suddenly, like an invisible hand had squeezed my stomach from the inside, and the whole contents of my stomach were unceremoniously squirted onto the avenue. Disgusting as this may sound, this was a good thing, because it meant the overall migraine experience would probably be short-lived. Usually at the onset of the vomiting, the visual disturbances clear away like clouds over Zuma Beach. So when I lifted my head and wiped my face on the front of my shirt, the blindness lifted, too. I pushed my mother's glasses onto my forehead, waiting for the next gush of vomit to rise, and looked around with clear eyes.

This was a much better neighborhood than mine. There were a couple of kids playing Wiffle ball on the lawn across the street; an orange-and-purple FedEx truck was making its round of deliveries; an old woman power-walked by my car, her gray head bobbing like a pigeon's. No one said a word. I thought the nausea had passed for a moment, and I almost got out of the car, but then I felt it again, that pressure rising up from deep inside me, and I retched for a full five minutes more, coughing and gagging and drooling like an animal.

Eventually, though, it stopped, and I was able to pull my head back in, wipe my face on my shirt once more, and look around for the exact address. There are usually a few moments of peace, relatively speaking, after I throw up, before the pain behind my eye starts to build, and I wanted to take full advantage.

I took a deep breath, locating the number above a door.

The house was a stucco duplex with a wide, manicured front lawn, a garden of decorative cacti, an old palm tree providing a finger of shade across the facade. I wondered why Angela had moved away from a place like this, if she had actually lived here, that is. It was so much nicer than my neighborhood. There were wild palms decorating the lawns, as well as two gigantic willows across the street, their long, whiplike tendrils tickling the dry grass in the hot Santa Monica breeze. I could even see a set of red swings with a slide and seesaw around the side yard. I pulled up without closing the door, parked the Cadillac in front of the walkway, and got out, pushing Mom's pink-tinted octagonals back down over my eyes to filter the garish light. From where I stood, it didn't seem like anyone was home. I walked across the lawn, stepped up to the front door, and noticed a pile of mail in front of it. I knelt down to sift through, finding mostly catalogs like Victoria's Secret, Williams-Sonoma, and Sharper Image, some of which were addressed to Occupant or Current Resident, others specifically to Jessica Teagarden.

Was that really her name?

And if it was, why had she told me her name was Angela?

There were only a few envelopes, one electricity bill, a couple of solicitations, and one thick envelope without a return address. It was the same shade of blue and addressed in the same blocky handwriting as the empty one I found in Angela's trash back home, the word *Jessica* emblazoned across it in letters a half inch high. It occurred to me that she probably had received the other blue envelope at this address, too, and had brought it with her, along with her old utility bills, to the apartment in West Hollywood. Whatever it contained, I knew, had something to do with her old life.

Furtively, I slipped the blue envelope into my pocket.

"Are you stealing people's mail?"

I turned around to see a boy, maybe ten or eleven years old, with an oddly shaped face. I gave him what I hoped would appear to be a friendly smile but probably turned out to be the usual grimace. "I was looking for Angela," I answered. Then I corrected myself, saying, "I mean, Jessica . . . Ms. Teagarden."

"She used to be our next-door neighbor," the boy announced. He had five or six heavy library books under his arm, plus a full backpack. "But she moved away."

"Oh." I stood up.

"No one lives there now."

"Really?"

"Not yet. I was hoping for some kids." He reached into the pocket of his jeans without dropping his books and fished out a single key on a shoe lace. "My mom's not home," he said. "She'll be back around twelve-thirty."

"She's at work?"

The boy smiled a bored, completely adult smile.

"Did you know her?"

He arched a single eyebrow and said this like a fifty-year-old man: "Are you referring to Jessica Teagarden?" He had the kind of cheekbones that made his eyes and nose seem almost concave.

I reached in my side pocket for the photo I had grabbed before I left the apartment, thinking I might at least be able to verify her identity. "Is this her?" In the picture, Angela half-sneered, half-smiled, holding that middle finger directly up to the lens. I could feel the migraine growing now, a piercing needle stabbing the back of my eye, the point touching the interior of my pupil.

The boy examined it, and his own gray eyes narrowed. "That's her, I guess . . . well, maybe . . . but why is she doing that?"

The inappropriateness of showing a ten-year-old kid a photograph of a half-dressed woman extending the fuck-you finger suddenly dawned on me. "That sure is a lot of books you have there," I said, slipping the picture back into my pocket.

"Yeah, well," he said, "I just came back from the library because I'm doing a report."

"What on?"

"The gecko."

"Interesting," I nodded appreciatively. "The gecko."

He dropped his books onto the ground. "Do you want to hear it?"

I blinked.

He turned his satellite-shaped face toward the sky, keeping his eyes wide. They watered, absorbing the light, then started to flicker. I was about to tell him it wasn't a good idea to stare into the sun, when he began speaking in a low voice, his lids half-closed. *"They are found in tropical regions all over the world,"* he said. *"Nocturnal, hiding in cool shadows during the day and foraging for insects at night, the gecko frequently makes his or her home in high tree branches . . . suction cups which can enable the gecko to walk across a smooth ceiling as if he is walking across the floor."* Suddenly, his eyelids fluttered wildly.

"Are you all right?"

He enunciated every syllable like a television voice-over actor. His face twitched, as though he were in the middle of a seizure. *"A highly developed sense of hearing . . . relatively unique in their ability to chirp or click. In fact, the very name gecko is believed to be a derivative of a Malay word which . . ."*

Now he paused, but his eyes kept pulsating.

"Hey!" I shouted.

He stopped, breathing heavily. The boy's eyes were still open, but his lips were trembling and he seemed to have descended into some sort of fugue.

I couldn't help but look around, thinking I might need to find some help. I even considered running back to the car and speeding away. "Are you . . . are you all right?" I asked again.

Thankfully, the boy coughed convulsively, and when he looked up, his eyes were clear. "What do you mean?" he asked. He seemed to have come to.

"You were . . . your eyelids were flickering, and you seemed to be . . . I don't know —"

He smiled hugely. "Oh, that's just what it's like when I'm *remembering*." He broke into an unselfconscious, high-pitched giggle, saying proudly, "That wasn't really my report. That was from the Discovery Channel."

"From TV?"

"I have an audiographic memory," he announced.

I didn't know what to say. "A . . . what?"

"*Audiographic.* That means I can remember everything I hear."

"Everything?"

"Absolutely everything," he answered. "And once it starts, it's kind of hard to turn it off."

"Do you remember anything about Angela . . . I mean, about Jessica?"

"Were you her boyfriend?"

I had to close my eyes. The light was killing me. "Yeah, I was . . . I mean . . . I am."

"I don't usually remember stuff like that. I have to care about it at least a little bit."

My head was starting to throb, the migraine assembling its powers, storm clouds gathering on the horizon. "Well," I said, "I really need to talk to her."

"You could ask my mom." He indicated the living room, an oasis of cool shadow. "She'll be home pretty soon, and you could wait inside."

I hesitated, thinking of the photo I had shown him, and wondered if the kid would launch into another science report. "You probably shouldn't invite strangers into your house."

He narrowed his eyes. "You don't look very dangerous." Then he pointed to my chest. "And you could use our bathroom to rinse the throw-up off your shirt."

I looked down. The front of my shirt was striped with greenish bile and orangey red smears of regurgitated spaghetti sauce.

Fantastic.

The boy opened the door for me all the way.

The interior had that afternoon feeling of no one being home. There was that stillness, a summer quiet. Motes of dust floated in the heavy air, revealing shafts of thick yellow that burned through the wooden blinds and cast hard zebra stripes of shadow across the floor. That film crew had been here before me to set up the scene, it seemed, the same one that had lit the parking lot yesterday. I pictured the gaffers inside this little duplex, standing around with their alligator clips and rolls of colored tape. I imagined that one of these walls was fake, concealing Universal's entire lighting department.

"I'm Angel," I said.

I was barely holding it together. In a few short moments, the course of the migraine had progressed from a slight stabbing pain to the feeling of a needle piercing my eye to the sensation of a shard of broken glass cutting through the back of my head.

"I'm Victor," the boy said pointing. "Bathroom's that way."

"Thank you, Victor." I stepped through a small hallway between the living room and kitchen and found a single toilet and sink in a closet-size space. There was a flaming intensity slashing through my cerebral cortex now, my medulla oblongata throbbing, the migraine coming on with full, merciless effect. I could feel it penetrating my frontal lobe like a surgeon's scalpel.

Inside the little yellow room, I pushed my mother's octagonal glasses up onto my head and examined my face in the mirror. My skin was practically transparent, the veins beneath my skin pulsating like an alien's. My eyes were even pinker, even more infant-fleshlike than usual, and deeply bloodshot from my being awake for so long. I ran some cold water over my fingers and placed them gently on my temples, trying to cool my boiling brain. This was the truly painful part of the migraine, and the fact that I hadn't passed out was actually a good sign. Things could only get better from here, I told myself.

There was a clean washcloth hanging on a silver hook, beige with a pattern of white stars, and I used it to wipe some of the vomit off the front of my shirt. Then I rinsed it, flicked the light switch off, and sat down on the toilet, putting my head in my hands and pressing the cloth over my sensitive eyelids.

I only wanted to think for a few seconds, to pull myself together.

I wondered again why Angela had left this neighborhood. This house was pretty nice, presumably the same as the one next door. It was a much more pleasant community out here than West Hollywood, too, with the ocean just a few blocks away, and the willow trees, and the well-cared-for lawns. If she lived next door, in a place just like this, why leave? Could it have been money? I knew Angela made plenty at the Mask. And despite the crappiness of my neighborhood, my apartment building didn't come at the cheapest rent on earth. It occurred to me that maybe Angela didn't fit in out here. Santa Monica is a daylight world, a place for sun worshippers and surfers, extroverts and exhibitionists. Perhaps she felt more at home in the West Hollywood world of darkness and paranoia.

I know I did.

I thought of the night I had seen her at the Velvet Mask, when she came out of the back room and looked around, that blank expression on her face. I didn't know if I should stand up and wave or just wait until she noticed me. I had decided to wait. For some reason, I thought it would be funny for her to discover me there, an ordinary asshole just checking out the girls. She had walked around one of the stages, moving in that languid, graceful way I had seen her move at home, until she finally noticed me. The blank expression filled in immediately, the same way it had the first time I had seen her. But this time it wasn't sympathy or understanding; this time her smile was instant, unyielding — it was happiness, and it sent waves of emotion through my body, something far beyond the desire I had been feeling, a sensation I could hardly identify.

I noted the bewildered looks on the faces of the Japanese salarymen and the drugstore clerks.

"Angel," Angela said, almost squealing, "you really came!" The waitress had brought my eight-dollar Pellegrino's, and I was sitting there with one of the cold bottles between my legs and the other on the table beside me. "I didn't think you would really show." She plopped down beside me, draping a thin arm over my shoulders.

"You made me promise," I said, laughing. "You made me swear to —"

"I know, but —"

"— God, so here I am."

"— I thought, I thought you were just saying it."

"So tell me what's what and who's who," I said. "Show me everything, because this is the only time."

Angela leaned against me. It was odd, but I felt the way I had felt as a kid with all those actresses, stylists, and production assistants. I felt like *someone*.

Her eyes, I noticed, were green tonight. "Okay," she said, "that's Virginia." She pointed to the dancing girl with flashing hair. "That's Ashley." She pointed to the emaciated blonde performing for the Japanese businessmen. "The DJ tonight is Alvin, but I don't really ever talk to him." Over in the corner was a booth with two turntables under a smoky cone of incandescence. A white guy in wraparound shades and giant silver headphones stood inside it. "Usually it's Eddie," she said. "But he was fired for bothering the girls." The music was harsh, pulsing, guttural, mindless screaming over a senseless beat.

I had to ask. "What's he playing?"

Her eyes grew wide. "You don't like it?"

"I'm just curious."

"ImmanuelKantLern," she announced. "They've got a new CD coming out."

"Immanuel —"

"— KantLern," she finished. "They run it all together in one word, isn't it funny? Immanuel Kant was a philosopher who —"

"I've heard of the philosopher." I laughed. "It's the rock group I'm not so familiar with."

She leaned toward me, whispering conspiratorially, *"I slept with the bass player."*

"You —"

"Joey. I met him at a party after they played at the El Rey." She raised her eyebrows.

I had to ask: "Are you his girlfriend?"

"Are you jealous?"

I felt a sharp prick of anger, a sensation I wasn't accustomed to, so I changed the subject, indicating the giant man in the silvery tie sitting beneath the exit sign. "Who's that?"

She laughed. "That's Lester. He looks mean, but he's sweet."

"He works here?"

A shrug. "He's the bouncer."

"Why is he dressed like a henchman from an old James Bond movie?"

"During the day he's a driver for a funeral parlor."

"Ladies and gentlemen," a loud voice said over the sound system, "coming to the stage of the Velvet Mask All Nude Gentlemen's Cabaret is the beautiful Gigi and the seductive . . . *Cassandra.*"

"Oh shit." Angela leapt up. "That's me."

———

"Hello?" a voice said. There was a knock, a hard rap against hollow wood.

There was another voice, saying, "He said his name is Angel. I think he's an albino."

I heard the first voice, now shrill. *"Are you Angel? Is your name Angel?"*

I lifted my head.

Oh shit. Oh Christ. I was sitting on a toilet in the bathroom of a stranger's house.

"Yes," I said, rubbing a hand over my mouth. "Yes, I'm Angel. I'm so sorry. I must've fallen —"

The door opened, and when my eyes adjusted, I could see the round, flat face of that ten-year-old kid and what must have been his mother, a woman in her thirties with the same strangely concave face, standing in the hallway.

"I must have fallen asleep," I explained.

She was in the middle of a panic. "What were you doing in there?" Her voice was sharp. "Do you have any idea how long you were —"

"I'm so —"

"— in there?"

"— sorry."

"Are you taking drugs?"

"No, no, absolutely not. I was, I had a migraine. I must've —"

"He was in there for, like, two hours." Victor's laughter was spiky, high-pitched.

"— lost consciousness." I was up now, and I would have moved into the hallway except that the two of them were blocking the way.

Victor's mother had her hands on her hips. Worry lines rippled across her forehead.

Victor just kept laughing.

"Please," I said. "I'm so sorry. I didn't mean . . ."

She gave me a hard look. "Well," she said, still unsure, "you certainly don't look dangerous."

"I'm so not dangerous," I told her, "believe me." I realized I still had the damp washcloth stuck to my forehead. "I'm the most un-dangerous person you will ever —"

She sighed, lips pursed, softening.

"— encounter," I said, rinsing it under the tap. "I know it must seem strange, finding me here like that. But I was . . . I was having a migraine, and your son, Victor . . . he was nice enough to let me use your bathroom, and I just . . . and I guess I passed out."

Victor's mom must have decided that a character as preposter-ous as me couldn't be telling her anything but the truth. "Well," she said, "are you all right now?"

"Absolutely, I'm fine, thank you."

She had light brown hair, straight, shoulder length. She had pink lips and sympathetic eyes. For some reason, I assumed she was a nurse.

I knew what I looked like: blue skin, pink eyes, white hair, wear-ing a puke-streaked shirt. I was a vampire, a mutant, and a grown man alone in the house with her ten-year-old son, maybe a child molester, possibly a drug addict, probably a criminal. I was lucky she hadn't called the police. I touched the top of my head and real-ized I still had my mother's octagonal pink-tinted glasses on, too.

Great.

She sighed. "Would you like a glass of iced tea, Angel?" Luck-ily, the altruistic impulse to rescue this pathetic refugee she had dis-covered in her bathroom was prevailing.

I took a breath and it came out ragged. Nervously, I folded the washcloth and placed it over the lip of the sink. "I'm so terribly sorry. I don't know what to say. I don't —"

Her voice had become gentle. "Come this way." She led me a few steps into a spacious kitchen, Victor chuckling behind us. I was his afternoon entertainment, I realized. He would be talking about this on the playground for weeks. "Sit down." Victor's mom was the kind of woman who performs well in emergencies, I realized. Maybe she really was a nurse. "And we'll get everything all straightened out."

There was an imitation mission table and chairs in here, just like the furniture in the living room. I pictured her in Ethan Allen with her arms crossed, biting her lower lip, deciding between the classic Hollywood collection and the eclectic *Friends* suite. I took a seat while she opened the refrigerator and found a carton of premade Lipton. She poured it into a blue glass and added a few ice crescents from the freezer. Sitting at the small wooden table on the stiff, uncomfortable chair, I rubbed my temples. At least the headache had mostly — not entirely, but mostly — faded.

Victor stood in the narrow hallway between the kitchen and the living room, rocking back and forth in his oversize Adidas and wearing an equally oversize grin.

His mother turned to him. "You have homework?"

He rolled his eyes. *"Mom."*

"Victor."

Seconds later, I heard those Adidas thumping up the stairs.

"Victor said your name is Angel?" Victor's mom said, turning to face me. She set the glass on the table.

"Yeah." Gratefully, I took a sip and let the coolness flow through my empty body. "And again," I said, "I'm so —"

"You're looking for Jessica."

"Well," I answered, "not really. I mean, I know she's not here. I just wanted —" I thought for a moment. What did I want? "I just wanted to find out something about her."

"Like what?"

"Like anything," I said.

"May I ask why?"

"Jessica is my next-door neighbor."

Victor's mom wrinkled her brow.

"She moved to West Hollywood," I said. "Into my building. But now she's . . . now she's missing."

She put a hand to her mouth, not in a shocked way, but in a slow, measured gesture to let me know she was concerned.

"Just to be sure," I said, reaching into my pocket, "this is the person we're talking about, right?"

When Victor's mom looked at the photograph, she furrowed her brow. "Was she mad at you?"

I looked at the picture . . . the half smile, the half sneer, the middle finger. I didn't answer, saying, "I think she's in trouble," instead.

"What do you mean?"

"Something happened. She . . . she called me, and from the sound of her voice, I could tell she was calling from the dark."

"From the dark? What did she say?"

"She just said my name, and then she was cut off."

Victor's mom narrowed her eyes. "How do you know she was in the dark?"

I remembered how difficult this had been to explain to those cops. "I just know," I said. "It's something I could hear in her voice. I could be mistaken, but I don't think so."

"When was this?"

"Yesterday, in the morning. I called the police, who didn't come until the middle of the night. They went into her apartment, but it just looked like . . . it looked like nothing had happened. I found a couple of envelopes with this address on it, so —"

She brought a hand to her mouth again. "She probably went on a trip, a last-minute thing. I'm sure it's nothing."

I shook my head, then looked up. "She brought me lamb stew."

"That's funny." Victor's mom smiled. "She brought me a pie."

"A pie?"

"When she moved in, Jessica came over with a cherry pie."

I pictured Angela at the door of their house, holding a cherry pie wrapped in a red-checkered cloth.

"Did you ever talk to her?" I asked. "Were you friends?"

Victor's mom thought for a moment. She leaned a wide, pretty hip against the counter and poured herself a glass of iced tea, too. "A couple of times when she first moved in, she came over for coffee."

"And?"

"She just seemed depressed, that's all."

"Depressed?"

Victor's mom shrugged. "Jessica always seemed like such a sad person, you know what I mean?" Her hair fell in front of her face, and she brushed it away.

I waited a few seconds, then said, "Not really." And I couldn't help but wonder why she was talking about her in the past tense.

Victor's mom looked at me. "How well do you know her?"

I went ahead and said it: "She's my girlfriend."

She nodded, but it was the kind of nod that contained doubt, the kind of slight movement of the chin that meant she heard what I said but didn't necessarily believe it.

"After she moved in next door," I told her, "she started coming over. It all happened pretty quickly, I guess, but . . . well, you know how these things go."

Victor's mom made a small *mmm* sound. Then she said, "Is it possible she got a part?"

"What do you mean?"

"Maybe she's shooting a commercial or something. Isn't she an actress?"

I didn't move. "She never mentioned anything like that."

"I don't know if she was ever in anything, but I just assumed . . . you know."

I shook my head. If it hadn't been for that photograph of Angela flipping the bird, I would have believed we were discussing a human being I had never met.

Victor's mom smiled one of those I've-seen-it-all smiles, then took a contemplative swallow, ice rattling in her half-empty glass.

I had been thinking of Angela as a burst of undivided light. But now I found myself picturing light shining through a prism.

An actress? This was a facet of Angela's existence I hadn't even known about, and one I certainly hadn't expected.

It must be a mistake, I thought.

Victor's mom developed an interesting look in her eyes at that moment, something between confusion and awareness, then turned to the counter and gingerly touched her forehead. She seemed about to say something more but then stopped.

Which was fine with me, because I felt a searing bullet enter my brain just then. It rested there, molten. I thought the migraine had faded, but now, unexpectedly, it had returned, reaching a whole new, ecstatic level. I got up and placed the glass in the sink, making a hollow metallic sound that rang through my being like a stone dropped down an empty well, and forced one of those unconvincing smiles onto my aluminum lips. I just wanted to get home, to get out of these clothes and back into my bathrobe. I especially wanted to remove my mother's pink octagonals. I had Angela's real name, at least, which was something to start with, not to mention that mysterious envelope in my pocket. "Sorry that I. . . . that I passed out in your bathroom," I said. "It's just that I have these migraines sometimes, and —"

Victor's mom cut me off with a motherly smile. "You don't have to explain." We had stepped over a line now, it seemed, had reached an impasse. There was nothing more she could tell me, and I could sense that she just wanted me the hell out of her house.

"Did you ever know Jessica by any other name?" I asked at the front door.

She eyed me. "Other than Jessica?"

"I only ask because she told me her name was Angela."

I waited to see if this would provoke a response, but Victor's mom just looked at me. "Why would she say her name was Angela when her name," she said with way too much certainty, "was Jessica?"

———

I remembered another night, a night when that cat was still out there stretching her back on the hood of that old Celica and squealing like a wraith. I remembered standing at the counter and pouring myself another mug of bourbon. It was just the whiskey now, no coffee at all. I had already swallowed a handful of meds, a blue one, two whites, Xanax, Adapin, I didn't care what they were anymore, I wasn't even paying attention, just as long as I avoided Reality. Angela had finished her Stouffer's frozen entrée and had placed the container on one of the stacks of paper beneath my desk.

Watching me from the floor, she sipped her vodka and bit her lip.

"She's still there," I said.

"Who?"

"That fucking cat."

"Is that what that noise is?"

Angela and I had had entire conversations about that cat, but now it seemed she didn't remember.

I took my mug of Jack and sat down next to her. She crawled toward me, pressing her body against mine.

"Why are you here?" she asked out of nowhere.

"Here?"

"This apartment, this crazy place." She waved her hand to indicate my desk, the books, the various drafts of *Los Angeles.* "Shouldn't you be —"

"After I dropped out of college," I said, "it was decided that I should have a place of my own."

"Why did you drop out?"

"Couldn't handle the pressure, apparently."

"What did you study?"

"Physics."

"What happened?"

"I freaked out, according to the authorities." I had never talked about this with anyone before. I don't even think I had ever said it out loud outside of Dr. Silowicz's office. When I recalled that era of my life, it was all textbooks, theories, equations. All I remembered were the things I had studied — the properties of light, stratified media, calculus, Heisenberg, Schrödinger, geometric optics, the compression of light by gravity, the influence of gravity on light in familiar systems, the agency of remote black holes in the deep recesses of space, the recognition of light as a wavelike phenomenon, the creation of an electron interference pattern one electron at a time, the inadequacy of common sense when it confronts quantum events . . .

"Freaked out?"

"I spent some time in a"— I searched for the right word — "*facility,* and then I was given over to the care of my psychiatrist," I confessed. "He thought it would be a good idea for me to move away from my family. He said I needed independence, a life of my own." I shrugged. "I found this place listed in an apartment directory."

"What's to prevent you from . . . freaking out again?"

I gave a little head jerk toward the kitchen, indicating the miniature city of plastic bottles rising like downtown Los Angeles from the counter, and answered, "Medical science."

———

The first thing I needed to do was get the sun out of my eyes. The migraine, though still painful, had become manageable, and since I didn't feel like wearing my mother's pink octagonals during the long drive back to West Hollywood, I made the short trip from Victor's duplex in Santa Monica to Venice Beach. I parked, then went on foot to purchase a new pair of sunglasses, knowing I'd find a pair out here for around five bucks. The sky was a deep blue, with watercolor clouds painted over the sea's hard horizon, and a yellow beach sloping down to the surf. There was a rushing in my ears, the sound of waves, undigitized, nonelectronic, and, to me, odd. It was what most people call a beautiful afternoon, bright and sunny, the kind of day I hate the most.

Walking in the sun, I shielded my eyes and tried to make sense of my conversation with Victor's mom.

I was unable, for the moment at least, to process it.

An actress?

Even though both Victor and his mom had identified Angela in the picture, this Jessica Teagarden person had to be someone else.

The beachfront was lined with people selling T-shirts, hash pipes, sneakers, religion. Luckily I found what I was looking for right away. A pair of black plastic, polarized wraparounds, they were asshole glasses, I knew, the kind that DJ had been wearing at the Velvet Mask, but they were fantastically dark and protected my eyes at the sides as well as the front.

I took Ocean, then Wilshire Boulevard all the way back to Hollywood before turning onto Sunset.

Rush hour, it was slow going, and definitely the long way, but I didn't feel up to the freeway right now and I was still tender from the migraine. Finally, I turned onto Hollywood Boulevard, then San Raphael Crescent, parking Mom's old Cadillac in the rear lot of my building and taking a moment to look around for the cat. I hadn't heard her since early yesterday morning, before dawn, when Angela had disappeared.

Where had she been for the past twenty-four hours, anyway? Had someone taken her in?

I noticed that the old man seemed to have vanished, too. His yard, normally so manicured, so artfully groomed, had become overgrown. The flowers still flourished, radiant blossoms in a rich profusion, especially the hyacinths, but the grass had gone wild and was starting to dry, brown patches forming here and there.

I gave up and went upstairs.

I closed the apartment door behind me and sat on the flokati directly in front of the television. Onscreen was the scene where the replicant named Roy steps into Tyrell's enormous bedchamber with a combined look of reverence and anger. Tyrell explains why he can't extend Roy's life. "To make an alteration in the evolvement of an organic life system," he says, "is fatal. A coding sequence cannot be revised once it has been established."

"Coding sequence," I murmured.

I suddenly remembered the envelope I had found in front of Jessica Teagarden's door in Santa Monica. I pulled it out of my pocket and tore it open, and into my hand fell a huge stack of hundred-dollar bills.

Jesus Christ.

There was a letter, too, a poem of some sort, fragmentary, erratic, printed out on a laser jet in characterless Helvetica:

When you're gone I disappear
When I see you I am resurrected

I wake up thinking of you
Go to bed dreaming of you

Breathe because you breathe
You are the blood in my veins
air in my lungs   taste in my mouth

This is a threat   a promise   a warning

You and I will be together
Picture a new life
We are in a car   I am driving
You are beside me
There is music   pulsating
White clouds in a blue sky
The green earth rolling

In this version we have escaped

I stared at the precise, blocky type and tried to imagine the mind that had composed this letter. I counted, and the bills added up to ten thousand dollars. *Ten thousand dollars.* I had been up far too long now. I was beyond bleary, having graduated to a state of complete derangement, and my stomach was a vacuum.

Someone had been stalking her, I realized. And then I thought of something even worse.

Angela had been kidnapped. This person, whoever had left this bizarre note, had captured her. That's why she had called, I thought.

I got up, slipped my robe on, and made myself a Stouffer's meatloaf with mashed potatoes and brown gravy. I also poured a deep mug of Jack and stared at the blue letter, pacing around and around on the flokati. It had to be one of the men who went to the Velvet Mask. He had developed an obsession.

"Let me give you a lap dance," Angela had said that night.

I shook my head. "You're out of your fucking mind."

"It's a thirty-dollar value."

"I'm gay." The idea of a lap dance in front of other people weirded me out completely, and I was prepared to say anything to get out of it.

She narrowed her eyes. "You are not gay."

"I am so," I retorted childishly, "I am very gay."

"Have you ever had sex with a man?"

"Please —" I shook my head. "Angela, I can't."

"You get a hard-on when I kiss you."

"That's involuntary."

"They're *all* involuntary." Then she laughed softly, saying, "Until you reach the age of sixty, and then you'll do anything to get one, including —"

"I can't" — I shook my head no — "I can't do this."

"Come with me." In the unearthly light of the club, her voice was quiet, smooth, as electric as the bands of neon that wrapped the stage. It intermingled with the sound of the grating, pulsating music and the low, slurred voices of the men who were drunk on the sight of naked women.

Angela tugged at my hand, and I resisted, saying, "Really, Angela, thank you, but —"

She led me into a small dark room with tiny booths and sat me down on a chair, throwing her legs over my lap and wrapping her dark arms around my scrawny white neck.

"Angela," I said, "don't." She had slipped a hand up the front of my shirt, lifting it away from my skin, even pushing her fingers down the front of my pants.

"Angela," she said back, mocking me, *"don't."* She breathed against my neck, her lips soft and warm.

I tried to squirm away, but she wouldn't let me. "There are people," I whispered.

"Of course there are people, you alien. This is Earth."

"People watching."

They weren't, really. It was too dark back here, and there were partitions anyway.

"Let them." Her hand made it all the way into my pants and her cool fingers curled around my penis.

I took an involuntary breath.

She hissed, "I want you to fuck me, Angel."

"But not here," I said, relenting. "Not right here, for Christ's sake."

"Tonight."

"Fine," I said. "But not —"

"You promise?"

I waited in the neon darkness of the Velvet Mask for what seemed like an eternity. It was actually five hours, until two in the morning. I waited while Angela, there known as Cassandra, took the stage in a continuous rotation with the others — Jennifer, Sandy, Tiger, Victoria, Ashley, Katrina, I had learned all of their pseudonyms — waited while she gave intermittent dances to the Japanese salarymen and drugstore clerks, the ad guys on commercial shoots, Midwestern conventioneers, and other assorted assholes, until finally she abandoned her own car and came home with me in the Cadillac.

———

In my parents' old house in Beverly Hills, there was a room that, as far as I know, no one ever entered but me. The walls of this room were lined with shelves, and the shelves were stacked with volumes of books that had been bought all at once, not because they were interesting but because they were decorator items. There was a full set of classics, from *The Scarlet Letter* to *The Short Stories of Ernest Hemingway.* There was the *Compleat Works of William Shakespeare,* of course, *Goethe's Writings,* and, most impressive of all, *The Great Books of Western Civilization,* which included Darwin's *Origin of the Species,* Newton's *Principia Mathematica,* and Immanuel Kant's *Critique of Pure Reason.* There were also two guide volumes, a *Syntopicon,* that came with the set and that led a would-be reader through the complex concepts of these significant works.

On the spine of the first of the two guidebooks were the words *Angel to Love.* On the spine of the second guide book were the words *Man to World.*

For some reason these titles fascinated me.

"Angel to Love," Angela repeated now. She reached across the gray leather interior of the Cadillac and placed a hand on my leg. I couldn't remember doing it, but at some point I must have told her about those books. "That's you," she said, laughing, "you're my *Angel to Love.*"

As a kid, I would actually touch my pink fingers to the gold-leaf lettering on their spines and repeat those titles silently, my blue lips moving. *Angel to Love, Man to World.*

I guess I wanted to be the *Angel to Love.*

But who was the *Man to World?* Could that be me someday? Was he the same person as the *Angel?* Could *World* be a verb like *Love?*

Inside the books was tiny black type that was way too official and grown-up to understand, and by the time I was old enough to actually read something like that, I had realized that these books were only props left over from the set of a movie my father had made and that no one in his right mind would ever actually read them.

Angela and I were currently inside our building, climbing the stairs. She was ahead of me, holding my hand and pulling me up each concrete flight. Now we moved into my apartment and she was slipping her shoes off. "Maybe I should take a shower," I said. I was shaking, the skin of my whole body tight against my skeleton. It was like I was cold, my teeth chattering.

"Come with me." She pulled me into the bedroom. "Come with me, my *Angel to Love.*"

I slept through what remained of the migraine and woke up just as the sun was descending, casting its last light over the western sky. Minutes later, I showered, dressed, and jumped in the Cadillac, making the short trip from Hollywood Boulevard to Sunset. At the Mask, the bouncer sneered and tried to stamp my hand. "What'd I tell you?" he said. "Everybody comes back." It had been two days now since Angela had disappeared, two days in which I had contacted the police, searched her apartment, questioned her old neighbor. In two days, I had virtually run out of options. I knew it was unlikely I'd find her here, but I thought *somebody* had to know *something.*

"I'm looking for Cassandra," I said, giving him my ten dollars. "Is she working tonight?"

He shrugged, peering sarcastically up and down the Sunset Boulevard sidewalk. "You see anyone named Cassandra out here?"

I pushed my new asshole glasses up onto my forehead and entered the darkness.

Inside, laser light refracted through the air, cutting the murky atmosphere and transmuting the faces of patrons and dancers into fanged, leering gargoyles. The music, as before, was dirgelike, molten rock, unrelenting, unvarying, probably ImmanuelKantLern again. It was the same DJ in the booth again. Wearing his huge silver headphones and dark wraparounds, he hovered over the turntables like a demented scientist over an evil experiment. The dancers thrashed in their squalid pools of hazy light as if in slow motion.

On the front stage, a tall woman with dark skin and a platinum wig gyrated crudely, her hips swaying hypnotically, while on the other, a prototypical blonde with long, tapered limbs peeled off her dress. Her eyebrows had been shaved, I noticed, then re-penciled at a contrived angle. The place was crowded with men — men in groups, men alone, men in pairs, men laughing, brooding, glowering . . . I looked around for the waitress who had served me those Pellegrino's the last time and discovered her offering a tray of sodas to a group of agitated, underage boys. "Excuse me," I said, approaching.

She wore the same purple minidress as before, but this time her velvet mask was pulled down. When she observed me through the almond-shaped slits, her eyes were cold.

"Remember me?" I asked.

"Pellegrino, right?" She flashed an icy smile and started to walk away.

"Actually" — I had to shout over the searing music — "I was looking for Angela."

Too quickly she said, "Angela isn't here."

"Do you know where she might be?"

"No," she said, already walking away.

"She's missing."

The waitress stopped and turned around. Across her face glimmered a look of what I hoped was concern, but because of the mask I couldn't be sure.

"I live next door to her," I went on. "She called me, and I could tell that something was wrong." I decided not to mention my theory about human voices and the dark. "And then I lost the connection."

"She hung up on you?"

"No. It just —" I wasn't sure I could explain this. "Was she here last night?"

I grabbed the waitress by the arm, and she looked at my hand as though it were a spider that had jumped on her.

I released her immediately.

"No," the waitress said. "She definitely wasn't here last night."

"The night before?"

She thought for a moment. "I think she might have been here for a while. But I only worked until ten, and we're open on weekdays until two."

"But you saw her? She was here?"

"I don't remember." She leaned toward me. *"Angel,"* she said, hissing my name, "I have to bring you something to drink. I can't just stand around talking like this . . . you know what I mean?" She glanced over to a yellow square of incandescence on the back wall. Inside it were silhouetted figures, and from the way she regarded it, I perceived a threat.

"You don't know what might have happened to her, do you?"

"What might have happened?" She shrugged and gave me that disingenuous smile again. "Maybe she found another client."

"Another what?"

She released a long breath, then turned and walked away.

I was too stunned to stop her this time.

Suddenly, this new thought made me feel even worse.

The ten thousand dollars I had found in front of her duplex . . . Could she have been accepting money from a man? Maybe a regular at the Velvet Mask? Perhaps he had fallen in love with her and she had taken advantage of him, accepting his gifts, and then something had gone wrong and he had become obsessed, so he had kidnapped her and put her in the trunk of his car or had forced her into a closet in his basement or had trapped her into a small dark place so he could keep her as his slave, and then she had called me, finding my number on her cell phone, she had called and said my name, knowing I would come and rescue her, just as I had rescued her in the pool, and then this man had discovered that she had the phone in her possession and took it away and hurt her and now she was waiting for me, desperately waiting for me to save her.

I looked around in a panic.

Behind me I noticed that Buddha, his name was Lester, I remembered, sitting on his stool under the exit sign. He was dressed in the same funereal suit as the last time I had seen him, the same long black coat, the same silvery cravat, and his face, as before, was simultaneously tranquil and scary. "Sorry to bother you," I said, coming closer, "but aren't you Lester?" Even though he wore that gloomy costume, there was something childlike about this guy, almost cherubic. I noticed a red scratch across his face, a scrape from his jaw to his cheekbone that I hadn't seen there the last time. I wondered if he'd had to bounce someone, if there had been a fight.

But Lester didn't respond; he hardly even looked at me.

A hand was tapping on my shoulder and a voice was saying, "He can't hear you."

I turned around.

It was a dancer, the timorously thin blonde with the penciled-on eyebrows who had been onstage when I walked in. Now she wore a sparkling green evening gown that clung grotesquely to her emaciated ribs. Her fake breasts were like half grapefruits that had been fastened to her pectorals. She had matching eye shadow and nails so long they curled under. Right now, one of those lavish nails pointed to her ear, and she yelled over the music, "Lester is deaf."

Deaf? Why hadn't Angela mentioned that to me? "Okay," I said, perplexed. "Maybe you can help me."

"What do you want?"

"I'm looking for a dancer who works here. Her name is Angela — I mean, Cassandra. Do you know her?"

"Cassie!" I was rewarded with a big smile of realization. "Sure, I know her."

"Do you know where she is?"

"No, no. Just, you know . . ." She made a swirling gesture that meant she only knew her from around here.

"When was she here last? Do you remember?"

She shook her head. "The other night, I guess. Monday, maybe Tuesday."

"What do you remember?"

Her face turned to stone. "She was here, she danced, and then she left."

"Did she leave with anyone?" I hesitated before saying, "A client?"

"What do you want to know that for?" She was teasing me like a schoolkid. "Are you her boyfriend?"

"I'm actually her fiancé," I answered seriously. We hadn't talked about that, of course, but I was telling myself now that when I found Angela again, I would never let her go. I would force her to marry me. I would take her away somewhere and keep her safe forever.

The dancer screwed up her face. *"Really?"*

"She called me. I think something may have happened. She said my name and then she was cut off. That was the last I heard of her."

The skinny dancer suddenly became very direct, her voice dropping by an octave and a heretofore absent gleam of intelligence appearing in her eyes. "She left with a guy."

"What guy?" This was him, I thought. This was the guy who was holding her hostage. "Can you describe him?"

She looked at me, then shot a glance at Lester. She obviously didn't want to say anything, or thought she shouldn't for some reason. "Just a guy."

"A white guy? A black guy? What kind of guy?"

This got a laugh. "Not as white as you."

"White, though?"

"White, middle-aged, gray suit, glasses." She made a sweeping motion with her long nails, indicating a table full of men. "They're all pretty much the same, aren't they?"

I looked around. It was true, many of the men in here *were* all the same. At least ten of them fitted that description.

White guy, middle-aged, gray suit, glasses.

I glanced back at Lester. His face was as inexpressive as asphalt. "You don't have any idea where they might have gone?" I asked the dancer.

"Guys like that take you back to their hotel," she said, "and guys like that could be staying anywhere."

"Can you give me an example?"

"The Four Seasons" — she shrugged — "the Mondrian, the Regent, L'Ermitage, Beverly Hilton, Château Marmont." There are a lot of business hotels in Beverly Hills and Hollywood, and she listed almost all of them. "Or maybe his apartment."

"Thanks," I said, then asked, "What's your name?"

She licked her teeth, and the bimbo character reappeared. "Baby," she said.

"I'd like to ask Lester if he saw her. Does he only understand sign language, or —"

"He can read lips," Baby said with a slow grin. "He understands everything we're saying right now."

Lester got up then, as if to prove her point, wearing just the trace of a smirk on his wide, sweet face, and put his hand around the back of my neck, gripping me like a beer can. His movements, which I was seeing for the first time, were graceful and lithe. He glided toward the rear exit, sweeping me along.

"I guess that's his way of saying it's time to go," Baby mocked.

"Why?" I choked. "What did I —"

She threw a quick look over to the phosphorescent square over the DJ booth. "Management," she said. "They don't like people asking questions." There was a more delineated silhouette in the window now, a person's head backlit in yellow, clearly inclining in my direction. The waitress was standing over there, too. She was pretending not to see me, I could tell, but I saw the stiffening of her body, that unmistakable posture of apprehension as I was being escorted to the door.

I threw up my hands. "I'm leaving," I said to Lester. "You don't have to throw me out."

His faint smile grew into a churlish grin. I think his eyes may even have twinkled in the laser reflections. The enormous man walked me the few steps to the rear exit and slammed the door forcefully behind me.

I was outside. The sky was completely dark now, and I stood in a pool of dim illumination that issued from a single bulb hanging over the Mask's rear parking lot. A few dancers were sharing a cigarette out here, and the air was cool, almost chilly.

"Excuse me," I said, "do any of you know a girl named Cassandra?"

They all looked at me blankly.

"Sorry," a blonde with a thick Russian accent finally answered, "you should ask inside."

"Thanks, anyway." I had parked the Cadillac only a few dozen yards away, and I walked to it now. The sound of the heavy music throbbed from within the building, but out here there was only a thin reverberation of some distant unpleasantness. I could smell a syrupiness in the air, too, like flowers blooming. Not hyacinths, I realized, like the blossoms that flourished in the old man's yard. No. This was the smell of lilies, honeysuckle, oleander. Or, it occurred to me, a breeze was carrying the dancers' cheap perfume across the lot.

On the other side of a chain-link fence were the limits of a suburban cul-de-sac, a patch of trees, a row of duplexes, houses, and apartment complexes, a neighborhood that covered all the territory between here and Melrose. The only light was starlight and the artificial glow of that weak incandescent bulb. Nevertheless I pulled my asshole sunglasses down over my eyes and slipped into the driver's seat.

A few slots over, I noticed a black limousine with an ornate gold-lettered logo on the door that said Horace & Geary, which I realized must be Lester's funeral home.

I had to think for a minute.

Why didn't they want me asking about Angela? I understood that men probably came around looking for dancers all the time — jealous men, libidinous men, angry men. It would make sense to throw them off the trail. And the dancers, too, women who were already on the run from something or they wouldn't be strippers to begin with, would be naturally reluctant to answer many questions. It was probably a simple force of habit that made these people reticent. I sat in the car and tried to envision a scenario that made sense. I imagined that Angela had gone back to a hotel with some guy the other night, the white man in a gray suit and glasses that Baby had described. Could it have been the same guy who left her the note?

I looked at the luminous analog clock in the ersatz bird's-eye maple dashboard and saw that it was nearly midnight. Since it was Friday, the Velvet Mask wouldn't be closing until four a.m.

Here is what happened, I told myself, remembering that stupid cop.

Here is what *transpired:*

Angela was being stalked by some crazy anonymous man. He had probably seen her at the Mask and started leaving those obsessive notes on her doorstep. It had become disconcerting, even frightening, and she had been forced to move, which is why she took the crappy apartment next door to mine on San Raphael Crescent, and which is also why that blue note had been left on the doorstep of her place on Orange Blossom — he didn't know she had moved. Unaware that he was her stalker, Angela had probably left the club with him on Wednesday. She had gone to his hotel. She was with him all night, and things had gotten out of control. He held her at gunpoint, put her in the closet or in the trunk of his car, which is when she had called me — just as I was staring out the window looking for that fucking cat.

I glanced up now and saw that the dancers who'd been sharing a cigarette had gone back inside. The door had been left open a crack and was releasing a neon glow and a dull throb of musical chaos from within.

The dashboard clock said it was two-forty-five.

How long had I been sitting here? Had I fallen asleep?

It was obvious what I had to do. I had to find the man in the gray suit.

White, middle-aged, gray hair, glasses — it wasn't much to go on. Half the men in the world match that description.

I started the car, pulled out, and made my way down Sunset.

And then I imagined her voice again, and the way she said my name. The darkness. I could still hear it. I could hear every little particle and wave of fear inside it.

I remembered the morning following the night I had seen her at the Mask. Angela had been standing in my kitchen, naked, her cinnamon-colored belly pressed against the sink. She lifted the miniblinds, and light streamed in, blisteringly white. Outside, the six-in-the-morning sunshine filtered through the waxy leaves of the old man's laurels.

"Can I open this?" she asked.

That cat was mewling out there, too, making those human but inhuman noises.

"No." I was incredulous.

Angela opened it anyway, and caustic illumination burst into the kitchen and into my overly sensitive brain. She even lifted the sash, letting in a sigh of coolness and the only fresh air that had entered the apartment since I had moved in, and with it came the cloying, rich smell of flowers — hyacinths, marigolds, hydrangeas, tulips.

"Do you smell that?"

"Smell what?"

She inhaled. "Flowers."

"They're hyacinths," I said. "The old man is growing them in the next yard." I had seen him out there a million times, tending to his garden, an old duffer in blue coveralls, a spade in his hand. The smell was heavy, yeasty, like summer pollen. Through the leaves of the laurel and the links of a gray metal fence, I could see his whole garden. The old guy spent his days watering and tending, weeding and replanting. At that moment, in fact, the sprinkler weaved back and forth in the stinging morning sunshine. He must have been up early to turn it on.

Angela hurried into my bedroom and was pulling on a pair of my cargo pants before I understood what was happening. She slipped one of my T-shirts over her head, too, pulling it roughly over her fake breasts.

"I want some," she said.

"Some what?" I followed her into the living room.

"Some of those hyacinths."

"Why?"

"I just do."

The door closed behind her.

About a minute later, I looked through the kitchen window and watched Angela stepping gingerly across the parking lot in her bare feet. She reached the fence, which was covered in a tangle of thick green ivy and purple jacarandas, then turned around to glance back at me. She swung her legs over in one swift acrobatic motion, but then the fabric of her pants caught on a piece of chain-link and she landed on the ground of the other side, *hard*. I thought she had been knocked out for a few seconds when she didn't move, and I held my breath until she got up.

She turned back with a flash of bright teeth and a sheepish wave.

"Jesus Christ," I said, knowing she couldn't hear me. "Be careful."

It was difficult to see much after that because I had to make out her form through the dark leaves of the overhanging branches. She was out of sight for a long time, long enough for me to consider putting on some clothes myself and, as much as I despised the light, going out after her. How would I explain this? I started to think the old man might have spotted her and that I would need some kind of justification. She's been drinking, I imagined telling him. It won't happen again.

But then the door of the living room opened and Angela came breezing in, her arms full of blue and white blossoms and her long fake hair plastered to the sides of her head. Somehow she had slipped through the parking lot without my seeing her.

She was drenched from standing under the old man's sprinkler, and my clothes conformed wetly to her body. She was smiling, too, arms full of those large petals of white and blue with heavy green stalks.

I don't know why — I wanted to say something, to tell her how beautiful she was — but I couldn't speak, and my eyes failed. Against the full morning brilliance flooding through the kitchen window, I couldn't see anything at all. I think I had been staring directly into the sun, and now I saw a migraine aura, vague, cloudy with radiance — gorgeous. Later, I knew, I would lean over the toilet and discharge the contents of my stomach in a series of chokes and spasms, but right now, this minute, looking into her face, the only thing I could see for some reason, I felt like I was looking directly into the heart of light. And that sensation, the one that began when I first opened the door to discover her standing there holding that casserole of lamb stew, had transformed, morphing from desire to happiness, and now . . . now this was something else entirely.

———

When I got home, the television was still glowing, *Blade Runner* was still running, Harrison Ford's beleaguered face was still navigating Ridley Scott's futuristic L.A. "More human than human is our motto." I sat down at my desk and thought for a moment, murmuring along with the dialogue, then went back out into the hallway and tried Angela's door again.

It was locked now, for some reason.

But I had to get in there. There had to be something I had missed the last time, some other clue.

I went back into my apartment and opened the cabinet beneath my kitchen sink, finding a hammer and a flat-head screwdriver.

Back in the hallway, I jammed the screwdriver against the lock on Angela's door, then slammed the hammer against it.

The flimsy lock broke easily, and the door popped open with a loud crack.

Quickly, I slipped next door and closed my own apartment door behind me, stashing the tools out of sight.

If anyone came up here, I'd play dumb and pretend I'd heard a mysterious noise.

Gosh, what the heck was that?

But of course no one came. I waited a few more minutes, then went back and entered Angela's living room, flicking on the overhead. It was the same as before: the same blue love seat, the same white rattan chair, the cookbook, gravy stained, resting on the kitchen counter. I went through the apartment methodically this time, trying to find anything, any evidence that might provide an indication of Angela's current whereabouts or the identity of whoever had written that creepy letter.

But I found only meaningless slips of paper, supermarket and drugstore receipts, un-filled-out magazine subscription cards. I searched through the drawers and cabinets in the kitchen, even looking inside that orange casserole dish, now scrubbed and resting in the sink. I lifted the cushions on the blue love seat and slid my hands beneath the upholstery. The couch was brand-new. There was nothing in it, not even dust.

In the bedroom, inside one of those Samsonites, I found a pair of jeans with shiny silver studs around the cuffs. I reached into the pocket and discovered a one-hundred-dollar bill inside it, still crisp. I wondered jealously what Angela had done for this money, then punished myself for being such a judgmental jerk. Or perhaps her stalker had given it to her, the white man in the gray suit. Perhaps there had been other envelopes full of other hundred-dollar bills.

I opened the closet and looked at those three dresses, one black, one green, one peach. They hung there like ghosts of Angela, and for a moment, I imagined taking her out in one of them, going to one of the restaurants my parents used to go to. Then I imagined the looks I would receive, all those eyes on me.

I don't know why, but since I was standing just inside the closet door anyway, I stepped farther in. I used to sit in closets a lot when I was a kid, hiding from the daylight, so maybe it was force of habit, or maybe I was regressing. In any case, the closet was nearly empty, and I simply pulled the door closed behind me.

A sliver of light issued from beneath it, a penetrating band of illumination.

I let my eyes adjust.

Is this what it was like when she called me? I tried to remember her voice. I said my own name, *"Angel?"* whispering it just the way Angela had, paying close attention to the hushed acoustics.

Could she have been in here?

After a few minutes I stepped out of the closet into the light of the bedroom, and as my eyes slowly readjusted to the ceiling fixtures, I saw through into the living room.

At first I couldn't believe it.

There was a man standing in the threshold of the front door. A tentative hand was touching the shattered lock. He wore a gray business suit with a dark tie and white shirt. His face was in shadow, but I could see that he wore glasses.

Glasses.

A white guy in a gray suit.

"Hey," I said, stepping fully out into the light.

Seeing me, the man in gray started, turned around, then slipped back into the hallway.

"Hey!" I shouted after him.

I didn't quite get his face. I had taken too long to react.

I could hear his footsteps, the hard slap of his shoes on the concrete steps.

This was the man Angela left with that night. It had to be. He must have come here and found that the door had been broken, then stepped inside.

"Wait!" I ran into the hall and jumped down entire flights, following the man in gray out to the parking lot. He jumped into an out-of-date white Honda and sped onto San Raphael Crescent, almost knocking over a trash can on the curb. His tires actually squealed on the pavement, leaving parallel smears of black rubber on the pale concrete. I remembered at the last second to look at his license plate, but it was too late, the man in gray was gone.

———

Any movie about serious subject matter is "dark." Any book in which someone dies is "dark." People are said to have "dark" sides.

It is always the "dark" underworld. People descend into the "dark-ness" of depression. Everyone is always going on and on about be-ing afraid of the dark, and darkness itself has become a kind of cultural metaphor for anything frightening or psychologically dis-turbing or even mildly unpleasant. But I have always found the darkness so much more welcoming than the light. The darkness doesn't burn; it doesn't sting your eyes; it doesn't require special lenses or shades. No one builds a shelter to shield himself from the dark. And while we need a certain amount of light to see, we sleep in the comforting dark; most people have sex in the dark; we like to eat in dark restaurants, watch movies in the darkness of the theater. Darkness is more calming, consoling, and much more soothing than the light. When we are truly afraid, we hide our eyes, seeking the protection of darkness. The safest way to hide from an enemy is under cover of darkness. We are born in the darkness of the womb and return at the end of our lives to the darkness of the grave.

For me, the best place to think has never been in the harsh light of day, but in the soothing dark of night.

All of which is to explain why I went back to sit in Angela's closet again.

I needed that darkness, that private muffled feeling of quiet, to experience just a little of what she must have felt when she called.

Whatever Angela had been terrified of, I thought, it wasn't the darkness, it was the menace of some other fear.

In other words, it isn't the darkness we fear — fear is the reason we seek the darkness.

The man in gray.

If that guy really was the man she left the Velvet Mask with, I asked myself, why was he looking for her now? Wouldn't he know where she is? Wouldn't he have been the one who put her in the trunk of his car or stuffed her under his bed?

But perhaps Angela had escaped and now she was hiding from him. Maybe she had hidden herself in a small dark place. I could feel the concatenations of my imagination beginning to overtake my sense of reason. Maybe she was hiding somewhere. I pictured a laundry closet in a hotel, the airless gap between a wall and a curtain, the filthy crawl space beneath a house. Or maybe he had never gotten ahold of her in the first place. Maybe she knew he was after her because of the letters and now she had disappeared, gone into hiding. Bewildering thoughts, glittering ideas, and lunatic theories slashed across my mind's movie screen like the coming attractions before a feature presentation, fragments of scenes, detached lines of dialog, the most unsubstantial suggestions of plotlines, which were portentous, I knew, of so much more than what was real. There in the darkness of her closet, my eyes began to pick up more and more detail. The blade of dim light that came from the crack beneath the door seemed to fan out like the spray of paint from an airbrush.

I forced myself to get out of Angela's closet and step through the chilly fluorescence of the hallway into my own apartment. I went to the kitchen to make myself a pot of coffee, slipping my sandals off and pressing the soles of my feet against the cool linoleum.

Through the slats of the miniblinds I searched around for that cat.

She was gone . . . still gone . . .

Like Angela, that cat was still missing. The sun was rising. The blue numbers on the coffeemaker told me it was half past five in the morning. I knew I couldn't sleep, but I didn't much feel like taking any meds.

I dialed Angela's cell number again, listening to her recorded message. "Hi, it's me," she said happily. "Leave a message, I'll call you back."

"It's me," I said into the phone. "It's Angel." I wanted to tell her that I would find her, that she didn't need to worry, that everything would be all right, but my voice got caught in my throat, and I couldn't make myself say anything else. Finally, I took a mug of black coffee over to my desk and sat down at my computer. I thought it might help to put down the bifurcated tree branches of possibilities, to plot out the potential scenarios using screenwriting software and to determine the best course of action. I must have fallen asleep, though, because several hours later, I found myself in my squeaky chair with my head resting on my arm and my hand prickly with pins and needles. My spine felt like it was made of lead.

Awake, I came to a conclusion.

———

When I was a little kid, my parents arranged to have a birthday party for me at the Four Seasons Hotel. There was a magician, a French clown, an enormous cake in the shape of a *Star Wars* battle cruiser. Practically every movie star's kid in Hollywood was there. This was before anyone knew how shy I could be, before my fears had developed into phobias and I had become a complete embarrassment. Anyway, I had known the party was coming, had even been excited about it, but the day it arrived, I felt only skin-crawling, teeth-chattering terror. I remember freezing up when a little girl walked up to me. She was holding a brightly wrapped package and offering an already famous smile. "Happy birthday, Angel," she said sweetly.

I couldn't respond. For some reason, I couldn't speak at all. I just stared at her, catatonic.

"Are you all right?" She looked around for an adult. "Is he okay?"

I don't know where my mother was at the moment, but Frank grabbed me by the arm and dragged me into the next room. "Listen, you little ghost," he whispered, leaning down, "I will tear those pink eyes out of your goddamned face if you don't go back in there and act like you're having fun." I still remember the grip of his hands on my arms. "Do you realize who that is?"

I shook my head.

"That's Drew *fucking* Barrymore."

Apparently, my father was trying to remake a Shirley Temple movie, and they desperately wanted Drew for the starring role.

Frank Heile.

My whole life, he has been taking me aside like that, threatening violence. He always liked to say he'd break every one of my pale limbs or snap my scrawny pink neck. Honestly, I have never been entirely sure of what he is truly capable of, but let me put it this way — Frank Heile is the character in the movie you discover is actually an escaped Nazi concentration camp guard; when Frank dies, I have always thought, the police will discover a shed full of snuff films; I have always imagined human remains scattered about his lawn, skeletons chained to pipes in his basement, bones poking up through the poured concrete of his swimming pool. This was the man who did my father's dirty work, his Robespierre, his Adolf Eichmann. This was the henchman who protected my father from the lawsuits of the people he stole his ideas from, the man who could destroy a promising acting career with a single phone call. Even my father used to kid about it. "Everyone should have a sociopath like Frank around," he would say. "It's good for business."

He never struck me — Frank never laid a hand on me — but even then, at six years old, I knew that if I wasn't nice to Drew Barrymore, I was going to get it.

"It's Angel Veronchek," I said now. "May I please speak to —"

"One moment, please."

"What is it, Angel?" His voice was hard, and he handled my name like a dirty towel.

I stood in the kitchen, cradling the phone against my ear, and poured myself a cup of room-temperature coffee. "I need your help," I admitted. I didn't much like asking Frank for anything. I didn't much like talking to him at all, was the truth, but I was desperate.

I crushed a number of anti-anxiety pills into the tepid coffee, then drank it down.

"What's the problem?"

His voice made me nervous, and I fingered a full, uneaten bottle of Reality. "I need you to help me find someone."

There was a pause, an impatient breath. Frank was writing something down. Then, "Who do you need to find?"

"It's a girl."

"A girl."

"You can't tell my father about this, all right? If you even mention it —"

"It will be our little secret," Frank said flatly. "Just tell me what kind of girl you're looking for."

"It's not a *kind* of girl, it's a particular girl." I had to breathe deeply to control my temper. Just talking to him made me furious. "A woman."

"Okay."

"Her name is Jessica Teagarden." I had trouble even saying it; her name still sounded so strange to me.

I sensed that he was writing this down, too. "Go on."

"She lives next door to me. Only . . . only . . ."

"Only what?"

"She's a dancer, a stripper. She works at a place called the Velvet Mask. Do you know it? On Sunset Boule —"

"I've driven by it."

All my life I had overheard Frank and my father discussing women as if they were desserts you could order from room service. "I know, you must find girls like her for people, so —"

"I get it, Angel," Frank said with a conspiratorial chuckle. "I just never thought I'd be doing it for you." I heard something in the background, some kind of movement, as though someone were asking him a question. Then he said, "A woman will call you. Her name is Annette. She's kind of a . . . casting director. You tell her everything you want, be as explicit as you like, and she'll set it up. I'll contact her directly and take care of the details."

"How do you know she can find her?"

"Believe me, Angel, Annette will find the girl you're look-ing for."

"Is she an investigator or —"

He laughed. "Don't worry about what she is, all right? Just trust me."

"You'll make sure nothing happens to her, won't you? I'm afraid she might be in some kind of —"

His impatience was increasing. "Nothing will happen."

I wondered if this Annette woman would really be able to find her so easily. But I knew that Frank's power crossed all boundaries, criminal, legal, ethical, personal, that the power of Hollywood is absolute. I decided to trust him. "Thank you, Frank."

There was a pause, and just as I was about to say good-bye, "Your father . . ."

I rolled my eyes. "Oh shit."

This came as a throwaway line, as though it had been over-rehearsed. "He's concerned about you."

"There's nothing to be concerned about."

"Just go and see him." Frank sighed a condescending breath, like he was talking to a child. "He's not a young man anymore. He's slowing down. And Gabriel —"

"Why would you bring *him* into this?"

It was so typical of Frank to bring up Gabriel. I could hear his insincerity through the telephone.

"He's improving, but —"

For some reason, my adopted little brother still wasn't speak-ing. I thought it was autism, *everyone* thought it was autism, but no one had the temerity to use the word in a sentence. "I have to go." I finished my coffee and meds with a hard swallow and already felt its calming effect. "This Annette person, she'll call soon?"

"Go see your father. That's not a request."

I couldn't take it anymore, so I hung up.

And just then I noticed a blinking number on the answering machine. One. One. One. One. The phone must have rung while I was asleep. Jesus Christ. How could I have missed that?

I pressed the button, hoping desperately it was Angela.

"Angel," a shaky old man's voice quavered through the little speaker, "this is Dr. Silowicz. You missed your scheduled appointment again, and I was just wondering if everything's . . . well, if everything's quite all right."

Silowicz.

I wanted to say that nothing was quite all right, you old fucker. Nothing has ever been quite all right in my entire life, and now it is much less quite all right than it has ever been.

But I didn't.

Instead, I called and asked if I could come and see him right away.

———

A relatively simple experiment, one I had even done several times before, it involved mixing two or three chemicals in a solution, then heating the solution in a test tube over the burner. I had found an old fountain pen in my father's desk and planned to fill its bladder with the resulting liquid. The idea was that you could write with it, and the blue, seemingly normal ink would stay visible for approximately ten minutes before it would fade away, right before your eyes. All you had to do if you wanted the now-invisible ink to become visible again was soak a ball of cotton in lemon juice and brush it lightly over the page.

I had the idea that I would write a secret journal, telling the absolute truth in disappearing words.

This was the summer before fifth grade, the year I started going to the Vancouver School. I had already spent all of July and most of August in the basement of my parents' house, playing with my Junior Genius chemistry sets. I wore a lab coat and protective goggles, and painstakingly illustrated my pointless experiments in a spiral notebook. The basement had originally been intended as a family entertainment area, a rec room with a big console television, stacks of board games, a Ping Pong table. But since no one ever went down there, I had turned it into my private laboratory, using the Ping Pong table as my work surface and the Atari game as the only source of light.

A blistering summer day, I remember, poisonously bright, and my father, as always, was shooting something or getting something into production or meeting with movie stars. Mom was out shopping or doing lunch or having plastic surgery.

As usual, I had been left alone.

I got bored with the disappearing ink experiment, however, and thought it might be interesting to add something unexpected to the solution. I reached for a random chemical. I had a large collection of plastic bottles assembled from several different chemistry sets I had received over the years, including a bewildering German set my mother's brother had sent from Switzerland. I don't remember what I put in there exactly, just that it was a crystalline white powder.

The solution, which was light blue, foamed for a moment, then settled, having become clear.

Fascinating.

Now I had to try another one.

This was something I used to do a lot of when I was a kid, adding random chemicals to a solution, heating it up just to see what would happen, and marking down the results. I don't think I had grasped the point of science yet, that you have to know exactly what you're doing, that you need an *objective*. This time I added something blue — it was cobalt, probably — to see if I could get that inky color to come back. But it wouldn't blend, the new chemical just settled on the bottom of the test tube. So I put a little rubber cap on it and held it over the flame of the burner with a pair of metal clamps, thinking it would melt.

Dr. Silowicz and I have spent hours discussing my lifelong interest in science. He always says it represents my desire for control. I've always held that it has to do with my fascination with the mysterious. Anyway, I kept the test tube over the burner too long, watching the solution inside it boil and rise, and I shouldn't have put the rubber cap on it, either, because the gas created by the heat of the flame expanded and the hot chemical solution exploded.

There was a huge noise, of course, a terrific *pop,* and then the sound of shattering, minuscule shards of glass and disappearing ink flying all over the rec room.

Luckily, I had been wearing my protective goggles and long-sleeved lab coat, like a responsible junior laboratory technician.

"Angel!" It was Annabelle again. Our housekeeper came rushing downstairs and pulled me away from the flame of the burner. After the tanning incident, the poor thing lived in dire fear of my burning myself. She was examining me all over, pulling off my lenses and brushing the tiny particles of glass from my lab coat and hair.

But I was laughing. "I'm fine, Annabelle. I'm all right. It's all right."

I looked around, expecting to see splatters of blue ink on the walls and ceiling and furniture.

But there was nothing, not a speck. Only tiny pieces of glass scattered across the Ping Pong table and the floor.

"I will clean," Annabelle said, turning around.

"No, no," I told her. "Annabelle, please, it was my fault. I'll clean up, okay?"

She eyed me for a moment, looking at me in a way that was both wary and affectionate, then left me alone.

I went around collecting the tiny shards of glass, scooping the minute particles into my hands. I cut myself, I remember, closing my fist too hard on a handful of slivers, and the chemicals stung the wound.

Then I blew out the burner and took a last look around.

Amazingly, there were no blue dots on the walls or furniture. Whatever I had added to the solution must have diluted whatever had made the ink blue to begin with, I thought. I put the chemicals aside and spent the rest of the afternoon in my bedroom, hoping Annabelle wouldn't mention the incident to my parents.

The evening passed. Night came.

I was nearly asleep when I heard my father's voice. Something shrill was forming there, something angry and foreign. My father's voice cuts through walls. It also cuts through skin, through human beings, through souls. I could also tell by its direction that he was in the rec room.

I heard my mother try to calm him down.

"Angel, goddamn it," my father bellowed, *"get down here!"*

I pretended that I didn't hear him, that I was asleep.

Then I heard him coming up the stairs, heavy-footed. I thought I could even hear his nostrils flaring.

The door burst open. The harsh hallway light gushed into the room like blood from a wound.

"Get the hell down in that basement and explain this."

I sat up, rubbing my eyes, pretending not to know what was going on.

"Now, Angel!"

My mother appeared behind him, saying, "Stop yelling." She came to the edge of my bed and sat down, putting a cool hand on my forehead. "What happened, sweetheart?" she asked. "Can you tell us what happened downstairs?"

This is the way it usually was with my parents: Milos yelling, Monique defending.

I looked at them both, one after the other. I was just about to say something, when Dad walked over to the bed, grabbed me by the collar of my pajamas, and dragged me out of the room.

"Milos," my mother said, "you're hurting him."

He dragged me all the way down the stairs, where I looked around, astonished.

Cobalt, and azure, and cerulean, and sapphire. And turquoise, teal, aquamarine, indigo, midnight. And peacock, robin's egg, steel, beryl, cyan . . . blue, blue, blue, blue, blue, blue . . . blue like Angela's eyes were the first time I had seen her . . . blue dots everywhere . . . on the walls, the ceiling, the furniture, the floor.

The entire room had been polka-dotted, stippled, dabbed, speckled, and dappled . . . vivid blue dots covering everything.

"They appeared," I said, amazed. "The color . . . it finally appeared."

Blue, blue, blue, blue, and blue.

Blue.

"Out of nowhere?"

"There was an explosion," I confessed. "Only they weren't here before. These dots . . . they were invisible."

"We'll repaint it," my mother was saying. "What is the big problem?"

"You shouldn't leave him alone." My father had gotten the anger out of his system, it seemed, and now marveled along with me at this inverse universe of stars.

I noted the chemicals I had used. They were sitting on the shelf, all grouped together like a bunch of delinquents in a 7-Eleven parking lot.

My mother looked at my father. "Are you through, Milos?"

"Monique —" He seemed about to say something more but then just turned and walked out.

My mother came over and put her arms around me, saying, "Don't you worry, little prince."

———

But in the middle of the night, I crept out of bed and snuck downstairs in my pajamas to wonder once again at the blue dots.

Without thinking, without even considering what I was doing, I quietly collected the chemicals I had used and brought them into the kitchen. I poured them all in a pan and warmed them over the stove. The smell was sulfuric and bitter, I remember, like burning plastic. I poured the clear contents of the pan into a large glass bowl and let the solution cool on the counter. I waited until I could comfortably place a finger in the liquid, then used a dishrag to soak up as much of it as I could.

I must have been half-dreaming.

I took off my pajamas, stripping naked in the middle of the kitchen, and applied the warm, soaked rag to my skin, first to my chest, then to my legs, then to my arms, even covering my neck and face and hair. I soaked up every last drop of the chemical solution with the wet rag and smeared it evenly over my white, pigment-free skin. I had the idea that if this solution could act as an appearing agent for the disappearing ink, it could do the same for the dormant chemicals in my skin. The melanin in my epidermal tissue would be activated somehow, I thought, brought to life.

It seemed logical at the time.

I stood there, waiting to become normal, waiting to develop skin tone.

"It seems he has created a stain of some kind," the doctor said the next day. My mother had discovered me in bed, wrapped in blue stained sheets. "It doesn't seem to be toxic"— he chuckled — "although obviously it's not washing off." She had rushed me to the emergency room.

"Is he going to stay that way?" I remember the warble of panic in her voice.

"It will wear off eventually." The doctor was smiling, amused. "It might take a week or two, it's hard to say."

My mother put her hands on her hips. "He looks like a Smurf."

I had only wanted my skin to have some color. I had only wanted to activate the melanin that I knew lay hidden inside it.

The doctor, a handsome blond man who looked like a news anchor, pushed himself around the room in an office chair on little wheels. He had examined me, asking if it hurt anywhere, if it stung. I had told him exactly what chemicals I had used, and he had decided that none of them were very dangerous. "I think the important thing to find out right now," the handsome doctor said, "is why Angel would want to do this." He looked at me intently, a smile across his movie-star features.

"Why, Angel?" my mother asked. *"Why?"*

I couldn't answer. My embarrassment prevented the use of my voice, and the light of the emergency room was far too bright to speak in.

My mother always responded to handsome men. "I don't know

what to do with him anymore," she said in a heavier than usual French accent, dabbing at her eye with a tissue. "He's so strange."

————

She kept me inside more than ever for the rest of that summer, making sure no one saw my insanely blue skin. She confiscated my chemistry sets and arranged to have a psychiatrist come to the house twice a week.

His name, of course, was Dr. Silowicz.

He wrinkled his brow, I remember, and asked a series of questions aimed at eliciting a particular response, one I felt I never got right, even though he told me there were no wrong answers. He also told me about the Vancouver School. He described the classes, the other kids, the snowy Canadian winters, even the private dorm rooms and the teak Scandinavian furniture.

And when I got there, I remember thinking he had described everything so accurately — everything, of course, but the bars on the windows.

The Vancouver School still seems like a dream, a hallucination that lasted years. It wasn't a peaceful fantasy, unfortunately. It was more of a confusing illusion, where classes led to encounter groups and psychological analysis led to calisthenics. There was art therapy. There was behavioral conditioning. There was psycho-aural stimulation, where we had to wear a blindfold and headphones for hours and listen to strange atonal symphonies. There was regression therapy, where we were encouraged to discover in the roots of our psyches the elemental, prehistoric urges inside ourselves. The staff filled our days and evenings with so much activity that the nights were all we had for privacy. In the late hours, the dorm came to life. There was a secret communication system that had been developed among the kids, a way to speak in knocks and coughs and whistles and little flashlights that glimmered Morse code–like under doors and through keyholes. That's probably how I became nocturnal in the first place. That's probably where I learned to appreciate a nighttime existence, lying awake in the small hours, eavesdropping on those covert conversations. We were allowed a single phone call home every week, which, for even the most stoic among us, was spent sobbing, pleading with our parents to take us back. The Vancouver School philosophy held that rigorous independence must be maintained and that too much parental contact was an indulgence that would only hamper our psychosocial development.

Mostly I remember the view from the window, the wintry Canadian landscape, a prospect of ice and snow, the nothing that wasn't there and the nothing that was. There were weeks-long stretches of time when no one would go outside at all. And at night I would kneel on my bed and look out at the barren moonlit meadow that reached all the way to a patch of frozen trees and an artfully concealed fence. I used to consider schemes of escape, foolproof plans that were always discarded, ultimately, because, once beyond that outlying meadow, freezing to death, like the rich improvement of our young minds guaranteed in the brochure, was a certainty.

There were plenty of other students at the Vancouver School, kids from all over the world, the freak children of the superwealthy. The illusion was that we were crazy geniuses, troubled prodigies who needed a secluded environment to thrive in. The truth was that we were the neurotic children of rich people, of parents who didn't want to be bothered and who believed that money could rescue their kids from whatever blue oblivion they were sliding into.

————

Usually when I visited Dr. Silowicz, I was like a talking machine that couldn't turn itself off. But today, for some reason, I was quiet; today I just lay on the Freud couch and stared at the cracks in his plaster ceiling, trying to find the words to describe what was happening to me, trying but failing.

His office was in the sunroom of his house, an old hacienda-style dwelling on the outskirts of Beverly Hills. When I came over, he always turned down the blinds to darken the room, leaving a single incandescent lamp glowing over his Eames recliner so he could see to scratch out his notes. I had been coming once a week for almost as long as I could remember. I saw him every summer when I came home from the Vancouver School and all through my one and a half years of college, and ever since, I had been seeing him regularly, sometimes as often as three times a week. "How are you feeling today, Angel?" the old guy asked after a prolonged silence. "What have you been up to?"

He was an ancient Freudian analyst, a believer in the talking cure and a doctor who had never once, I'm certain, pronounced a single one of his patients cured. He sat in his modernist leather chair in the corner, his feet propped on the ottoman, a yellow notepad resting on his tweedy lap. His body appeared crumpled, like a discarded paper bag. Silowicz shaved his face but always missed a few patches, leaving stubbly white hairs poking out here and there. He had been old when I was in the fifth grade; he was ancient now.

"I met someone." I hadn't told him about Angela. I hadn't seen him since I'd met her all those weeks ago. I had just kept canceling, one week after another, unable to make myself go anywhere for fear of missing Angela even for an hour.

Silowicz stiffened, interested. "You met someone, you say?" His voice was crackly, wheezy.

"A few weeks ago." I was lying on the couch, my head protected from the germs of other patients by a white paper towel. "That's why I haven't been in to see you."

"What kind of a someone?"

"A woman. She was my neighbor."

"Tell me about her." There was excitement in his voice. "I mean, if you don't mind." He cleared his throat. He was shocked, I think, but didn't want to interrupt me.

"She's been coming over to my apartment every night." I touched my face, drawing an imaginary outline across my features, caressing the bridge of my nose with my fingertips. "And then she called me."

I let some silence pass so Dr. Silowicz would know it was okay to speak.

"This, uh . . . this is upsetting you?"

I looked over. "What do you mean?"

"You're crying."

I touched my cheeks and felt something wet. *"Shit,"* I said.

"Fuck." I reached behind my head for the paper towel and wiped my eyes with it.

Dr. Silowicz handed me a box of Kleenex.

It wasn't the first time I had cried in his office. I had shed enough tears in here to irrigate the Valley.

"Continue," he said, "if you don't mind. What happened when she called you?"

"She called from the dark," I went on. "I could hear it in her voice. She was inside the trunk of a car, or a closet, or some kind of box, maybe a Dumpster. Or maybe something worse. I could hear it. I could hear the darkness in her voice." I turned to look at him, but he gave me nothing. This thought suddenly jumped into my head. "Or maybe a cage."

"What did she say?" He cleared his throat. "When she called, what did she —"

"She said my name."

"Your name?"

"Yes."

"Your full name?"

"My first name."

"I see." He cleared his throat. "She said 'Angel.' What else?"

"Nothing else," I said. "There was nothing else."

"She hung up?"

"The connection was lost. There was a click."

"A click. I understand."

"So I called the police."

"The police?" I could hear the leather of the Eames chair squeaking as he leaned forward. "You called the police?"

I took as much air into my lungs as I could and then, as I exhaled, said, "I'll be needing something powerful for this, Dr. Silowicz. I think I'll be needing something —"

"Can you describe her?"

"Describe her?"

I described Angela as precisely as possible: the way her eyes kept changing colors, the long, thin limbs, the color of her skin, the way it glowed from all that sparkly lotion. I tried to press into words what Angela was like, trying to make Dr. Silowicz see her image, her presence in a room, the way she smelled like cigarettes and flowers and spices and sweat. I wanted him to understand the way her focus centered on an object, wanting it but not caring, desiring it and then giving it away in the very same instant. I even showed him the picture, the blurry photograph I had taken of Angela making that obscene gesture with her middle finger. I kept trying to press her into words, but the whole description was interrupted by wheezing, tubercular sobs.

"Her name," he said after a while. "Angela. It's the female version of your name, isn't it?"

"Her real name is Jessica," I said, "Jessica Teagarden." I had been about to tell him about the letter and the ten thousand dollars, but then I decided against it, thinking it would only confuse things.

"You say she's a dancer?"

"Just for a while," I said defensively. "Just until she gets it together. She has a lot of other prospects, a lot of other . . ."

"Go on."

"I asked Frank to help me find her," I said. "He's got a casting director on it."

"I'm sure she'll turn up," Silowicz said. "If anyone can find her, Frank can."

"I'm going to marry her," I blurted. "When I find her, I'm going to ask her to marry me."

There was a pause as my psychiatrist considered this new chapter in my mental disintegration. I could hear his pen scratching something on his yellow pad — he was trying desperately to get it all down. He usually wrote nothing, but today Silowicz was transcribing every word. "What would you think," he said cautiously, "about spending some time . . . about taking a break?"

"What are you talking about?"

"Going somewhere, you know, where you can get some rest?"

"Why the hell would I want to rest? Rest from what?"

"It's just an idea."

I blew my nose.

"Do you think you might want to talk about your mother today?"

"No."

"What about . . . what about the monster?"

I sighed.

The monster. This was something Silowicz and I had spent hours discussing. When I was a little kid, I must have been around four or five years old, I used to have these nightmares. All kids have nightmares, I know, but mine, I think, were particularly vivid, probably because of all the sci-fi horror movies I had been subjected to at such an early age. Anyway, I used to dream about this monster. Fangs, blood-red devil eyes, lizardy skin, a long tendril of a tail that dragged and flicked whiplike behind him, the monster was something between a demon and a space alien. At night I would lie in bed and listen to him thrashing through the other rooms, making his way through the house. I could hear him destroying the furniture, crashing through the walls and doors. I could hear my mother screaming as he viciously ripped out her throat. Four, five years old, and I was certain there was a bloody crime scene down the hall, my mother's mangled body in shreds on her seafoam carpet, her neck torn open and her mouth agape.

I never saw the monster directly, but sometimes he would come into my room at night and stand over me, drooling and respiring. I was never able to open my eyes and would lie there trying not to breathe, listening to him hover at the threshold of the door.

Later, when I got older, I asked my mother. "I thought there was a monster," I said. "What was it?"

"You used to call me in the middle of the night and say it was in your room." She laughed. "I told you he wasn't real, that you were only imagining, having bad dreams." She brushed the hair away from my face. "You argued with me."

Dr. Silowicz had been trying for the past several sessions to get me to recover this memory. He thought the monster represented something important. The idea of an intruder, he told me, was indicative.

"Indicative of what?" I had asked.

"Of a feeling of being violated perhaps." Silowicz always had everything all figured out. "Of insecurity. Perhaps if we locate the true source of this insecurity, you may learn to feel more confident now, at this stage in your life." Whenever he made a point, he read-justed his skinny old-man legs on his swiveling ottoman. "What else do you remember of this . . . of this monster?"

"Just the way he would destroy the house, coming up the stairs after Mom, his claws scratching on the walls."

"And what would he do to her?"

"He destroyed her, too. He mangled her."

"How?"

"I don't know. I could hear it. I could hear him tearing her face apart. I always imagined he was at her throat with his claws and his fangs."

"At her throat? Like a werewolf?"

"I guess so."

"He tore her face apart, you say?"

"Yes."

"It was around this time that she had her first plastic surgery, isn't that true?"

It was. "I guess so."

"And when he came into your room?"

"He would stand in the door and watch me."

"Why do you think he spared you?"

"Because I didn't move."

"You believed that if you didn't move, he wouldn't eat you?"

"I guess maybe I thought he couldn't see me." I shrugged. "Fuck. I don't know. I was just a little kid."

"And where was your father when this monster came?"

"A good question."

"A monster," I remember telling my mother. "Standing there."

I pointed to the corner of the room. "And he tore your face off. He went into your room, and —"

"A dream," my mother said through her newly taut skin, her cool hand on my forehead. "A bad dream, my little prince."

———

But today I didn't feel like talking about that stupid monster. Today I wanted to sit there and cry pathetically about Angela. I had the idea that if I cried enough, I might eventually get it all out.

"You really felt something for her," Dr. Silowicz whispered after a while, "for this . . . Angela."

"She might be dead," I told him. "It's like you're not even listening. It's like you're —"

"I'm going to give you something."

"For you not listening to me?"

He cleared his dry old-man throat. It sounded like someone crushing a handful of dry leaves. "For grief."

———

If I had ever taken Hapistat before, I couldn't remember, though it seems that over the years, I've taken pretty much everything at one time or another. Right now I sat in my mother's Cadillac in the parking lot of the pharmacy and examined the bottle. "Common side effects," it said, "include dry mouth, constipation, blurry vision, difficulty urinating, increased sensitivity to the sun, dizziness after standing up quickly, weight gain, sleepiness, increased sweating, confusion, agitation, and nausea."

I read a particular phrase again: "increased sensitivity to the sun."

Fucking terrific.

But as long as it didn't impair my memory, it was fine with me.

It indicated one every eight hours.

Naturally, I took four. I had decided that Frank would find Angela, anyway, so I was free to overmedicate again.

They were dry, bitter, round pills that dragged slowly down my throat, getting caught against the sides of my dehydrated esophagus.

But I drove home feeling the immediate effects of the drug like a vine of relief creeping through my body, the tendrils of emotional redress threading themselves around my veins and weaving their way through my circulatory system.

The closest thing in memory to this sensation was the moment I saw Angela in the Velvet Mask.

Hapistat.

Happy, happy Hapistat.

My vision became blurry, and by the time I arrived at my apartment building, I was pretty sure I shouldn't be driving anymore. Truthfully, I even had trouble removing the key from the ignition. For some reason — I guess because I was under the influence — I started looking around for that stupid cat. Where the fuck had she gone? I tried to remember the last time I had heard her mewling out here. It was strange, but Angela and the cat had disappeared around the same time, maybe even at the same moment. I hadn't seen the old man out here in quite a while, either, come to think of it. I leaned over the back fence, the one Angela had climbed over to steal the hyacinths, and tried to see if I could find her in the flower beds.

Marigolds, tulips, gardenias, pansies.

But no cat.

I knelt down on the pavement and looked under all the SUVs and sedans. Far away, under a beat-up old Mustang convertible that never seemed to move from the same spot, was a cat-size lump.

Maybe that was her.

I got up and walked over to it, thinking she might be sleeping.

I knelt down on the rough, oil-stained concrete and lowered my head.

It was the cat, all right. Her body had been mangled, and her rear legs were twisted into an impossible position, even for a quadruped. She had been hit by a car coming through the lot, obviously, and had dragged herself under this old Mustang to die.

I think I would have cried again if it weren't for the Hapistat.

Anyway, I couldn't just leave her lying on the pavement.

I scrounged around for an empty plastic bag in a garbage can and then went back to the Mustang, dragging the cat out from under it by the tail. I didn't much like touching her. She was probably covered in fleas and currently, I imagined, insects of a more macabre variety. I slid her broken remains into the plastic Vons bag and, standing, wondered what the hell I should do with her. I couldn't just throw her in the garbage. I looked across the chain-link fence of the parking lot to the old man's yard next door. It had become overgrown in recent weeks, the flowers and grass a rich profusion. The old man had gone away, it seemed. Or maybe he had died. Or perhaps he had just lost interest and was sitting inside watching TV.

It must have been the Hapistat, because I found myself a few seconds later flinging the supermarket bag with the dead cat inside it over the fence and following it myself, climbing as quickly as possible, where I found myself in a universe of magic and wonder, with pixies flying through the air and fairies dancing a joyous welcome about my ankles . . .

Not really.

Really I found myself digging a shallow grave for a dead cat with a spade I had found leaning against the shed. I slipped her out of the plastic bag so she would properly decompose, covered her remains with dirt, and tried to make the surface look the same way it had before. I was like a character in a bad mystery movie burying a body in a shallow grave.

Finished, I placed the spade against the wall where I had found it and slipped back over the fence into the parking lot.

Thankfully, no one noticed me.

Ashes to ashes, dust to dust, I thought.

I am the resurrection and the life.

Upstairs, I poured myself a ridiculously deep mug of bourbon and started off with one long swallow, hoping to dissolve any of the remaining Hapistat from the sides of my throat and any remaining memories of that cat from my brain. I washed my hands thoroughly in scalding water, scrubbing my fingers like a surgeon, then slipped out of my clothes and into my ratty old bathrobe.

I sat on the floor in front of *Blade Runner,* catching the opening. The darks and lights of Ridley Scott's futuristic vision glowed through a brown smear of murky smog. It was a vision that had grown outmoded, amazingly, one of those cases where the actual reality had surpassed the prediction. Onscreen, fireworks exploded sadly in the faraway distance. A floating electronic banner advertised life on the off-world colonies. I must have been hungry, because I suddenly remembered that lamb stew. I thought of the Stouffer's chicken with mushroom gravy and wild rice dinner entrée Angela had eaten that first night she was here and of how we had talked for hours.

"Mom?" I said.

"Angel?"

I had called her, I guess, and was now lying on the fuzzy black wool of the flokati with the telephone pressed to my ear.

"Oh, sweetheart," she said, "what's wrong?" I hadn't heard her voice in so long.

"How are you, Mom? How have you been?"

"I bought the most beautiful things," she said. "Margaret and I went to Fred Segal, and they have the most beautiful —"

"I fell in love, Mom." I was just trying it, just saying it to see if it registered.

"— dresses, and they have the most exquisite set of luggage, with pony hair and apricot-colored handles, tortoiseshell, I think —"

"I fell in love with a girl," I said. "But then she left me."

"Sweetheart?" she said. My mother had the thrilling, musical voice of an old movie star. "Darling? My little prince?"

"Yes?"

"Will you come see me?"

I pictured her face the last time I had seen her. My mother had undergone so much plastic surgery over the years that I believed she might actually have become a replicant. Onscreen, Rick Deckard floated through the futuristic Los Angeles in his hover car. I lay among the dead and drying stalks of hyacinths Angela had strewn everywhere and put the phone on my chest and felt my mother's voice speaking into my body.

"Would you like to go to your grandmother's?" she was saying. "To Switzerland?"

"Mom?"

"We could stay for as long as you want. Zurich is so beautiful this time of year. There's no snow at all."

"Come on, Mom."

"We could go shopping. You could help me find a necklace, Angel, my Angel, my sweet, sweet Angel . . ."

"I told you I was in love, Mom."

"I know. An Angel to Love, you're my —"

"But then she disappeared," I said. "She said my name and then she disappeared . . ."

I don't remember how our conversation ended, or even saying good-bye, only that I slipped into a dream. I was living on one of the off-world colonies from *Blade Runner*. There was an open desert in a vast, permanently lit landscape and a sky in which twin suns whirled slowly in elegant figure eights. I encountered thousands of people like me, beings with skin so white they looked like marble statues. Moving stiffly, rigidly, as though in a trance, their white, naked bodies glided past in elegant columns. I approached one of those beings and lifted my hand to touch its mouth. And when I did, his face fell open, revealing the diodes and wires and servos beneath.

And I woke up coughing, imagining a mouthful of orange dust.

I rose from the floor slowly, like one of the marble characters from my nightmare, went to the bathroom for a shower, then brushed my teeth until I spat blood.

My skin felt sensitive and rough. I went back to the kitchen and made myself a pot of coffee and an English muffin. I had to take the muffin out of the freezer, so naturally it didn't cook evenly in the toaster oven. I ate one bite, then threw it into the trash. Disgusting. Something was wrong with the butter, too — it was rancid, having gone bad like everything else in my life. I looked through the miniblinds into the parking lot and remembered Angela stealing those hyacinths. She had left them on the rug, all over the living room floor. They were dead now, had gone bad, too.

Standing at the window . . . this was exactly what I had been doing when the phone rang, I remembered, when she said my name, when she disappeared . . .

In the parking lot below were the usual cars. The afternoon light illuminated the dull asphalt, and the sky, though blue, appeared empty and far away.

The phone rang.

Holy fuck, I thought. It was happening again.

It was happening exactly the same way it had the last time. "Yes?"

"Angel?"

"Speaking."

"Angel . . . this is Annette." A pause. "Frank asked me to call you?"

I breathed. "Oh, Jesus. Did you find her?"

"Of course I found her, dear."

"Did you talk to her?"

"I don't talk to the girls. That's up to you."

"But how . . . how did you —"

"How we find the girls is our business," she sang.

I don't think I have ever felt greater relief.

So I had been wrong, I thought. Angela was fine after all. It had all simply been exaggerated in my overactive imagination; as usual, it had been blown grotesquely out of proportion. Maybe she had been busy, I started to think, and hadn't been able to return my calls. Maybe she had broken her cell phone, which would explain why she wasn't answering it when I called. Maybe she had dropped it the moment she called me. She said my name and the phone slipped out of her hands onto the floor and shattered, and she had meant to call me back to tell me where she had gone but couldn't because my number was programmed into it and she didn't know any other way to reach me.

Crazy, I know — I even knew at the time — lunatic theories.

And the note . . . perhaps she had moved to get away from whoever had written it . . . a stalker, maybe even the man in gray. She was hiding somewhere until the whole thing blew over.

"Here's what you need to do," Annette was saying. I heard the telltale sound of a cigarette being inhaled, something I remember my mother doing on the phone before she quit. It made me think of Angela, too. There was still a half-empty pack of Marlboros on the counter. There were still crushed cigarettes of every kind all over the place — Kools, Salems, Merit Ultra Lights. "I want you to check into the Mondrian no later than seven o'clock. Do you know where that is?"

"Sure," I said, "on Sunset."

"And you don't even have to bring any money because Frank has taken care of everything."

"Good old Frank."

"You shouldn't have any trouble getting in there, but if you do," Annette said, "just call me." She gave me a local number, sucking on her cigarette between the area code and exchange. Annette's voice was smooth and raspy, like a disc jockey on a late-night jazz station. "Most likely, there will be a guy who answers. Just tell him that you're Davidson and that you really need to see Astrid."

"Astrid?" This confused me. "I'm looking for Angela."

"That's just another name, dear. You'll get the girl you want, I promise."

I went to my computer so I could take all of this down. "Anything else?"

"You'll need the code."

"The code," I repeated.

"It's Black Hole Sun."

"What does that mean?"

"I have no idea, sweetie. I think it's a song."

"What happens then?"

"What happens then," Annette said smilingly, "is that Astrid —"

"Angela."

"Right. *Angela* should be over right away. If she can't make it, someone will contact you. But Davidson is one of her best customers, one of the best customers around, actually, and that hotel, and so forth. . . . Trust me, she'll be there with bells on."

"She'll be expecting someone else," I said nervously. "She'll be expecting someone named Davidson."

"What you do when she gets there is up to you." Annette laughed, ignoring my concern. "As far as I know, you're a film-maker looking for a particular type of . . . talent for your next project. I just put people together."

"Of course," I said.

"And tell Frank I said hello."

———

A rectangular blue pool, pillows strewn here and there for the hipsters to lounge on like the nobles of the Roman court, the Sky Bar at the Mondrian had been once upon a time Hollywood's chicest meeting place. But now it was filled with second-rate beautiful people, stars who had lost their sparkle, pornographers, one-hit wonders, commercial directors, and last year's rock stars. The interesting thing about it for me was that no one gave me any strange looks. In my black clothes and wraparound shades, pale skin and metallic hair, I probably struck these people as an interesting affectation, just another deviation in the endless variety of Hollywood jerks. If I was here, I must have a reason for being; I must be *someone.*

The sun was piss yellow, beating down on the smattering of wannabes and onlookers who gloried in the vicious light, beads of sweat forming on their gorgeous foreheads and sensuous lips. I was throbbing with confidence from the handful of Inderols I had swallowed before leaving the apartment, not to mention my firm belief that Frank could take care of anything. I found a seat at the bar and ordered a vodka and orange juice, Angela's drink. Just to taste it reminded me of her, sweet and acidic, cool and warm all at once. Facing the bartender, I shielded my eyes from the reflections that flashed off the array of liquor bottles behind him and basked in my own source of illumination, medical courage, and some liquid courage, too, together forming an artificial yet powerful self-possession.

I would see her, I told myself drunkenly. In a matter of hours I would see Angela again.

When the light finally collapsed, I went upstairs and punched in the number Annette had given me, repeating the code, "Black Hole Sun," and telling the man who answered that my name was Davidson. I didn't know what I would do when she got there, but I was certain that once Angela saw me again, she would explain, that everything would be revealed. I imagined her arms around my shoulders, a rushed, embarrassed apology, her face pressed into the hollow of my collarbone. She would be so happy to see me. She had been afraid to make contact, I told myself, for fear of implicating me in whatever trouble she had gotten herself into. It was all so easy, so simple.

I waited, and at exactly ten o'clock there was a knock.

———

Observe. Hypothesize. Predict. Experiment.

This is the scientific method, by the way, the universally agreed-upon process of discovery designed to prevent our own thoughts and beliefs from influencing our interpretation of the world around us.

I believed, for instance, that Frank Heile could do anything, that his power was absolute and that his knowledge was virtually omniscient. I believed, therefore, that when I heard that knock at the door of my hotel room, I would discover Angela on the other side of it.

I had observed, among other things, that Angela was gone, that she was missing. I had formulated a hypothesis to explain it, that she had probably gone into hiding and was afraid to contact me or go back to our building because she feared that her stalker — the white man in the gray suit, no doubt, or whoever had written that note — would find her again. If this was true, I told myself, she must be taking cover somewhere, most likely in some underworld hideout, where only a person like Annette could find her. And here was the experiment, to see if she would really arrive.

But even as I heard the knock on the door, I could feel the twists and contortions of my logic. Even as I turned the handle, I knew that my desire had overcome my sense of reason. Even as I opened the door, I could plainly imagine a chart outlining the distortions and perversions of my thinking.

In short, my observations were inaccurate, my hypothesis was insane, my prediction was wrong, and my experiment was flawed. I would be, I freely admit, the world's worst scientist.

She was tall like Angela, with long straightened hair like Angela's, but she had a different body type entirely. While Angela was all skeleton, all bone and hair and teeth, this woman was all muscle, meat, and flesh. She was brown-skinned like Angela, too, but much darker, almost purple. She wore a virtual rainbow of makeup, all the way to her brows, of pink, fuchsia, and rose, beneath which were big, round eyes and long, thick lashes. Her lips were dark at the edges, light in the middle, three gradations of red.

"You're not Angela," I informed her.

"You're not Davidson," she said back. She wore a full-length satin skirt, I noticed, the color of red wine, with matching heels and a thin white sweater cut way too low.

"I don't —," I began. "I mean, it's not personal."

"Can I come inside, or are you going to leave me out here in the hall?"

I stepped aside.

"Fucking Frank," I said, looking up at the ceiling. "Fuck, fuck, fuck."

I detected an accent in her voice, the softest lilt, just from the way she said, "I'm starting to get used to people not being Davidson."

"Sometimes it's really him?"

"Sometimes."

West Indian, I thought. It was the way she held a split second too long on the vowels. She walked all the way into the suite and looked around. She was planning her escape route, I imagined, locating the telephone, noting the emergency exit. She probably thought this was some sort of trap. She was smiling, too, a courteous, empty smile, a *welcome-to-Burger-King-how-can-I-help-you* smile.

"I'm Destiny," she said now. "But you can call me Angela if you want to."

"Do you dance at the Velvet Mask?"

"Sometimes."

That was why she was here, I realized. Annette had simply requested the black girl who danced at the Mask. "You don't know a girl named Angela who dances there?"

She shook her head.

"Cassandra?"

"No."

"What about someone named Jessica Teagarden?"

Destiny studied me for a moment, taking me in. "I don't know anyone with a name like that."

"How much are you?"

"Pardon me?"

"How much did Frank pay for this?"

She sat down on the edge of the white couch. They had upgraded me to a suite, I think because they recognized my father's name, and right now we were in the living area, which contained a white couch, a white chair, a white desk, gray walls, light gray carpeting, a film of white sheers covering the night-black windows and through which I could see the faint lights of the city glimmering like slow-motion fireworks. It occurred to me that this room even contained a matching white man, an albino all in black. "All I know is what *I* get," Destiny said after a moment. "I don't ask questions, and I don't know anyone named Frank."

"Fucking Frank," I said.

Through the window, an enormous, building-high advertisement towered over Sunset Boulevard. It was for the new CD by that band, ImmanuelKantLern. The name of the band itself was a portent for our times, I thought. Kant can't learn. He can't teach, either.

Whatever idealism had ever existed in the minds of our most brilliant philosophers has been forever obscured. The name of their new CD was *Jokes On You,* and the members of the group towered over Los Angeles, staring insolently over the flickering city lights.

I wonder what Kant would have said about my reasoning.

Destiny used the slightest movement of her chin to indicate the minibar. "Do you mind if I have a drink?"

Without asking what she wanted, I poured another vodka and orange juice, using a tiny bottle of Absolut and an individual-size Minute Maid. I dropped a handful of ice cubes into her glass, and it sounded like the beginning of a nursery song. "I'm sorry," I said. "You're very . . . you're beautiful. It's just that I was expecting someone else."

When I turned around, Destiny was sitting on the couch just as she had been a moment before, only she had taken off her skirt and top, which she had laid neatly over the arm of the white chair. She wore a bright red thong and three gold chains, one around her neck, one around her ankle, and one around her waist. Her breasts were a half shade lighter than the rest of her, but still fantastically dark. "Whatever it is Angela does for you," she said quietly, "I can do it, too."

"That's not the point."

"Just tell me what it is."

"This was Frank's idea." I handed Destiny the drink. "That you're here, I mean. This is because he thinks it's possible to replace one person with another, like a new actor playing someone else's role." I tried to think of all the sequels Frank and my father had made.

"In tonight's production, the part of Angela," she said, smiling, "will be played by Destiny."

"Exactly."

"I'm a very good actress."

Earlier, I had placed my things on the counter of the kitchenette. Right now, I found the photograph of Angela and held it up for her. "This is Angela. This is who you're supposed to be."

"Hmm," was all she said, taking the picture and placing it on the coffee table. Then, "Why don't you come sit by me? Forget about this other girl, and come over here." Without looking at the glass, she brought her drink to her waxy lips. When she sipped it, her eyes didn't lower at all.

I made myself a vodka and orange juice, too, and sat down next to her, awkwardly holding the drink between my legs.

"What is your name, anyway?"

"Angel," I confessed.

"Angel was expecting Angela?"

"It's just a coincidence."

She shook her head. "I don't believe in coincidences."

"With a name like Destiny," I said, smiling, "I guess you wouldn't."

"I have never seen anyone as white as you, Angel." She looked me over. "Are you an albino?"

I nodded.

She glanced down at her drink. "What did Angela do for you?"

I thought for a second. "She talked.'"

"What did she talk about?" Destiny edged closer.

"Destiny," I said, "that isn't your real name."

"No." She laughed. "Of course it isn't."

"Where are you from?"

"You can hear my accent?" She sighed. "I try to hide it, but I'm not doing a very good job." She let it get thicker. "I'm from Barbados. Have you been there?"

"Maybe when I was little, I think, a million years ago."

"It isn't fair," she said.

"What's that?"

"That you're wearing clothes and I'm not. Do you think that's fair, Angel?"

"I don't really think I should, you know —"

"Why not?"

"You're not the right girl."

It had something to do with all the meds I had been taking, not to mention the drinks I'd had at the bar, not to mention my disappointment at Destiny for not being Angela — or, I should say, at Angela for not being my destiny — but I set my glass on the coffee table and removed my cargo pants and long-sleeved shirt, placing them on a small marble-topped table behind the white couch. Now I wore only a pair of baggy gray boxers.

"She gave me a lap dance," I said, sitting back down, this time closer.

Destiny smiled. "I thought you said she only talked."

"Talking," I said, "was her principal, was her primary —"

Destiny leaned all the way into me and cupped her left hand over the front of my shorts. She put her lips against the skin of my cheek, right next to my ear, and said, "I don't want to hear any more about this girl named Angela." She found my erection beneath the fabric. Angela had done precisely the same thing, I remembered. Do they all do this? "This will be covered," Destiny said, "all right?"

"Covered?" For a second I thought she meant insurance. I imagined forms to fill out in triplicate, envelopes to find stamps for, a bristly haired man in pinstripes offering me a handshake and an expensive pen to sign with.

But then, like a magician producing a coin from the air, Destiny revealed a square of silver with a flourish of her hand, a round shape inside it.

"Oh," I said.

She tore the little packet open and unveiled a blue prophylactic. She tugged with one hand on the elastic of my boxers. "Take these off."

I slipped them off and placed them on top of my other clothes. As usual, I was surprised at my hard-on. What had produced it? The vodka? The memory of Angela? Hormones? She reached forward and placed a hand over my testicles. She used her thumb and forefinger of her other hand to make a circle and then slid the blue condom on, leaning forward and simultaneously taking my now-blue-latex-covered penis into her mouth. She reached up and touched my chest with her sharp, pink fingernails, pushing me back onto the cushions. "Relax," Destiny said, releasing her lips.

Her nails felt like razor blades against my skin, but her mouth was warm and wet even through the latex of the condom. Her hair, black and heavy, fell over my lap and divided into mathematical sections on either side of her pointy spine. I noticed the individual vertebrae standing up through the skin. I thought I'd like to touch each one and reached over to place my fingers against them, imagining the white skeleton of her body. There were hard muscles there, too, tense and flexing, connected by visible tendons.

Destiny opened her mouth and dropped her head all the way down, then pressed against me with her lips and pulled up. After a few repetitions she started making these weird, insincere noises inside her throat, moans and cries that were obviously only for effect. I let my fingers trace the outline of her spine, reaching almost all the way to her waist. I touched her head, holding her when she pulled away, and said, "Can you stop, please? Destiny? Can you stop for just a minute?"

It felt like she was going to pull my dick off.

She sat up halfway. "What's wrong?"

"This isn't what I wanted."

She shook her head. "This is what everyone wants, Angel."

"Not me."

"Did Angela do this for you?"

"Yes," I said, "but —"

"I can't do anything without the condom," she warned me, shaking a finger. "I won't." She had lifted herself up completely now but still had her other hand on me.

"That's not — I mean, that's . . . I'm not even, not even —" I was stammering. "I don't think I even want this."

Destiny looked at my lap, arching an eyebrow. My blue penis was still standing straight up in her hand.

"Do you want to fuck me?" She indicated the bedroom with a quick movement of her eyes.

I *did* want sex, but I wanted it with Angela. I wanted her voice, her warm lips against my ears, the crazy things she told me, all those weird evasions and equivocations, her eyes, whatever color they might happen to be that night. "Can't you just talk to me for a while?" I had been deluding myself again, hadn't I? Living a fantasy instead of paying attention to what was real.

"Talk dirty?"

"Well," I said, "no, not dirty."

"What do you want me to talk about?" She released my blue penis and reached for the drink she had placed on the floor by her feet.

I thought of something. "The sun," I said, "where you're from, the island where you're from, what is it like? Is it bright?"

"The sun?" She took a swallow, ice cubes rattling. "It's very strong, extremely . . . strong."

"What does it feel like," I asked, "against your skin?"

Destiny regarded me. "It feels like . . . like warm honey is being poured over you."

"Describe it." I was looking at her, looking directly into her eyes. They were deep brown, with minuscule flecks of greenish yellow.

"It feels like you are being cooked," she said, grasping the perversity of my request. "It feels like the air is filled with heat, and if you are out in the sun in the middle of the day, especially in the summer, it feels like stinging heat, like it will melt you . . . like you're in the fire." Her voice had become more and more island, curving softly around the vowels. "Like you're inside the oven."

"What color is the sun? I mean, where you're from. What color is it?"

"Orange." She looked around, struggling to find the right words. "Bright, bright, bright, like . . . I don't know, it's so bright."

Red. Orange, I thought. Bright yellow. Burning.

"Do you know what it is?"

"What *what* is?" She had placed her drink on the floor again.

"The sun, what it's composed of."

She didn't answer. She reached for my blue penis again and squeezed it, moving her hand along its length.

"Hydrogen," I informed her. "It's hydrogen burning. And the light," I said, "is a form of electromagnetic radiation. Visible light, the orange and yellow and white light of the sun . . . it's all just part of the same spectrum that contains everything, even us. We're made of light," I went on, "did you know that? And what we are, just depends on the speed at which we're vibrating." I'm not sure where this was coming from, thoughts coursing through my deranged brain and automatically pouring out of my mouth, memories from textbooks and bits and pieces of information I had gleaned in college and from articles in the science page of the *L.A. Times*.

"You are made of light," Destiny said, "aren't you, Angel?"

"Everything in the universe is vibrating," I told her, and she was standing up, leading me by my blue latex penis into the bedroom, "at different speeds." The last time my penis had been blue, I thought, was when I stained myself with the disappearing ink solution in my parents' kitchen. Destiny sat down on the bed and pulled me toward her, taking it into her mouth again. Blue, blue, electric blue. That had been Angela's color, the color of Angela's eyes the first time I had seen her, the color of her aura. "Even matter," I said, "is vibrating. If you look closely enough, matter itself is only movement through time and space."

Destiny leaned back against the bed and pulled me toward her. I could hear her heels dropping onto the floor. She pulled her red thong off, slipping it expertly over her legs in one smooth balletic motion. "In Barbados, when the light touches the waves," she told me, "it looks like broken glass, it looks like the sea is made of diamonds."

I crawled forward onto the bed until we were lying against one another. "That's refraction," I said, "and reflection."

She pulled at my body until I moved on top of her. She opened her legs and guided me. "It's okay," she said. "Just push . . . just push it in." I pressed my eyes closed and pushed my penis into her.

There was resistance at first, a dryness, but then it slid in, all the way inside.

"There was a girl in a restaurant today," Destiny went on, "who was wearing a necklace, all diamonds. They were probably fake, you know, but she was sitting at the bar and kept turning her head." Her voice had become melodic.

"Yes?" I was moving in and out of her to the rhythm of her speech.

"And when she turned her head, the diamonds of her necklace caught the light of the sun." Destiny was guiding me into her, holding my waist in her hands. I felt the sharp hardness of her nails on my skin. I felt the soft insides of her, even through the blue condom, the wet darkness of her body. I kept my eyes closed. I imagined it, the light moving across a necklace, each stone catching a momentary fire. I felt myself, my own body, glowing white. I pictured Angela with that armful of hyacinths. She was soaked in a blinding morning radiance, her hair wet. I stiffened my back involuntarily and leaned into it, into Destiny, but thinking of Angela, only of Angela, pushing my body up on my arms, tilting my face to a brilliant, imaginary sun.

Destiny had a hand on my eyes now, nails touching my eyelids, the skin of my face, my lips. "You can't go out, Angel," she said, "can you?"

"Out?"

"In the light. You can't go out in the light. You'll burn."

"I'll glow," I said. "I'll turn phosphorescent."

She laughed. "You're doing that now."

———

Vapor illumination beamed across Sunset Boulevard from the chemical-yellow street lamps. The temperature had dropped, and the lights of the city had turned unreal. I waited for the car valet in the cooling air. Upstairs, I had abandoned Destiny to the white room, the white sheets, the chatter and clink of the B-list partiers at the Sky Bar below, and to her own destiny, whatever that might be. I felt as if I had stepped out of my body and into another. I was someone else, calm, untroubled, even tranquil. It was the sex, I knew, and it wouldn't last.

In the Cadillac, I drove down Sunset, then over to Hollywood Boulevard, where tourists and drug dealers mingled with shoppers and rock-and-rollers, where kids with rings through their noses and old ladies in oversize sunglasses loitered dementedly through the neon streets.

I couldn't bring myself to go home just now, though, so I kept on driving.

Farther over, on the backstreets of West Hollywood, people shopped for groceries and sex, they drank in bars, living out their Charles Bukowski lives in miniature, everyone a low-level, polite transgressive.

I turned around and drove through Beverly Hills, my old home, where sleek limousines chauffeured hotel guests and movie stars to the see-and-be-seen restaurants like Chaya, the Ivy, and the Palm, places my mother and father had been going for years. In these restaurants, I knew, young men paced importantly back and forth with cell phones pressed to their ears while the starlets who were their dates waited gorgeously, accepting the licentious stares of the less glamorous like nobility receiving the entreaties of the poor.

I drove through downtown, too, where Angela had taken me swimming on the skyscraper rooftop that night — how long ago had it been? only a few weeks now — and saw the inevitable empty streets and avenues, where homeless people pushed overloaded shopping carts through the coarsely shadowed lanes, where gleaming black-and-white police vehicles patrolled ceaselessly, shining flashlights down desolate alleys. I drove around and around, trying to locate the health club she had taken me to that night. But I had been blindfolded when she took me there, and for some reason I couldn't remember leaving.

The sun came up.

I've always liked to watch the morning light drape over the slanted roofs of the ersatz châteaus and phony Tudors of Los Angeles, have always loved the way it falls evenly across the red-tiled verandas of the imitation villas and throws into brilliance the low, boxy structures that are the only honest examples of architecture here and look like nothing at all.

In Beverly Hills, palm trees spear the sidewalks like great cocktail toothpicks, their height exceeded only by the smog-blackened telephone poles and brown, terraced hills in the filmy distance.

Here, even the shadows are pale.

An ostentatious, tacky glow reveals the city's daylight colors of asphalt, tar, desiccated green, and pale, fleshy gray. The streets are wide, but never wide enough. Cars clog the avenues and boulevards. Lights change, but no one moves.

During the early hours, the audacious L.A. sun advances imperceptibly, but still progressing faster than the traffic.

Downtown, the smog is absolute. In the morning a rich gray-brown mist settles thickly at the base of the perpendicular cityscape, thinning gradually as the eye rises skyward. Orange light filters through the desert dust, the exhaust fumes of a million engines rising, the diesel and high-octane vapors expanding through an atmosphere that almost never breathes. Toward the airport, the oil derricks pump the liquid earth, their great heads rising and dropping back to the ground like giant mechanical birds. A blazing disk behind them threatens to send the whole city up in flames.

The freeways twist, curling one under the other.

Off-ramps, merging lanes, and cloverleafs spiral outward and in, doubling back on themselves like Möbius strips. In an all too apt metaphor for my life, a portion of highway soars over a patch of dry grass and suddenly dead-ends over nothing at all.

I kept driving, creeping my way through the morning traffic, going all the way out to the water, turning down Ocean until I arrived in Venice. I parked the car, then walked down to the beach. I slipped off my sandals, rolled up my trousers, and let the entire Pacific crash against my legs.

I dreamed, as I have dreamed all my life, of standing on the beach in the full daylight sun. I imagined myself with normal skin and dark, light-absorbing eyes. I stood just far enough away from the Santa Monica Pier to watch the silhouette of the roller coaster reveal itself against the horizon while the disk of the sun ascended over the brown mountains of Malibu.

I would never find her, I thought. She was slipping farther and farther away. Angela had left the Velvet Mask with a white man in a gray suit, and the following morning, she had called me, desperation shot through her voice, hoping to be rescued.

Victor's mom hadn't been able to help me, and Destiny turned out to be the wrong girl entirely.

I had failed.

Even Frank had failed.

And I didn't have anything left to go on but that twisted note.

I had read it over so many times by now that it was practically committed to memory. *I wake up thinking of you / Go to bed dreaming of you.* Whoever had written it had clearly developed an obsession with Angela and had imagined a real relationship existed between them. *When you're gone I disappear / When I see you I am resurrected.* There was an implied closeness, an understanding, however misbegotten, that she was in love with him, too. But how would I find the author? Was there any clue in the handwriting on the envelope? It was just blocky letters in dark ink, a style anyone can write in. And what about the paper itself? A medium blue, cheap stuff, and available pretty much anywhere, it was actually quite similar to some of the paper I had used a few months before for a recently completed draft of *Los Angeles*.

I tried to remember Angela. I tried to remember more than just her voice on the phone. I pictured her eyes. I imagined the feeling of her nails on my skin. But it was growing faint, the memory itself. Already the memory of Angela was fading.

"Memories," Rick Deckard says in *Blade Runner*. "You're talking about memories."

We never actually forget something, I once read; it just becomes increasingly difficult to find it in our disordered brains. Once a piece of information enters the human mind, it is simply a matter of locating it, a process of retrieval achieved by either *recall* or *recognition*. In recall, events and information are simply reproduced. Try it. Consider the newspaper article you read yesterday, its beginning, middle, and end. Remember fifth grade? The first day, the middle of the year, Christmas break? Recognition, on the other hand, is a matter of seeing something you've already seen before. Oh yeah, you say, I remember that. Go through your high school yearbook and look at the pictures. Remember her? And him? It all comes back. She was nice to you. He broke his arm playing soccer. That's what I needed, I thought: *recognition*. I needed to hear her voice.

———

The same FedEx truck was making its rounds; the same old woman power-walked down the street, arms pumping like pistons, hand weights tightly gripped; the same sprinkler sprinkled; it even seemed like the same kids were playing that same game of Wiffle ball. It could easily have been the same day, the same afternoon, the same everything — everything, of course, but me. When I arrived at Jessica Teagarden's former duplex in Santa Monica, it was all the same as before, but, luckily, I wasn't puking. This time, I had re-membered to wear my asshole shades, and I wasn't trapped in the violent throes of a vicious migraine.

I stopped the Cadillac directly in front of the walk and imme-diately identified Victor's unique, dish-shaped face in the window.

Seconds later the door opened and he was calling my name.

"I need to ask you something," I told him.

There was the same stillness inside, that cool, heavy smell that I recognized this time was lemon furniture polish. I could hear the perpetual sigh of forced air. As usual, the scene had been pre-lit, props set up beforehand by that make-believe lighting crew.

"You want to come upstairs?" Victor asked. "I've got a micro-scope."

"Sure." I followed him up, taking the stairs two at a time, and turned down a little hallway.

He slipped into a miniature, shelf-lined room that contained a neatly made bed jammed into a corner and a tidy desk of white particle board. Above the bed were obsessively organized shelves containing books and science kits; a familiar Junior Genius chem-istry set was displayed prominently above the headboard.

"Yeah." Victor noticed me looking at it. "My mom's afraid some kind of toxic chemical is going to fall in my mouth in the middle of the night."

I laughed.

"But I keep telling her that they're not going to put anything very poisonous in a kid's chemistry set."

"Did you make the disappearing ink?"

"I made it." Victor shrugged. "It was boring." He pulled a kid-size chair away from the desk and sat down.

I took a seat on the edge of his bed. "My mother always thought I would burn up in the sun," I confessed.

"You probably will," he said, turning to look at me. "What did you want to ask me anyway?"

I thought for a moment. "Did you ever overhear anything about Jessica Teagarden? Did you ever hear any conversation your mom had with her, or even about her?"

"Like from when?"

"From any time," I said. "Your mom said she came over for coffee. Do you recall anything about what she said? Were you here? Were you in the house?"

Slowly, Victor moved his tongue around in his mouth, considering the idea like it was a piece of candy. I imagined that his wide, flat face was a satellite, ready to receive the signal. "Yeah," he said tonelessly. "I guess so."

I leaned forward. "I thought you said you can remember everything you hear."

"Sometimes it doesn't just come, you know? It has to" — Victor made a slashing gesture across his face — "start flashing."

"What do you mean?" I asked. "What flashes?"

"I see them, white flashes in my eyes. Like, like . . . headlights at night."

"Is there any way to control it?"

"You can start it sometimes, you know, but it's hard to know what you'll get."

I recalled the way he had stared into the sun the last time I met him, repeating the voice-over from the nature documentary. "You were able to tell me about the gecko," I said, "remember?"

"Yeah, but that's what I was remembering then."

"How does it usually start?"

"If I press down on my eyes," Victor said, "or sometimes when I sit too close to the TV."

I looked around the bedroom. There was probably a chemical in that science kit that would launch Victor into an epileptic fugue, I thought, but I certainly didn't want to chance that.

Then I noticed the lamp on his desk. "What about when you look into a light bulb?" I asked, lifting the shade.

"I don't know." He shrugged. "I don't think I've ever tried that."

I was taking a chance, I knew, but it was all I had. "Stare at it."

"You really want me to?"

"Why not?"

Victor squinted against it, involuntarily closing his eyelids.

"Keep your lids open," I said, "even though it hurts, even if it stings."

He faced the bulb and held his eyelids open with his chubby fingers.

"Are you getting anything?"

He just blinked, and I could see tears welling up.

"Think about Jessica Teagarden, try to picture her face."

He shook his head and looked away. "This is just hurting my eyes."

"Keep looking."

"It burns." He shut his lids.

"Open your eyes."

I suddenly remembered standing in the darkness, wearing that blindfold, right before I opened my own eyes, and seeing the shimmering blue pool on the health club rooftop.

"Keep them open."

Victor stiffened, his whole body going rigid. Then his head twitched, and he said, *"If a short-sighted, mucus-covered messy eater which grows up to three meters long doesn't sound like the ideal diving companion, think again."* Victor's eyes hardened, turning away from the bulb, and he stared straight through me. *"When you understand the moray eel, you may well start to love it, says marine biologist Gavin Anderson . . . in a stunning array of colors, with a slippery mucus-covered body and a head full of glistening white, razor-sharp teeth. At first sight, a moray eel can send shivers down your . . ."*

Victor went on this way for a full five minutes more, repeating the narration about moray eels. He even slipped in a couple of commercials, one about mattress discounts and another about a teeth whitener.

I shook him by the shoulders. "Victor," I said, "I need you to remember Jessica. Try to remember something about Jessica Teagarden."

I needed Angela.

I needed to hear her voice. I knew Victor must have heard her say *something*, but the kid only went on repeating a bland nature documentary, and these memories, however perfectly recalled, were perfectly useless, an exact audiographic recollection that came to nothing, just a purposeless recitation of facts, a trivial collection of data that, at best, only served to take him out of the present and turn him into a drooling imbecile.

I left Victor in his perfectly tidy junior-scientist bedroom, feeling like I was leaving a piece of my own scientific childhood there with him. He was practically catatonic now, spittle running down his chin, repeating those boring things he had heard on television. I had needed him to remember Angela, needed him to repeat her voice, but all he was able to find inside his head were pointless facts about a vicious sea creature.

Memory wasn't helping, I realized. Memory itself had failed.

———

A few minutes later I was driving home. There had to be something I had overlooked, I thought. I still hadn't spoken to any of my neighbors. Maybe someone had a forwarding address; maybe it was that simple; maybe somebody even had Angela's new telephone number. I imagined dialing, the phone ringing, her voice answering. I parked in my usual spot in the parking lot and started looking around for that cat before I recalled that I had buried her in the old man's backyard.

Christ. I was really out of it.

All I wanted was a warm shower, to crawl under the black sheets, and to sleep through this nightmare.

I stepped through the doorway of my apartment and immediately started pulling my clothes off.

I stopped though, my shirt suspended over my head.

To experience fear requires a matter of milliseconds. That's because the emotion comes from the amygdala, the deepest, darkest part of the human brain, and evolutionarily the oldest section of our minds. It controls autonomic processes, too, like breathing and the beating of the heart. Sometimes this reaction is called fight or flight. Adrenaline courses through the bloodstream, blood pressure soars, the heart rate increases. The reaction of fear, it seems to me, can come from one of two main sources: the unknown or, even worse, the known.

In this instance I experienced both.

"I made myself a cup of coffee, Angel," a voice said. "I hope you don't mind."

Frank was sitting at my desk, taking a long last drink from my coffee mug.

I pulled my shirt back down. "Jesus Christ," I said. "You could scare someone half to death doing that."

I noticed someone else in my apartment, too. Standing in the kitchen, a young man in expensive glasses.

Both he and Frank were dressed in what could only be described as Hollywood-entertainment-lawyer clothes. Frank's tie was shiny pink and his suit was chocolate brown, with wide lapels and widely spaced pinstripes. The young guy wore a jacket so black and a shirt so white he was graphic, like a piece of human typography.

"How did you get in here?" I wanted to know.

"You must have left the door unlocked."

"I don't think so." I shook my head. "In fact —"

"It's immaterial." Frank got up, a big man with a deep voice, and my swivel chair squealed in relief. "We're here, aren't we?" He stepped toward me, gripping his hands around my upper arms and digging in with his fingers. He used to grip me like this when I was a kid, too, I remembered, his voice low and threatening.

I squirmed away. "It was the wrong girl, Frank."

"I know, Angel. I'm aware of that."

"This . . . *Annette* person just sent someone who was vaguely like Angela. The only resemblance was that she was black. That's not exactly —"

"It was probably just a misunder —"

"I still need to find her. I still have to —"

"Before you do that," Frank said, "you have to come with me to your father's. Right now. You can spend some time with your little brother and catch up with Melanie, and it will mean a great deal to Milos." Frank's face was usually tanned and hairless, with sparkly green eyes and an overly stylized fifties-movie-star coif. But at the moment, he just looked old. His eyes had gone fish gray, his complexion sallow; it even seemed that he hadn't shaved this morning.

"What's this about?" I started waving my arms around. "You break into my apartment, you —"

"This is about your father wanting to see you," he said flatly.

"He sent his fucking lawyer." I shook my head, then indicated the young guy standing in my kitchen. Fair, thin, pink-skinned, with the overly eager look of an incipient marketing executive, he couldn't have been more than twenty-five. "Who's this, anyway?"

"This is Marcel, my new associate."

The kid in the impossibly black suit smiled abashedly, then moved toward me, hand extended.

I ignored him. "You couldn't come alone? It's fucking ridicu —"

"Angel," Frank said, "you're coming home with us, all right? Do you have everything you need?"

"This is like a scene from a bad movie."

"Everything is like a movie, Angel." Frank smiled like he was talking to an idiot. "Don't you know that by now?"

"First of all," I began, "you come here completely unannounced. You break in —"

"Are you listening, Angel?" Frank raised his voice. "Your father wants to see you."

"I'm really not in the mood to see him at the moment," I said. "Or you."

He let out a heavy breath. "We can tell you what happened to her."

I stopped.

"The girl you're looking for. Your father and I can tell you what —"

———

Only minutes later we were sitting in the back of Frank's limo. The young associate who had been introduced as Marcel had gone to sit in the front with the driver, so it was just me and Frank, the two of us resting on a sea of pliable automotive leather.

"Tell me," I said.

"I'll let your father give you the details."

"Jesus." I sighed. "You tell me you know something but not what it is."

"I'm telling you what he told me to tell you."

"You don't have a mind of your own?"

He smiled a Grecian Formula–model smile. "Not when it comes to Milos Veronchek."

"And didn't I ask you not to tell him? Didn't I specifically —"

"It's not what you think," Frank said. "Angel, it's —"

"Did Silowicz say something?" I asked angrily. "Because that is a breach of doctor-patient confidentiality, that is a very serious —"

"No." Frank shook his head vehemently. "No. Your father already knew. When you mentioned her to me, he already knew all about her."

"How?"

"When you went to the club —"

"Hold on. You've been *following* me?"

I knew Frank and my father monitored my spending, but had they actually resorted to following me around the city?

Jesus Christ.

I was staring at him now, trying to burn his face off with my eyes. "You're having me tailed, is that it? Is it your fucking associate? That Marcel guy, is that his —"

"Angel." Frank closed his eyes. "Just wait, okay? Your father will answer all of these questions."

I sat there stonily, tracing my finger along a seam in the leather of the seat. The limo's interior was dark gray, almost charcoal. As long as I remembered, Frank had traveled in limos, never driving anywhere by himself.

"Don't you drive, Frank?" I asked out of nowhere.

He looked at me. "What do you mean?"

"How come you always take a limo?"

"I like to work while I'm in traffic. I use the phone. I do my reading." He paused, thinking. "I drive on weekends."

"What do you have?" I didn't even know why I was asking. I just wanted to know something personal about him.

"Pardon me?"

I wanted to know because I had never known anything about Frank's life beyond that he worked for my father, that he paid all the bills, oversaw our family finances, organized practically every aspect of our lives, the architect behind my father's evil empire. For some reason, perhaps my advanced state of fatigue, I had actually developed a perverse curiosity about Frank. "What do you drive on the weekends, Frank? I mean, when you're not working."

"I have a Porsche," he admitted.

I laughed, not at the fact that he had a Porsche, but at the fact that he didn't want to tell me, at the fact that he was embarrassed. It was like Darth Vader was blushing.

I pressed him. "What color, Frank? What color is it?"

"Red," he confessed.

"How long have you worked for my dad?"

"Since before you were born. You know that."

"How many years?"

I could see by the way he looked up at the ceiling that Frank was counting the decades. "More than thirty-five, Angel, almost . . . Jesus, more than forty."

"You have other clients?"

"Not like your father."

"Not like my father," I repeated.

He laughed like Ed McMahon. "No."

"You don't see the absurdity of this?"

He blinked.

"You're a lawyer," I said, "a fucking attorney. You should be at the courthouse. You should be suing somebody or defending a criminal. You should be doing something important, something legal, or even illegal, but instead, you're being sent to pick up your client's son, like you're some kind of houseboy. Don't you see how pathetic —"

"Your father," Frank said evenly, "is my most important client."

"Would he do it for you? Would he go pick up your son for you?"

Frank shrugged. "I don't have any kids."

I sighed. This was getting nowhere, and the feeling was becoming familiar. "That's not the fucking point."

"Then what is the point, Angel? Why don't you tell me?"

It's a long way from West Hollywood to Malibu, and the traffic, especially at that time of day, and especially since Frank's driver took all the most obvious streets, moved tediously, like a swarm of ants stuck in a puddle of evaporating Pepsi. I was exhausted, depleted, having driven all over the city myself last night. The day had become harshly bright, and even through the tinted windows, the light felt like acid against my skin. I wore the same clothes I had been wearing since I had come home from Victor's, black cargos, a long-sleeved black shirt — it seemed so long ago now — and I was grimy, polluted, covered in sweat and salt. Even in the air-conditioned splendor of Frank's limo, I felt suffocated. Those hot winds were blowing again, and a fine, particulate dust was making its way into every pore of my being. I watched the corrosive light trace the asphalt horizon. The sun glowered through the smog, creating a gloomy haze over the flattened pavement.

I was staring out the window, having given up, when Frank slapped my knee. "And here we are," he said.

The limo pulled into the long drive that led to my father's all-glass, ocean-view house. I could already see a servant moving toward us, ready to open the door and escort us inside.

I got out and followed him across the granite-tiled causeway toward a house made entirely of glass and steel, where every interior millimeter was exposed to blinding natural light.

Frank walked behind me, and we both stepped through the front hallway, passing the cavernous living room of museum-quality midcentury modern furniture, where an artificial stream ran beneath a plate-glass floor. We walked directly back to the rear patio, which faced the Pacific and featured a black, perfectly rectilinear infinity swimming pool that soared out over the waves like a gleaming piece of polished onyx.

My father was seated on a lounge chair with his brown, bumpy chest on full display, an amber glass of iced tea clenched in his manicured fist. He opened his arms, gesturing like a beneficent king at my arrival. Melanie and Gabriel, meanwhile, sat nearby in a plastic, blow-up baby pool, the ever-present nanny abiding quietly at their side. Gabriel, no longer a baby, sloshed morosely in the shallow water.

I looked at my dad, then back at Frank.

Melanie got up and came toward me. Whenever she saw me,

she was compelled to give me a motherly hug. She put her wet arms around my shoulders, and I felt her soft lips graze my cheek. "It's so nice to see you, Angel." Her display of affection was simultaneously condescending and imploring, I thought. She wasn't sure if I was above her or below her in the family hierarchy, and I wondered what perverted logic she used, a relatively attractive young woman, to have sex with this repulsive old man.

Or maybe they didn't have sex, I thought. Maybe that's why they'd had to adopt.

Halfheartedly, I hugged her back, then took a seat under the shade of an umbrella, and waited sullenly for Dad to speak.

A million years ago, Milos Veronchek came to this country with his parents from Brno, an obscure city that is currently part of the Czech Republic. He tells stories about sleeping on the floor in the single room he'd shared with his parents when they first arrived in Brooklyn. His mother died of a mysterious illness shortly thereafter, probably an untreated respiratory infection, and my grandfather had simply disappeared, making Dad one of those street urchins you see in photographs of the early twentieth century. Picture a soot-smeared face with hard, coal-black eyes, an ugly boy wearing a floppy black hat and newspapers wrapped around his feet. That's my father.

Anyway, the story has a happy ending. He ended up in a progressive program designed to rescue kids from the streets and was sent upstate to an orphanage near Rochester. He was never adopted — he was never cute enough for that, believe me — but by the time he was fourteen, Dad was working full-time for Kodak. I've never been very clear on the events of this early, pre-Hollywood part of his life, except that he worked his way through every department in the company, learning all there was to know about cameras, lighting, and film, and that at some point he started directing technical demonstrations. On one such project in the fifties, they actually flew him out to Los Angeles to sell Hollywood on a new color process.

He never returned, of course, finding the Los Angeles sun too seductive to leave. He quit Kodak and took a job in the lighting department at Universal. By the sixties he was a young producer and technical advisor who had worked on nearly a dozen movies. By the seventies he had become one of Hollywood's biggest directors, at the helm of western epics, disaster films, and car-chase features. The last movie he directed was a caper story about a retired jewel thief who has to pull off one last heist so he can save his brother's failing grocery store. It wasn't a bad script, I guess, but it never found itself. Was it a comedy, a drama, an action picture? No one knew, and it was universally regarded as one of the biggest turds of the decade, virtually ending the careers of its entire cast, including a former Academy Award nominee.

Dad turned to producing after that, putting together a string of minor commercial failures until the advent of the star vehicle, a concept he practically invented, and that made him one of the biggest movie producers in history.

He had always been successful, my father, but this made him into a monster. I have no idea how much money he has now — hundreds of millions, maybe more. His movies have become larger and larger, and his Eastern European face has developed a permanent smirk, a countenance that is at once arrogant and disbelieving, amazed at his own magnificent good fortune and basking in it. He's like Gatsby, only without the aspect of tragedy. Everything he touches turns to gold, platinum, diamonds — and, in my opinion, shit.

"Do you want to know my secret?" he once asked me.

I shrugged. I didn't want to know his secret. I have never been interested in the business side of moviemaking.

"I don't care," he said. "I don't tell the writers how to write. I don't tell the actors how to act. I don't tell anyone how to do anything. I just put them all in a room and say, 'Make a movie!'"

My dad is completely bald now except for a shimmering ring of gray stubble around his head and these bushy-white Leonid Brezhnev eyebrows that curl up like flames. "I'm just happy to be here," he says all the time, "happy to be a part of it." His skin, like all Hollywood megaplayers', is ludicrously tan, even shiny. He is only around five foot five, much shorter than me. I inherited his mind, my mother always insisted, if not his physical features. I share his technical proclivities, his interest in science and math. Sometimes he drinks, and when he is drunk, he tells me that he loves me, that he loved my mother, despite leaving her, despite the fact that he treated her like an unwanted possession, and he says that I never have to worry like he did, that a true father would never abandon his son, that he will leave me his fortune, and that I'll be rich forever.

In the matter of our skin, of course, we are opposites. He is always outside, my dad, always standing in the bright Los Angeles sun, his dark brown eyes open wide to absorb the sky's golden intensity.

I could feel those eyes staring at me for a full minute before he finally shouted, "Angel, that is your brother over there!"

I looked up and saw Melanie smiling expectantly, pitiable.

Then I looked at the kid, Gabriel, a dark cherub in bright pink swimming trunks, a glum expression on his round, permanently sullen face. I didn't know what to say; I guess I was supposed to hug him.

"So you can't even greet him?" My father, not a bad actor himself, appeared genuinely hurt. "You can't even say hello?"

"Dad, come on."

"Angel."

I turned to face the kid, offering a quick, "Hello, Gabe."

The boy slapped the water and turned his sulking face to the sun. He wasn't even aware of my presence. The truth is, he had no idea what the hell was going on.

Dad modulated his tone to a sing-song, having won. "So, Angel, how have you been?"

I thought for a moment. "I'm not sure."

"Do you need anything?"

This made me crazy. "I thought you were going to tell me about Angela."

He laughed and coughed at the same time. The sound of the cough was strange; it was dry at the surface, but there was something gelatinous and tremulous at its source.

"Are you sick?" I asked.

"I'm old. This is what happens when you're old."

"You're only as old as you feel," Frank said obsequiously.

"I feel old," my father said.

Suddenly, Melanie squealed. "Are those dolphins?" She picked up Gabriel and held the little kid over the railing that faced the water. I could see his vacuous eyes scanning the air in front of him. He was panicked, completely confused. Did he even know what he was looking for? Or did he believe his mother was dangling him over a cliff for no reason?

These people are deluding themselves, I thought. This kid is retarded.

"Dad" — I looked around — "are you going to tell me what happened to her or not?"

He threw a glance to Melanie, and she hurriedly clutched Gabriel to her chest and disappeared into the house. He was always doing this, sending people away with a look, like a pasha who could make things happen with an arrogant clap of his hands.

Now my father brought one of those old brown hands to his chin and pretended to think for a moment. "Angel," he said thoughtfully, "you're in trouble."

"I'm fine." I shook my head. "I'm absolutely —"

"That girl."

I felt my own hands, white and fragile, grow cold. "Obviously," I said, "you've been following me. I'm under some kind of fucking surveillance. So the least you could do right now is tell me what you know."

"Angel, please," my father said, "we're just making sure you're all right, and usually you never leave that rattrap of an apartment, which I still don't understand, but when you started going out to that topless place . . ." His voice had become lilting over the last phrase, a sliver of his Czech boyhood shining through.

I stared at the black pool, incredulous, and then out at the reflective ocean beyond it.

There was silence, furrowed brows, concerned faces. Frank and my father, the two of them always together, they were like a tag team of parental dysfunction.

"This girl," Frank said, "this is the one who works at the Velvet Mask, am I right?"

I looked at him. "What do you mean?"

"She's the one you're after, right?"

"As opposed to who?"

Frank closed his eyes, exasperated. "She dances under the name Cassandra?"

"Yeah," I said. "I told you that already, Frank. But that's . . . that's not really her name. What do you know about her?"

Slowly, my father said, "We know . . . we know enough."

"Something happened to her," I said. "Something happened, didn't it?"

"Let her go." Frank's voice was soft.

"Angel." My father leaned forward in his chaise longue, clearly straining. "Listen to me. *Listen.*"

I remained silent, waiting to hear what he would say.

"We know you've been . . . looking for her, so we did some investigating ourselves. We have resources . . ."

"This Cassandra, she is not a good person," Frank interrupted. "She has a criminal history. She has been brought up several times for possession. She has been arrested for solicitation . . ."

"She's a dancer," I said defensively.

"Ten years ago this woman was arrested in Orange County for her involvement in an extortion racket," Frank said. "There have been numerous drug charges, domestic violence, assault . . . She's got a file as long as my arm."

"She's a lowlife, Angel," my father said. "What do you want with a woman like that? There is nothing wrong with you that you can't find a decent girlfriend. Melanie can set you up. She knows a thousand nice girls. And if you want a woman for a night, call Frank."

I sighed, putting my face in my hands. "Can't you just tell me where is she?"

My father and Frank glanced at one another. They knew. Everyone knew where Angela was but me.

This came from my father: "She has a boyfriend. She went away with him somewhere. We don't know where."

"A boyfriend?"

"A musician," Frank said. "She left the country. They left the country together."

"She left the country?"

"Far away." My father nodded.

This was clearly bullshit.

I looked at Frank, then back at Dad. "Why would you do this to me?"

My father made a sympathetic face. "We just wanted to make sure you found out what happened to her, that's all, and that you knew she was all right. That way . . ." Now he started to chuckle, as though we had put the whole thing to rest. "That way you can go back to doing whatever it is you do all night in your shitty apartment. What is it? Are you still writing?" He didn't wait for an answer. "Why don't you move in with us? This is a beautiful place to write a screenplay, with the ocean, the beach —"

"But she called me. She called and said my name, and then —"

"And then what, Angel?"

"She was cut off. But she was calling from the dark. She was terrified. I could hear it."

"So she changed her mind," Frank offered, shaking his head. "Maybe she decided she didn't want to talk to you after all."

"How do you know that?" I stared at my hands. They were white, of course, and beneath that, pink and blue, the color of my veins, the color of flesh beneath the skin. There was also a small dot of something purple forming on my skin, just over the knuckle of my middle finger. I hadn't noticed it before. It would become cancer later if I wasn't careful, I thought. Maybe it was cancer already. Maybe I was dying. Maybe it had metastasized throughout my entire body and I only had a few weeks to live. I suddenly felt like an actor in a tragedy. "She told me she . . . she told me she loved me." I felt ashamed as soon as it came out of my mouth.

"Girls like her," my father said, "they say that kind of thing . . . they don't really mean it."

I shook my head. I pictured my own funeral. I imagined Angela staring down at my coffin, my alabaster face serenely offering itself back at her. I looked out at the Pacific again, at the cold ocean waves. Sometimes two of them collided with each other, an interference pattern forming as they crashed onto the golden beach. "But why would she just leave her apartment and all of her things?" I asked. "And I know for a fact that someone has been stalking her. *I saw him.*"

"Who did you see?"

"A man," I said weakly. "He was wearing a gray suit."

Frank and my father were looking at each other. I could tell they believed I was crazy.

"Angel," Dad said, "let it go."

"Let it go?" I said. "What the hell are you talking about?"

My father shrugged. "There's nothing else to know."

"What's her boyfriend's name?" I asked.

Frank shook his head.

"What country did she go to?"

"Angel," my father said, "please stop this, for your own good."

I had no clear sense of reality anymore. All I could do was look at the light, which fell in soft blankets of orange and silver over the water and sand in the distance. Beyond us, I could see a haze of smog rising over the rocky hills of Malibu Canyon. But here on my father's veranda, the sun beamed hard, unimpeded rays, leaving clean, razor-sharp shadows on the speckled granite.

I pictured Angela, her seal-wet body in the cool water of the pool, her fake hair slick against her head.

Had that even happened? Were those memories even real?

This wasn't right, I thought. Whatever Frank and my father had found out about Angela couldn't be the whole story.

She wouldn't have just left.

And her voice.

And the letter . . . and the money . . .

I thought I'd have better luck asking Frank these questions privately later on.

Plus, I felt sick.

Somehow, I managed to get up and move inside without saying good-bye. Melanie, of course, having relocated to the living room, followed me to the door, holding the squirming Gabriel against her hip.

"Don't you want to hug him?" She held the kid toward me, his arms flailing. "Your little brother?"

"How old is he?" I asked.

"He's almost four already. His birthday is only" — she seemed embarrassed to remind me — "three months away."

"He's still not talking?"

". . . a few words . . ." She shrugged, as if it were her own fault.

I gave in, leaning toward Gabriel and inhaling his baby smell, then pressed my cheek against his.

There was spit on his skin, and I felt that smear of viscous liquid. I had nothing against this kid, this little boy they kept insisting was my brother, but I also knew that, at this point in time, there was nothing I could do to help him. He was stuck with these people.

———

I sat in the back of one of my father's limousines, directing the route, riding all the way past the red cliffs of Malibu into the heart of Santa Monica, taking Wilshire into Beverly Hills, up Doheny and, finally, over to Sunset Boulevard. I watched the sun flash and glow off the polished metal and painted fiberglass of the Los Angeles traffic. Suddenly I pictured Frank's associate, Marcel, following me. Had he come into the club with me that night? And what about those criminal charges they said Angela had?

Someone was clearly mistaken — Frank, probably. He had been misinformed.

Or he was lying.

Not far from down on Sunset was the Tower Records, and on

impulse I asked the driver to stop. I jumped out of the car, slipped through the automatic doors, and went directly to the new rock section. I found the display for ImmanuelKantLern. Their new disc was stacked under a poster of the band, a group of sullen young men standing around in an empty parking lot at dawn's first light, each member staring off in his own mock-profound direction.

My father had said she went away with a musician, and this was the only group Angela had ever mentioned.

Back in the limo, I tore the plastic wrap off the CD and looked closely at each member. They all had spiky rock-and-roll hair, numerous tattoos, weird piercings. Each member of the group had the last name of a famous European philosopher. There was Timmy Schopenhauer, Jason Montaigne, Eddie Hume, Jared Burke.

I looked at the bass player, Joey Descartes, the one Angela said she had slept with. He wore an adolescent sneer on a thirty-year-old face.

After a few minutes, the driver took me over to Hollywood Boulevard, then pulled onto San Raphael Crescent.

"Hey," he said as I was getting out, "you're Milos Veronchek's kid, right?" He was a lanky young man with soft brown hair and ruddy skin.

I hesitated. "Yeah."

"I feel stupid asking you this, but"— his face was apologetic, as though expecting a punch —"do you think I can give you a screenplay, and if you like it . . . I mean, seriously, dude, only if you like it, you could pass it on to your dad?"

I had no reason to be mean to this guy. "Sure." I shrugged.

"But you know, I don't see him very often. It might be a long time before I'm out there again."

He looked up at my apartment building, obviously wondering why I lived in a place like this if my father was the great Milos Veronchek. "I just thought that if I could just get this screenplay to someone like your dad, you know, then maybe I could get an agent." He leaned down and pulled out a manila envelope. "And if I could get an agent . . ."

The next step was obviously fame, stardom, wealth beyond the dreams of avarice; his expression indicated the world of possibilities that would follow.

"I'd be happy to."

"You gotta try every angle," he said, handing me the envelope, "even if it seems desperate. You know what I mean? Like Tom said in *Risky Business*" — he laughed — "sometimes you have to say, what the fuck?"

———

Inside, *Blade Runner* played on the television, the characters murmuring at low volume. My desk waited; the computer screens glowed as if in anticipation. The stacks of colored paper remained on the floor: red, orange, yellow, green, violet, blue, hot to cold, the visible spectrum of colored light. I dropped the limo driver's screenplay onto the floor, emptied my pockets onto my desk, slipped into the kitchen, and poured myself a deep mug of bourbon. I took a long, hard swallow, followed it with a couple of tabs of Ambien, then brought the mug with me into the bathroom, where I was finally able to pull my clothes off without interruption. I brushed my teeth, spat the usual bloody pink foam into the sink, and when I took another sip of the whiskey, I felt that malicious sting and, after a moment, a welcome numbness.

In the kitchen, I dialed Frank's cell number.

"Hello?" he asked.

"Frank," I whispered, "are you still at my father's?"

"I'm in the car," he answered flatly.

I brought my voice back to a normal volume. "Tell me the truth."

"The truth, Angel?"

"Where is she? Did she really go away with that band? Is it ImmanuelKantLern?"

He sighed. "If that's what your father said —"

"Jesus Christ, Frank, I'm not asking what my father said. He's not God, is he? Just because he says something doesn't make it true. I'm asking *you*, okay? I'm asking you if she really went away with that fucking band."

Frank allowed a moment to pass, a theatrical demonstration of how little he appreciated me talking to him this way. "We're talking about Cassandra, right?" he answered finally. "The girl from the Mask."

"Yes. The girl from the Mask," I said. "Why do you keep asking me that?"

"I just want to be sure."

"Tell me. Just fucking —"

"According to our information, yes, she went away with that musician."

"The guy from ImmanuelKantLern."

He breathed heavily. "I guess that's what they're called."

"Frank, I'm hanging up now."

"Angel —"

When I thought about it, it actually made sense. Someone had been stalking her, so Angela had hooked up with her old boyfriend. She would go away with him for a while and come back when it was safe.

In the living room, wearing my old robe, I inserted the ImmanuelKantLern disc, *Jokes On You,* into the stereo, listened once, perplexed, then played it again, hating every dragging beat, detesting every artless measure. There was something awful about this music, something degenerate and sleazy. It had the guise of sincerity, but I detected a cynicism beneath its surface, as though the band were playing down to its own audience.

Jokes On You, all right.

But maybe I had become out of touch. Maybe I was just too old.

The main thing was the bass line, a burning, unrelenting depth of sonic distortion that reached lower than the human ear could apprehend. The vocals were trapped somewhere between rapping and singing, and the guitar whined, sniveled, and complained. I had to strain to hear anything redemptive in it at all, finding only an angry satisfaction, a bitter agreement with the band's alienated, anarchist posture.

On the computer I checked out ImmanuelKantLern.com, discovering the schedule of concerts for their current world tour. Right now, it said, they were in South America. My father had been right — it had to be them. For the next two nights, as a matter of fact, they were playing in Rio. Perhaps she had gone off with them to South America and couldn't get through to me. Maybe that's where Angela had been calling from when she was cut off. Could she have been on the plane, ascending into the brightening sky, I wondered, while the small cabin darkened?

I took the mug of Jack and dropped down onto the flokati. Dead hyacinth petals were strewn everywhere, now brown and wilted, filling the room with the smell of decay.

"You only think you're white," Angela had told me one night. "You know that?" This was a continuation of a conversation that began early in our relationship and meandered through subject matter like Mulholland Drive through the Hollywood hills.

"You keep saying that. Why do you keep saying that?"

"You're white on the outside, Angel, dark on the inside."

"I don't like those symbols." I took a sip of bourbon. "They're too reductive. And besides," I said, "I thought you told me I was orange and red."

"Everything's a symbol," she said, raising her head so she could see my face. "Everything's a symbol, jackass. This is a world of symbols for another world."

"What do you know about other worlds?"

There was a flash of anger across her features, like fast clouds passing over the moon. "I know this world is bullshit."

"There is a theory about other worlds," I told her, suddenly excited to be talking about something I knew. "It comes from the uncertainty principle. It comes from the study of light."

Angela sighed, rolling her eyes.

"For every optional circumstance, for every quantum uncertainty, another world breaks off," I went on, "so every optional world exists." I held her gaze to make her listen. "This isn't science fiction. There are actual physicists, true-to-life scientists, who believe this."

Angela took a swallow of her vodka, then took a long drag on her cigarette, leaving a trace of pink lipstick on the white filter.

"There are other worlds," I told her, "and this one is only as real as the rest of them. All worlds are equally viable."

She seemed older to me at that moment, the lines and creases around her eyes deeper than usual. "Are we going to have sex," she asked, "or not?"

I fell asleep on the rug, remembering Angela, trying to, anyway, listening to the music of ImmanuelKantLern, with the empty mug in my hand and the dead blossoms of hyacinths distributed around my exhausted body like flowers around a coffin.

Sometime in the middle of the night, I crawled off to bed, wishing I could crawl off to one of those other worlds.

THANK YOU FOR CALLING VARIG AIRLINES," AN ACTUAL WOMAN
finally answered. "How may I assist you?"

"I need a ticket." This was the following morning, minutes after I woke up.

"Where would you like to go, sir?"

"To Rio de Janeiro."

"And when would you like to depart?"

"Right away."

I packed nothing, thinking I would pick up whatever I needed
when I got there. Besides, I told myself, I was only staying for one
day. I could get a change of clothes and a toothbrush anywhere. I
suddenly realized I would need my passport. Shit. Where was it? I
searched frantically through every drawer in my apartment, finally

discovering it in an old silver box at the back of my closet. Then it occurred to me that Frank would see the charge for the ticket on my credit card — Christ, it would stand out like an anarchist flag — and he would immediately inform my father.

Fuck it, I told myself. Fuck Frank. And fuck my father. I'm thirty-two years old, I thought. I can do whatever the fuck I want.

Fuck all of them. Fuck everything.

As my father's limo driver had reminded me, sometimes you have to say, what the fuck?

I showered and threw on a fresh set of clothes, stuffed as much of the money I had found into my wallet as I could, as well as the note, and then, just as I was about to lock the door behind me, it dawned on me that this would be an extremely long flight, that I'd want something to read. I grabbed the nearest book off my desk, not even bothering to see what it was, and slipped into the hall.

In the Cadillac, I noticed that the day was overcast, the sky asphalt-white. The atmosphere was close, overheated, and the palm trees drooped like beaten dogs. It was an airport day, there's no other way to describe it.

I drove the fastest way possible, on the freeway, discovering that the traffic had yet to jam up.

At LAX, I waited no longer than five minutes before the flight started boarding, and I was placed in the first first-class seat.

I reached into my pocket to see what book I had grabbed.

Crap.

I was stuck with a copy of *In Search of Schrödinger's Cat: Quantum Physics and Reality.*

I flipped it open, reading an epigraph from the great physicist himself on the first page: "I don't like it, and I'm sorry I ever had anything to do with it." He was speaking about the uncertainty principle, which is the idea that, at its most elemental level, light is both particle and wave, and that whichever one it happens to be at any given moment depends entirely on the observer. I had been reading through this book in the weeks before Angela had disappeared, reacquainting myself with some of the ideas I had been obsessed with in college. Erwin Schrödinger had set out to disprove the uncertainty principle through the application of common sense with a thought experiment about a cat.

He imagined a cat inside a box. He also imagined that inside the box was a sealed phial of poison, and suspended over the phial of poison was a hammer. Hooked up to the hammer was a photosensitive device that registers whether a single photon of light exhibits wave properties or particle properties. If the photon is a wave, let's say, the hammer does nothing, remaining suspended over the phial, and the cat lives. If the photon is a particle, on the other hand, the hammer smashes the phial, and the cat dies instantly. (For this experiment to work, you also have to imagine that the box is soundproof, which is a weak spot in the whole scenario, I know, but there it is.) Anyway, the only way to find out what happened, whether the result is particle or wave, is to open the box.

In the meantime, what's going on with that stupid cat?

The answer, and Schrödinger himself thought this was ridiculous, is that the cat is neither alive nor dead. She is alive *and* dead. It's what physicists call a superposition of states.

Ironically, and much to Erwin Schrödinger's great disappointment, his thought experiment was actually used to *prove* the idea of the uncertainty principle, not to discredit it. Moreover, an additional theory suggests that the world itself splits in two, one world in which the photon is wave — and the cat is alive — the other world in which it is particle — and the cat is dead.

Two worlds. Two cats. Both existing simultaneously.

Only by looking inside the box does one of those worlds collapse.

That's what I had been trying to explain to Angela that night, that there are multiple worlds, alternate realities constantly splitting off for every instant of subatomic indecision. If you look closely at the light, I told her, you will find uncertainty there, doubt, the ultimate vacillation at reality's core. Which direction it goes depends, the uncertainty principle informs us, on the observer.

Light, it turns out, is only what you make of it.

I recalled another day/night/morning/evening. This time it was a whole handful of dry, cube-shaped pills.

"There are two kinds of artists," Angela was saying, "the kind who manifest their darkness from the present and the kind who bring it up from the past. Which are you?"

"I'm not an artist," I answered. "I'm a scientist."

"I thought you were a writer."

"When did I tell you about my writing?"

"You're writing a screenplay," she answered, pointing toward a stack of blue paper. "It's called *Los Angeles*."

On the television was the scene in which Rick Deckard sips from a clear drink, and a thread of blood issues into the viscous liquid. He sits at a piano and thumbs through photographs, reliving old memories. "Well, I'm not a writer anymore." I had started talking crazy because of all the meds I'd been taking. "I'm an elec-tromagnetic scientist." I could feel the effects of too many anti-depressants in my legs. My veins had filled with helium, and I knew that if I tried to get up, I would float away. "Help me," I begged. I was made entirely of rubber bands.

"An electromagician?" Angela placed her glass on the floor be-side her and reached for my hands, standing, pulling me up to her level. "Are you a dark electromagician, Angel, or a light one?"

I was leaning on her shoulder, and she was leading me into the bedroom. "I told you I don't like that kind of symbolism."

"You're all about that kind of symbolism."

"I am the embodiment of that kind of symbolism," I said. "I know this. I am aware of this. Of this I am all too painfully aware." I dropped onto the bed face first. "But that doesn't mean I support it."

Angela slid beside me, her cool slender legs touching mine.

"Electromagnetism, the full spectrum, light to dark." I tried to explain to her the history of light, some of the important things I had learned in college — Newton's theories, Fresnel's findings, the chain of events that led to Maxwell's discovery of electromagne-tism, Einstein's ultimate insight into the essentially dual nature of the universe. Because from there —

"Can I kiss you?" she asked.

— from there came Schrödinger, and Heisenberg and his un-certainty principle, the Multiple Worlds Theory, and all the rest.

"Go ahead and kiss me," I said, giving in.

Our conversation went on like this. Still in my mind were shreds of language, scraps of dialogue that appeared and reappeared with Angela's image, her face, her body, her limbs wrapped around me, her lips against my neck, my chest, against my lips.

And always, always, that cat.

Crying, screaming, wailing.

We were in the living room, on the flokati, in the kitchen pouring drinks or microwaving dinner entrées. We were in the bedroom, in bed, limbs tied together, the cat mewling desperately outside.

"What do you like, Angel?" she kept asking. "What do you want me to do?"

The cat was screaming.

"Just this," I said. "Just you."

"What do you want, specifically? *Specifically.* Something concrete, something particular."

Wailing, mewling, caterwauling.

"I don't have specific," I told her. "I'm all generalities. I'm all abstractions."

She lit a cigarette, and when she closed her eyes halfway, I could see the crescent of eye shadow there, that smile of mascara.

On television was the scene where the actor named Morgan Paull interviews Leon. This is early in the film, the first moment of violence. "Maybe you're fed up," Morgan says. "Maybe you want to be by yourself. Who knows? You look down and you see a tortoise, Leon, it's crawling toward you."

"What is it?" I asked.

"What is what?" Angela said.

"What is it that you're after? What do you want from me?"

Angela shook her head, eyes still closed.

"Answer the question."

She made a gesture. "I am . . . enigmatic."

"I'm not exactly a prize," I said. "I mean, look at me."

"Yes," she said, smiling. "Look at you."

"I'm a freak."

A squeal of agony emitted from the parking lot.

"You're my little prince."

"I have psychological problems."

"Like what?"

"I have agoraphobia. I have social —"

"What is the one where you're afraid of the truth?" Angela traced her finger along the length of my nose. "Because *that* is the illness you suffer from."

On the plane, taxiing out onto the LAX runway, I thought of the way I had buried that goddamned cat in the old man's yard. In this world, she was dead, that was certain. Perhaps she was still alive in some other world. Just then the airplane's wings lifted us into the air, and the flight attendant, a platinum blonde who had once been Barbie-doll sexy, was asking if I would like something to drink.

"You remind me of my mother," I told her.

"That's a compliment, I guess." She had a Southern accent and wore so much makeup that her base powder cracked like old concrete around her features.

"She was a famous model," I informed her. "She was a French movie actress."

The flight attendant smiled impatiently. "Would you like something to drink or not, sweetheart?"

"Do you have bourbon?"

"Uh-oh," she said, smiling, "a whiskey drinker." She turned around and came back with a miniature bottle of Jack Daniel's and a small glass.

My seat was next to the window, and I watched the asphalt of L.A. fall away beneath the plane, and then the steel water of the Pacific, gray and blue with flecks of white twinkling across it like flashbulbs at the Olympics. We turned, banking sharply to the south, the whole plane veering sickeningly to one side. Flying has never bothered me, but there was something about this, the spontaneity of it, I guess, and the fact that I couldn't take it back, that made me uneasy. I felt my stomach turn one way, the plane veering in the opposite direction. It wasn't the flight, I guess; it was the decision.

I sipped the Jack Daniel's and it tasted like bananas.

I took a quick inventory of the items in the pockets. They contained the Schrödinger book, my passport, and my wallet. The inventory of my wallet included thousands of dollars in one hundred dollar bills, that crazy note I had found on Angela's doorstep, my credit cards, and my California driver's license. The inventory of my apartment included a table, a chair, a fuzzy black rug, stacks of books and CDs, two computers, a large-screen television set — which was still on, incidentally, still playing *Blade Runner* over and over — a stereo, an electronic wave-generating device, a closet full of clothes that were essentially identical to the ones I was wearing now, a bed with black sheets and red blankets, red towels in the bathroom, a toothbrush, and a closet-size stackable washer and dryer. The inventory of my life included a famous father, his young wife and adopted baby, a mother who's face had been rebuilt in plastic, a psychiatrist, a sociopathic lawyer, a missing girlfriend, and a rock star whom, somehow, no matter what, I had to find in Rio de Janeiro, even if it killed me.

"Do you happen to know," I asked the man sitting beside me, "where musicians stay when they go to Rio?"

"Musicians?" He had dark hair with gray temples. He wore a rumpled suit and a red silk tie. His face was pocked with ancient scars.

"You know," I said, "like rock stars."

"Like Madonna?"

"Sure." I shrugged. "Like Madonna."

"They might stay at the Copacabana Palace. It is very expensive." He thought for a moment. "Are you a rock star?"

"Me? No." I laughed. "No, no. I'm looking for one."

This piqued his curiosity. "Which particular rock star are you looking for?"

"It's a group. ImmanuelKantLern," I said. "I'm going to see them tonight."

"Ah," he said.

"And I was hoping to stay in the same hotel. Have you heard of them?"

He furrowed his brow. "There is much about modern music I do not know." He gave me a polite smile that made me realize he believed I was insane and that he really didn't want to talk to me anymore. "I prefer jazz."

I looked down into my glass and saw that my banana-flavored Jack Daniel's had somehow disappeared.

I tried to look out the window, to appreciate the fading light of the sky from this altitude. But there was nothing to see, only fluffy clouds like a commercial set in heaven, a blue sky, and a yellow-gold sun. I half-expected to see a fake angel suspended on wires.

After an hour, the sky became excruciatingly bright. A white sun shone like an everlasting camera flash. I closed the shade and rubbed roughly at my sockets. I found my asshole glasses pushed up onto my forehead and slipped them down. I kept repeating in my mind the image of Angela coming into the apartment with her arms full of hyacinths. I kept hearing the grating, antisocial music of ImmanuelKantLern. Reading about the Multiple Worlds Theory — *"both cats are real. There is a live cat, and there is a dead cat; but they are located in different worlds"*— I fell into a somnambulant haze, then woke up when I felt the hand of a flight attendant gently shaking my shoulder. Instantly I realized that I had an erection and had been dreaming about Angela dancing onstage at the Mask.

Jesus Christ.

I flinched, embarrassed. I wondered if I'd had that hard-on the whole time and berated myself for not keeping the tiny airplane blanket over my lap.

I realized, too, that I had forgotten to bring any medication.

I lifted the shade and looked out the window again. We were descending through a Technicolor sunset, the falling light filtering through clouds of orange and pink and a thousand hues of gray. It seemed fake, a painted backdrop brought in by the effects department. It also occurred to me that this whole airplane could be fake, one of those props my father used to make disaster movies. Some kind of motor was causing it to shake slightly, providing the illusion that we were flying.

I had the absurd idea that Angela would be waiting for me at the gate, that she would greet me, arms wide, when I stepped off, saying, "Angel . . . Angel . . ." just as my mother used to say when I would come home from the Vancouver School. Angela would be wearing blue contacts, and her skin would sparkle the way it had on the first day we met . . .

But no one greeted me.

At baggage claim, I used a courtesy phone to make reservations at the Copacabana Palace. Then I stepped onto the sidewalk and immediately found a taxi.

"Excuse me," I asked the driver, "do you speak English?"

A small man in a yellow baseball cap turned to look at me. He made a pinching gesture with his fingers, meaning *a little,* and said, "My English . . ."

He might be young enough, I considered, to know where the concert was. I leaned forward. "Have you ever heard of ImmanuelKantLern?"

He nodded excitedly. "ImmanuelKantLern! Yes! Rock music!"

"Can you take me to the concert?"

"Concert?"

I wasn't sure if he understood. "They are playing tonight. Somewhere in Rio." I waved my arms around like a fan in the audience. "A concert."

"They are rock . . . concert," the driver said.

"Can you take me?"

"Yes, yes," he said, finally understanding. "I take you." We sped away from the curb.

It was already almost nine o'clock. The concert was scheduled to begin at ten, according to their website, and I was beginning to worry that I'd miss it. Perhaps I'd be staying in the same hotel and I could find that Joey Descartes fucker there. I wasn't sure how I would approach them, but I imagined that Angela would turn to me, and that whatever had caused her to leave me for him would melt away as she rushed into my arms, moving in exquisite slow motion, her eyes glossy with tears.

I also imagined the look on that bass player's face.

We drove, first through the industrial wasteland that separates all airports from all cities, then into a literal urban jungle, threading the car through the small streets and avenues lined on either side by terraced apartments and enormous, quivering trees. We finally came out onto a wide, pale beach, waves catching the faint light of the moon in the satiny water.

"Ipanema," the driver reported.

He drove along this beach for several minutes, then turned into the city again, where great vines climbed over fences, and thick branches rustled over densely shadowed alleys. Eventually he stopped in front of a crowded sidewalk. I looked up and saw a high wall stretching half a city block, with several sets of double doors opening onto the street.

"Can you wait?" I reached into my wallet and pulled out one of those hundred-dollar bills.

He understood immediately. "I wait. Yes, yes. I wait for you." The driver indicated with a sweep of his arm the area in front of the concert hall, and I stepped out.

I could hear pulsating music coming from inside, and I wondered how I might get in. I went to the first set of double doors. They opened easily onto a long hallway throughout which were gathered tight knots of teenagers. One of these knots was crowded around another set of doors. The music coming from inside the concert hall was unbearably loud, rhythmically brainless, falling like hot lava into my ears. The air was no cooler in here, and the stifling, nauseating odor of thousands of human bodies penetrated the atmosphere. I began to walk toward the door before I noticed the two bouncers who guarded it. One of them held his hand up and gave me a look, the one that means *hold it, pal* in any language.

"Do you speak English?" I asked, trying to make an innocent face.

He spoke again, and whatever he said made the other bouncer laugh.

"English," I said stupidly. "American."

He put a hand against my chest and pushed. I needed a ticket, he was telling me.

I reached into my pocket for my wallet, not thinking how dumb this was, and pulled out three of Angela's crisp hundred-dollar bills. "Can I buy one?"

He took the money and turned to the other bouncer, saying something sly, no doubt, and slipped the bills into his pocket.

I stepped forward again, hoping he'd let me through this time, but once again, he pushed me, fingers positioned like a huge spider against my chest.

I turned imploringly to the other bouncer, who only laughed, flashing an open, pitiless grin.

Outside, a handful of kids were selling T-shirts. They rushed up to me, speaking in indecipherable incantations, instantly identifying me as a sucker. I sidestepped them and walked around to the edge of the building, where I found an alley lined with putrid garbage cans. Here, a group of people passed a joint from hand to hand. I walked through them and discovered a parking area in the back, just beyond a high chain-link fence, which separated the alley from the rear of the concert hall, and there it was . . .

A long, white limo.

A couple of security guards loitered nearby, smoking cigarettes. This was the vehicle that would take the band back to the hotel, I realized.

I turned around and hurried back, coming out into the street again. I saw the driver on the other side. He was parked in the wrong direction, standing against the taxi with his door open, flirting with a couple of shiny-haired girls.

"Hey," I said, approaching.

He immediately opened the back door for me. "Hotel?"

"No," I said. "I want to wait."

"Wait?"

"For the band."

His expression told me that he didn't understand.

"ImmanuelKantLern." I mimicked the act of holding a steering wheel. "We'll follow them, okay?"

"Ahhh." The driver tapped his temple with his forefinger.

We waited for another half hour, listening to the clamor inside the concert hall. The crowd cheered maniacally for every song, adding an extra element of violence to the evening's already savage pitch.

Then, after several encores, the music finally stopped.

"Are they leaving?" I asked.

Just then, we saw the white limo pulling away. The driver turned the ignition and waited briefly as the limo turned onto our street. Then he slipped directly behind it into traffic. We tailed the limo for several blocks, then turned onto the beach in Ipanema. It stopped in front of a pale modern building, and the driver pulled up directly behind it. I jumped out and caught a glimpse of the group as they slipped inside. The door was held open, and the handful of young men with colorful clothes and crazy hair moved quickly into the lobby.

She was there. She was with them. I couldn't see her face, but I definitely caught a flash of Angela's fake blond hair.

"Angela!" I yelled. "Wait!"

But the door was already shut behind them.

I came up to it and leaned on the handle. It started to open, and a man stuck his head out from behind it. "Can I help you?" he asked.

"I need to . . . to see the band — the guys who just went in there."

"ImmanuelKantLern are attending an invitation-only party," he said coldly. "Can I see your invitation?"

I sighed. "But it's important."

He smiled a very American bullshit smile. "If you have an invitation, then you can come inside. Otherwise —"

"Otherwise?" I thought for a moment he was about to suggest another way in.

"— get the fuck out of here."

I thought about bribing him, but then remembered what had happened with the bouncers. I didn't care about the money; it hadn't been mine anyway. I just knew it wouldn't work. Besides, the door had already closed and had the look of a door that was not likely to be opened again anytime soon.

I could wait until they emerged, if they ever would, and try to accost them then.

Or I could try again tomorrow.

I knew from the schedule on their website that they were playing at the same concert hall in less than twenty-four hours.

"Can you just take me to my hotel?" I asked the driver after walking back to the taxi. "The Copacabana Palace?"

He started the engine and drove away. "It's about maybe . . . twenty minutes," he said.

We turned onto the beach again. I hadn't noticed the bars and clubs, or the people walking up and down the broad sidewalks before. There were small kiosks surrounded by crowds of people — people dancing, partying, drinking. In the distance was the ocean, smooth waves lapping an iridescent shore under a glass-eyed moon that seemed to be hanging in the wrong place in the sky. We turned into the city, weaving through the tree-lined streets and tiled boulevards, and then, after penetrating a long, busy avenue, emerged onto another beach, where a wide road separated a phalanx of high-rises from a pearly crescent of sand. I tried to remember if I had ever been here before. It would have been with my parents, if I had, in the hushed, air-conditioned seclusion of whatever the most expensive hotel would have been at the time, and they wouldn't have dared to take me outside in a climate like this, not during the day, anyway.

I remembered cool evenings in places like Rio when I was a kid, recalled standing at the window of the hotel and wishing the sun would descend a little more quickly, wishing I could speed up the tape. I'd run back and forth from the curtains to my mother in her bed, saying, "It's almost all the way down," anxious, panicking, repeating, "Mom, we're going to miss it, we're going to miss it," as if the night itself would slip by.

"We won't miss anything," she would say. "There's nothing to miss."

I'd tug on her hand, pleading, *"Mah-ahm."*

Finally, a wan smile would cross her lips, and my mother would get out of bed and squeeze into a pair of jeans, sandals, and an elegant tank top. We'd walk through the hotel, passing the bar, the restaurants, the people coming in for the night, and I would run with my arms wide toward the water.

"Angel," she would call after me, "be careful!"

I'd run straight into the ocean and let the waves splash against my body, crushing me up to my bony, albino chest.

After a day in the sun, the water would still be warm and soft enough for me to wade a little way out.

My mother would remove her sandals and dangle them in one hand. She might even roll up the cuffs of her jeans and wade in herself, calling after me, "Angel, Angel, be careful, little prince. . . . Don't go out too far."

And when the sun descended completely and there was no

more light in the sky, and the stars had come out to shine like pinpricks of pink and yellow, she would call me back in, saying it was time to get dressed, that we were meeting my father for dinner.

I held on, of course, staying in the water, in the cool, wet sand, experiencing something close to what other children take for granted, until I heard in the tone of my mother's voice that I could no longer press my luck. She would wrap a rough towel around my body, pulling me in to her, and I'd take her hand again and walk back to the hotel, wherever we happened to be — the Caribbean, Hawaii, Spain — defeated by the brevity of the time I'd had outside but also elated by the water and cool evening air.

My mother might say she would take me to the pool after dinner if I was lucky, if I was good, if I played my cards right.

———

The driver pulled up to a white, rectangular building that looked like a multitiered wedding cake. Bright yellow windows shone over a mosaic sidewalk. A uniformed man opened the door for me; he wore shiny gold buttons across his chest and practically genuflected, speaking in a heavily accented English: "May I please welcome you to the Copacabana Palace?"

I gave my yellow-capped driver a couple of those hundred-dollar bills, thanked him, and slipped out of the car, walking into the gardenia-scented lobby.

The walls were paneled in marble. The light fixtures were gold. On every table were silver punch bowls filled with polished apples. At least ten employees hovered around nervously, including a young man down on his knees wiping the floor with a lace hand-kerchief.

"I made a reservation earlier," I said, approaching the desk. "My name is —"

"Mr. Veronchek, of course." The clerk was an older, distinguished-looking man in a suit that seemed slightly too big for him. His hair was about thirty years too young. "We have a suite waiting for you, sir."

"Thanks," I said, relieved.

"Can we take an imprint of your credit card for incidentals?"

"Absolutely." I handed it over. "I was also wondering if you could help me get a ticket to a concert."

The toupeed man behind the counter looked up and smiled. "There are many wonderful musical performances in Rio," he said. "We have classical music, a national opera house, and, of course, Samba, which is —"

"ImmanuelKantLern," I interrupted.

He paused. "Excuse me?"

"It's a rock band. They're playing here tomorrow night. I tried to see them tonight, but I couldn't get in."

His smile soured. "Very well, sir. I will make the arrangements and have a ticket waiting for you in the morning."

"Thank you."

"Can you —" He sighed. "Can you please spell the name of this group?"

I spelled it for him, painfully calling out each letter and explaining how they ran it all together.

Then he looked down at his computer and frowned.

"Is something wrong?"

"Your card," he said quietly, "has been rejected."

I shook my head. "That's impossible."

"I'm sure it is a mistake. Do you have another?"

This is what had happened at the supermarket a few days before Angela had disappeared. I had called Frank's office about it but realized now that no one had ever bothered to clear it up. These cards had huge limits, and I hardly ever spent anything. Was it possible that someone had let a payment lapse? Or maybe they had made a mistake at the bank. Thankfully, my other Visa worked, and a minute later, I followed a young man through the marble hallway, then around a pool that glowed like a liquid moon and past a bar where a handful of wealthy Europeans spoke quietly to one another while a guitarist plucked a whispery bossa nova.

We crossed through a pink candlelit restaurant and stepped into a gold-paneled elevator.

I walked like a griever in a funeral procession.

Finally, the bellman opened a door for me and started to show me the room.

I gave him a huge tip — those hundreds were the only bills I had — and begged off, saying, "I'll be fine, please . . . you can go now, thank you."

He stepped out backward.

I dropped onto the bed, simultaneously pulling off my damp, sweaty clothes.

I thought of ImmanuelKantLern's new CD.

Jokes On You.

I didn't lie awake and listen to the South American waves, I didn't dream, I didn't get up once during the night to gulp water from the faucet. I only slept.

I slept the black, pharmaceutical-free sleep of the completely defeated.

The joke was on me, all right.

————

I had spent the first part of my life in hotels like this one, enshrouded in the perfumed comforters, behind the heavy curtains. I had lived in rooms like this all over the world, in fact, in Europe, New York, California, South America, the Caribbean. Every Christmas growing up, I accompanied my parents to some new exotic destination . . . St. John, Bora-Bora, St.-Tropez, the Seychelles . . . , and all I remember, of course, are the rooms, the pearl carpeting and faux-French furniture, the curtains drawn to protect me from the sun, the candlelit restaurants at night, where I sat with a book while my parents ate in silence or my father entertained, his voice booming. I have probably been to Paris twenty times, but I have never been up in the Eiffel Tower. I have been to New York fifty times but have never walked through Times Square. There was a point in the middle of the night when I woke up and felt that old familiarity of waking up in a hotel, the controlled atmosphere, the ambient hush of the carpeted halls outside the door. I have been everywhere, is the truth, and nowhere.

When I woke up in the morning, I felt metallic, my limbs hanging like dumbbells from my body and my skin like aluminum foil. The room was freezing, the air conditioner set to chill. I ordered a grapefruit and a pot of coffee from room service and wrapped myself in one of the fluffy white robes I found hanging behind the bathroom door. I had strewn my clothes at the foot of the bed and now, picking them up, noticed they were still damp from last night's sweat and severely wrinkled from the million hours on the plane.

I should have brought something to wear, I realized. A change of underwear, at least.

Eventually I got in the shower. The maid came in, and when she heard me in the bathroom, she must have turned around and left. The first thing I did when I got out was check to see if the money was still in my wallet, having been told so often about all the crime in South America.

But there it was. Thousands of dollars in crisp hundred-dollar bills. The note was in there, too, the blue letter I had found on Angela's doorstep. *Breathe because you breathe / You are the blood in my veins / air in my lungs / taste in my mouth / This is a threat / a promise / a warning.*

I slipped into my wrinkled, dirty clothes and took the elevator downstairs.

In the hotel gift shop, I selected the items I would need: toothpaste, toothbrush, a clean shirt, underwear. I thumbed through a meager rack of tropical shirts and swimming trunks and finally chose a solid red short-sleeved shirt. When I turned back around, I saw a brown-eyed girl giving me a wide, easy smile. It wasn't the plastic Los Angeles greeting I was so accustomed to — this was open, direct.

She rang up the items and asked in a Portuguese accent if there was anything else I needed.

It was at that moment that I noticed the jewelry case. The thought jumped into my head that if I bought something for Angela, it would mean we would be together again. It was magical thinking, an act of faith, of almost holy belief that she was waiting for me, that the voice I had heard on the phone, whispering in the dark, would speak to me again, full of breath and light, flesh and blood.

A gift would demonstrate my feelings for her, too, when I saw her again. It would show her how serious I really was.

The shop girl waited patiently behind the counter while I examined the jewelry. There were glowing garnets, flashing emeralds, vulgar rubies.

I examined necklaces, bracelets, earrings . . .

I pointed to a diamond surrounded by deep blue sapphires on a platinum band.

"Oh —" The girl beamed from behind the counter. "The sapphires . . . they are so beautiful."

I handed her my card, the one that worked.

Moments later, dressed in my new red shirt, the black velvet box containing Angela's ring tucked snugly in the lower right side pocket of my cargo pants, and my teeth freshly brushed, I approached the concierge, who was already reaching into a drawer.

"Your ticket, Mr. Veronchek." He gave me an envelope, and I slipped it into the pocket next to the velvet box.

A bellman stepped forward. "May I call a taxi for you?"

I pulled my asshole sunglasses down over my eyes and followed him outside.

The sky was a plush shade of blue, with clouds scattered across it like white scraps of paper strewn over an open field. The beach was carpet beige, a tasteful hue from an expensive set design, and the water that had been so black in the moonlight glowed emerald where the waves absorbed the rays of the sun. As the eye traveled out to sea, the waves turned to cool aqua and finally became a glittering silver. An orb of liquid fire, high in the sky, dripped through the air. It painted the modern high-rise buildings yellow-white, splashed against the street, and bled onto the mosaic tiles of the sidewalks.

A taxi appeared in front of me as if on cue, and I slipped inside. I had told the bellman I wanted to go to the concert hall where ImmanuelKantLern was playing. He repeated the address to the driver, and we pulled onto the wide black-and-white-tiled street.

On the beach, teenage boys gathered in groups, kicking soccer balls. There were girls out there, too, hundreds, wearing the smallest bikinis, with gleaming black hair and, even from here, flashing white teeth. We drove beyond the beach and into the city, weaving swiftly through concentrated but quick-moving traffic until we finally stopped in front of the huge concrete edifice where I had tried to get in last night, a bland, unadorned expanse of office gray, so different in the light of day.

The taxi driver pointed to the glass entrance.

I gave him one of the hundreds and waved away his astonished response.

She was here, I thought. I could feel her. She was somewhere nearby.

"Angel," I imagined her saying, smiling hugely, the way she had smiled for me that night at the Mask, "you found me . . ."

The concert wouldn't start for hours, but I planned to take in the layout during the day, find out where the back entrances were, discover where the equipment trucks were loaded, maybe even locate Angela before the show.

I stepped around to the front of the building, passing the row of double glass doors, and noticed a wall lined with parking spaces.

I walked around to the back, to the loading zone. There were already a couple of trucks parked there, as well as a huge tour bus. I looked up at the windows, which were dark and reflective, so I couldn't see anything inside it, but I heard some music emanating, a familiar dirty pulse.

I walked to the front of the bus and lifted my hand to knock on the door.

"Hey, hey, hey, hey, hey." It was a voice coming from behind me. "You again?"

I turned around and saw that American with long gray hair falling out of a white Panama hat. This was the same guy from last night, the one who had told me about the invitation-only party.

"I heard music," I said. "I thought —"

"You thought, you thought. What do you want?"

I took a risk. "I'm looking for someone."

"Who?"

"I'm looking for a girl named Jessica Teagarden. Sometimes she calls herself Cassandra."

The man stepped forward. "Why would I know her?"

"She's the girlfriend of . . . of one of the guys in the band."

"I'm the road manager." He laughed and lifted his hat, revealing a shining bald head fringed by long gray hair. He ran his fingers over his scalp and placed the hat back down. It reminded me of Mike, that cop who had come to my apartment the night after Angela disappeared. He actually seemed like the same actor playing a new role. "And there aren't any girlfriends on the road with the band. Believe me, I would know."

"I really need to find her, and I think . . . I think she may be here. I came all the way . . . all the way from Los Angeles." The guy wasn't reacting, so I reached into my pocket and pulled out my wallet. "It's very important. It's actually a matter of life and death."

Slowly, I counted out five hundred-dollar bills.

"Well" — he started looking around guiltily — "the band's doing a radio interview at the moment, and they won't be back for quite some time."

I counted out a couple more and held them out, offering an encouraging look. "Will you help me?"

"You a freak?" he asked, taking the money. "A weirdo? You gonna make a fool of me?"

"I just want to find —"

He cut me off, pocketing the cash. "Joey's been kind of paranoid lately, but I'll see what I can do." The road manager pulled a cell phone from his pocket and punched in a number. He walked away and started speaking quietly into the phone. I even thought I heard him say the name Cassandra, but I couldn't be sure. I also noticed that the noise coming from inside the bus had momentarily stopped. He paced back and forth, speaking quietly for several minutes, then clicked off and turned around. "The guys are coming back about an hour before the concert. He'll meet you around nine. Is that all right?"

"Does Joey know where she is?"

He screwed up his face. "I didn't get into all that."

"Okay," I said. "But exactly where should I meet him?"

He reached into his shoulder bag and pulled out a shimmering rectangle of plastic. "This is a backstage pass." He presented it like a mayor offering me the key to the city. "Just come around here at nine." He pointed to a gray metal door. "And the guard will let you in."

"One hour before they go on?"

"One hour."

"Nine o'clock?" I didn't want to get anything wrong.

"Exactly at nine."

I imagined walking up to a door and before I even lifted my hand to knock, she was opening it. I thought of her face, the tiny wrinkles at the corners of her eyes, that look of understanding . . .

"Thank you," I said, backing away. "Thank you so much." I walked back around to the front of the concert hall and found myself crossing the busy four-lane avenue.

There was a little park across the street that I thought might be a good place to wait. I found a spot in the shade of an old magnolia and sat down on the damp, tropical grass. I wrapped my arms around my legs and propped my chin on my knees, staring out at the flashing sea. I could see the water, the sandy beach, kids kicking soccer balls, girls frolicking in the sun. I was buoyant, ecstatic, waiting and watching the light ripple and shimmer off the surface of the water. It was already almost three in the afternoon, and the sun was a furious, raging ball of flames. From behind me came the heavy sounds of traffic, the whine and roar of engines that seemed different somehow, higher-pitched, than the automobile engines in L.A.

"Angel?" a distant voice said.

I looked up.

"Angel?"

I couldn't fucking believe it. It was that junior lawyer, the one who had been with Frank back in L.A.

Marcel.

"Angel?" He was coming toward me, about thirty yards away now, wearing khaki pants, a pink golf shirt, a blue blazer. Even in South America he was wearing expensive, entertainment-lawyer-on-his-day-off clothes.

I jumped up and took off, running across the small expanse of park through the waxy magnolias directly into the oncoming traffic.

I didn't look back to see if he was following me — I just ran, my legs practically breaking beneath me, and almost caused a major accident.

When I finally turned around, I was blocks into the city, breathing hard, my ankles sharp with pain, and dripping with sweat.

What the fuck was *he* doing here?

Frank must have sent that prick down to get me. He had probably come on the next fucking plane.

I kept walking, looking furtively behind me, until I came to a café. I slipped inside and moved all the way to the back, taking a seat in the most shadowy part of the room. Even though I was sweating like an animal, I ordered a cappuccino from the waitress, and drinking it, minutes later, watched the young lawyer slink by the window. He even came to the door and looked around inside.

I put my head down and tried to stay out of sight. He didn't see me, luckily, and eventually turned around and disappeared. I imagined the conversation Frank and my father must have had when they discovered I was in South America. I had paid for the concert ticket with my hotel bill, so it probably wasn't listed on the credit card. No. The concierge must have told him about the concert, and Frank's assistant must have come here after speaking to him, then simply walked around the perimeter of the concert hall and spotted me below the magnolia in the little park.

I sipped my steaming coffee and slowly chewed through the two dry cookies that had come with it. The café was ancient, with small, round, marble-topped tables and molded cane chairs. There was a dark wooden bar, lacquered a million times over, and a hissing espresso machine. The tile floor had been worn through to the concrete beneath. It was crowded at the moment, which was fortunate, and which was why Frank's assistant hadn't been able to see me. He was on the phone by now, I imagined, notifying Frank that he had found and then lost me, that I had run away, but that he was hot on my trail.

I finished my coffee, left another one of those hundreds on the table and stepped outside, careful to look around the corner. Marcel would be waiting at the concert hall by now. I only hoped he wouldn't find out about my backstage pass, and that I could locate Joey — and Angela — before the concert.

I walked through the labyrinthine streets, careful to watch for Frank's creepy assistant, and finally made my way back.

Once more, but far more carefully this time, I stepped around the gray building.

It was late afternoon now, and the sunlight was harsh, burning. I could feel it stinging my skin, clouding my eyes. I should have picked up some sunblock at the gift shop, I thought. I was so stupid. Humid weather has a way of magnifying the rays of the sun, actually making them fiercer as they refract through the microscopic beads of liquid condensation in the air. It made me think of the neon lights piercing the dim atmosphere of the Velvet Mask, searing through the vulgar darkness. How long was it since I had been there? I felt as if I had traveled a million miles, and that it had been a thousand years since I had received that call.

I slipped into the concert hall parking lot for the second time that day, where I noticed more activity than before and that the enormous bus had been moved off to the side. Once again I heard music. I slumped down against the wall in the small space between the building and the bus and thought for a minute.

Frank's assistant wouldn't find me here. It wasn't possible. I had the backstage pass in my hand, as well as my ticket. I had everything I needed.

All I had to do was wait.

Just then, the door of the bus opened and the road manager stepped out. Thankfully, he didn't turn his head and see me, and he walked straight into the building, leaving the door of the bus open behind him. No one else came out, but I heard a noise coming from inside, a familiar, soaring cacophony — it was the music of ImmanuelKantLern, if you could call it music. I got up and walked carefully to the door, taking that first step off the ground. There was the driver's seat, empty, and a heavy curtain separating the back of the bus from the front. I ascended another step, the racket becoming even louder.

"Hello?" I held my backstage pass forward like an amulet. "Hello?"

I pulled the curtain aside and looked down the narrow aisle. There were bunks, shelves with mattresses for sleeping on the road, but no one in them. The music was coming from all the way in the back. Someone was smoking back there, too. I could smell the fresh cigarette burning and the old tar and nicotine that had been soaked into the upholstery. I moved slowly, one step at a time, until I pulled another curtain aside.

There he was.

Eyes closed in an expression of pure rapture, Joey Descartes was playing a black Fender, sitting on a built-in couch. A cigarette dangled from his lips. On the floor by his feet was a small electric amplifier. He had blond hair cut in the current rock-star style, carefully messy, with muscular shoulders and a hairless chest. Shirtless, his skin was pasty, almost as pale as mine, and he wore antique leather pants. There was a red tattoo of a heart, not a Valentine heart, as you'd expect, but a ventriculated human heart, concretely enough, inked over his own. I waited until the song was over, a repetitive dirge that never altered its consistent throbbing pulse, one note that never modulated or wavered.

Then I took another step forward.

She was sitting across from him, a paperback novel open on her lap.

It was Angela.

But it wasn't Angela.

"Angela?" I asked, knowing it was the wrong girl but still some- how wishing she would transform herself into the right one.

It was as though an actress were playing Angela in the biopic based her life. She had the right outlines, the right clothes . . . she was all the right colors . . . but her facial features, especially her eyes, were all wrong.

Everything was wrong.

The fact that I had come here was wrong. Her identity was wrong. What I thought I was doing here was wrong.

She looked up at me, whoever she was, confusion written across those gorgeous features.

"Angel," she said, "what are you doing here?"

I stared back at her. "Who are you?" I asked. "How do you know my name?"

"Who the fuck are *you?*" Joey shouted, and at the same time, he came toward me, wielding his black Fender like a club.

———

There is another kind of darkness, one that has nothing to do with the absence of light. It is the darkness of being unconscious, of time gone, of memory lapsed. It is interesting, isn't it, that the absence of memory is called a blackout, that sleep itself is remembered as darkness and awareness as light? These are more than just metaphors, I believe, and have more than a symbolic significance. It is a glimpse into the actual, it is the way the instrument of our consciousness measures the universe itself. Am I in darkness or in light? Am I awake? Am I alive?

And then there was light. I *am* awake, I thought.

I opened my eyes all the way and found myself alone in a space approximately the size of an elementary school classroom. No windows, no furniture, only four blank walls, a concrete floor, and a ceiling inset with lifeless fluorescent lights. I checked the metal door and found that it was locked. I didn't know if I had been unconscious for hours or only minutes or even seconds. The bass player must have really clocked me with his Fender, and then someone must have deposited me here. Automatically, I touched the light switch by the door and let the light fall away. I needed the darkness. I brushed my fingertips against the wall and guided myself to the spot farthest away from the door, then slid down to the concrete and wrapped my arms around my knees.

Sitting in the dark, I whispered my own name. "Angel." I said it the way Angela had said it on the phone and listened to see if she had been in a room like this when she called. But the word echoed strangely back to me, as if the darkness itself were responding. I waited for my eyes to adjust. There wasn't even that usual sliver of yellow bleeding around the cracks in the door, which would eventually illuminate the whole room. No. This darkness was absolute. This was darkness itself. Just as it had been when Angela blindfolded me, there was nothing to which my eyes could react, no photons, no particles or beams to find their way in. My extreme light sensitivity wouldn't help me here. I kept saying my own name, "Angel," saying it over and over so I could hear its echo, until eventually I heard the whispery voice speaking all on its own.

It was her. It was Angela. She was speaking to me, calling from the dark.

"Angel."

I waited.

"Angel, can you hear me?"

"Yes," I answered, "I can hear you. I'm here, I'm in the dark with you." I scanned the cloud of black in front of me. But my eyes might as well have been closed. "Where are you?" I asked. "Tell me where you —"

"I've been waiting for you," Angela said. *"Waiting."*

"I'm so sorry."

"You said you would rescue me." It was the same faint voice she had used on the phone, hushed, fearful. *"You told me you would come for me, that you would find me, that you would come."*

I got up and moved around the room, fingertips tracing the smooth walls, a hand reaching unsteadily in front of me. "I know," I said. "I'm looking for you. I'm looking everywhere. I'll find you, I promise. It's just —"

"It's so dark," Angela said. *"Angel, it's so dark in here."*

"Don't be afraid," I begged, my arms reaching out. "Please, Angela, don't be afraid."

"I'm so alone," she said. *"Where are you?"* Her voice was growing fainter, as if she were slipping away.

"No," I told the darkness. "I'm here. Every second, Angela," I said, "I'm here with you. I just can't —"

"Angel," she said, *"what is the darkest place?"* Her voice was almost completely gone now, barely audible at all.

"I don't know," I said. "I don't know what you mean. Please, Angela —"

Then the door opened like a rock that had been rolled away from a sepulcher, and a Brazilian security guard said something in bewildering Portuguese.

Lying on the floor, the side of my face pressed to the concrete, I looked up at him. He waved toward the hallway outside, and with some difficulty I pushed myself up and stepped into the light. He dragged me by the arm through the brightness of the corridor, then eased me out the back, releasing me in the tropical night air like a trout thrown back into a stream.

It was night.

I realized now that I had been somewhere inside the concert hall. After knocking me out, Joey probably didn't want to bother with the local police and had me locked up to keep me out of the way.

I walked past the trucks and the ImmanuelKantLern tour bus without looking back and found myself after five quick minutes in the very center of Rio. It had rained, a tropical burst, and the streets and sidewalks shone slickly, reflecting the gleaming traffic lights. The buildings leaned toward me as though in a German Expressionist painting. I had become off-balance, and the sounds of the city were distant, incomplete. My neck, arms, and face had been burned in the afternoon sun, and I was dizzy from hunger, starving because I hadn't eaten anything since those two little cookies at the café. I wanted to go back to the hotel, but wasn't sure if I was headed in the right direction, and at first I tried to use the sound of the ocean to guide me.

It was somewhere to my right, I was certain.

No, wait, it was ahead of me.

Fuck. I should have found a taxi at the concert hall, but now it was too far behind to go back. I turned down one small street after another.

Where was I?

On either side were apartment buildings, windows flickering like the eyes of jack-o-lanterns. The streets seemed to be getting denser, smaller, with no main avenues presenting themselves.

Then I saw him. "Hey!" I shouted.

I couldn't believe it. Walking up ahead of me, his head down . . . there was no doubt about it.

He turned to look at me but kept walking, increasing his pace.

"Hey!" I said again, and took off after him.

What the fuck was he doing all the way down here?

I started to run, and he started to run, too. I followed him half a block before he turned down a narrow alley and disappeared into the shadows.

I ran through the alley and came out on the other side, panting. Where did he go?

Then I saw him just beside me. He was crouched down, hiding in some bushes, waiting for me to pass.

I stepped forward, acting like I didn't see him, then jumped into the bushes and grabbed him by the collar. He thrashed against me, but I was able to pin him down.

"Who are you?" I said. "Why are you following me?"

The man in the gray suit didn't answer, staring back at me with terrified eyes.

"Why are you looking for Angela?" I said. "Tell me."

"Please," the man said with a heavy accent. "Please."

I reached into the inside pocket of his jacket and pulled out his wallet. Flipping it open, I saw an I.D. card of some kind, as well as credit cards from the Bank of Brazil, and even what appeared to be a local bus pass.

This was just some Brazilian man, I realized. Just as Angela had been replaced by a stranger, so had the man in the gray suit.

I got up.

He rose, wary, brushing himself off.

I handed him his wallet. "I'm sorry," I said.

I didn't know what else to say. I had just attacked a complete stranger.

He backed away then, pushing through the bushes, and hurried down the street. He would be looking for a cop, no doubt, and no one would be easier to identify than a red-shirted albino in the streets of Rio.

I hurried under a cover of trees, kicking the dead leaves of succulents beneath my feet. I had to get back to the hotel, I thought, to make my way back to the airport, to get the hell out of this country. I turned one corner, then another, looking for something that would lead me to a street where I could find a taxi. Finally, I saw what I thought might be a wider avenue up ahead.

But within seconds I was against a wall, the serrated blade of a kitchen knife pressed hard against my throat.

They had come out of the shadows like thugs in a movie, one of them tossing his cigarette to the side, the other with a hand seemingly idle in his pocket. Right now one of them — he couldn't have been older than fourteen — tore through my pockets, quickly finding my wallet. He spoke rapidly, in an unidentifiable dialect, but I clearly understood his amazement at discovering the thousands of dollars in there. I had given a lot of that money away by now, but there was still plenty left. Christ. It was so fucking dumb. What the hell was I doing, carrying all that cash in the middle of the night in Rio de Janeiro? It was textbook stupidity. The kid with the knife to my throat wore a studied maniacal look. He tilted his head so I could see the psychotic whites of his eyes. It was deliberate, I knew, meant to provoke the greatest possible fear, and a director would have said it was over the top.

Then, for some reason, I became absorbed by the interference pattern of a street lamp shining across the park. There was a row of thick trees there, and behind them two sources of light. One was a chemical yellow, the other a bright white neon. The two beams of illumination overlapped. They didn't blend, exactly. Instead, one seemed to occlude the other, and inside the area of interfering light was a fascinating pattern of oblongs and crescents, an effect physicists call a moray.

The scene was lit. The cameras, I imagined, were rolling. I waited for the director to yell "Cut!" and for my muggers to ask if it had all been too much.

"No, no," Ridley would say. "That was perfect, absolutely terrific. But let's do it again just to be safe."

I felt the blade of the knife pressing harder against my throat, and the whole time, I kept my eyes on the intersecting patterns of light. This is just a scene, I told myself. This is merely a moment in a movie. Ridley and his crew were right over there, concealed by the darkness, hiding behind their equipment. Not coincidentally, I began to think of an experiment Isaac Newton had conducted with knives. Newton, at least in regard to physical optics, is associated more than anything with the prismatic decomposition of white light. In one historic experiment, he created a wedge-shaped slit with two blades. Then he shone a beam of light through the slit. On a white piece of paper a few feet away, he created a diffraction pattern. Light, he learned, *curves* around an object, it doesn't move in the perfectly straight line that common sense dictates; instead, it curves the same way ocean waves curve around a rock.

Particle or wave?

Red. Orange. Bright yellow. Burning.

They couldn't have been more than teenagers, these kids, though on their faces, even in this dimly lit park, I could read a lifetime of experience. I lost my fear, strangely enough, and felt envy instead. Unlike me, these boys were consumed with purpose, with a clear, attainable mission. They needed money, and they would do whatever they had to do to get it. They would kill me if necessary.

One of them kicked my feet out from under me, and as I fell to the ground, I felt the knife tip nick the high point of my cheekbone.

I waited for the blade to come down, like Anthony Perkins's butcher's knife in *Psycho,* my hands flying up involuntarily to protect my face.

But when I opened my eyes, the boys were gone.

They had taken all the cash but, thankfully, had left my wallet and its contents on the ground. In their excitement, they had also failed to notice the ring box I had stashed in my side pocket.

I took it as a sign.

I suddenly developed an animal-like sensitivity to the sounds of traffic and followed my ears to a wider avenue, and then to the broad street that ran parallel to the beach.

I started walking, which is when I felt something wet and looked down.

Christ. I had pissed in my pants.

I stepped across the street in front of the beach and shuffled into the sand. There were people strolling up and down the sidewalk, and the lights of high-rise hotels glowed cheerily. I went down to the water and splashed a handful of salt water against my face. I was bleeding, and I was worried I wouldn't be able to get a taxi now that my face was covered with blood. I wouldn't have much luck getting one if I smelled like urine, either, so I stepped fully into the water and rinsed myself off.

I was slipping in and out, I admit, my mind sprinting from one idea to another, my thoughts colliding, the rational with the irrational, the impossible with the likely. I knew that some of these things were real, that some of them weren't. I knew that some of my thinking was based in fact, that some of it was just insane. But I could only move forward. I could only continue the search. I had to find Angela. I had heard her calling me from the darkness of the concrete room beneath the concert hall, so I knew she was nearby. I had heard her again, and while a part of me knew that it was only a dream, just a manic hallucination, I also believed that it meant she was alive somewhere, that Angela was waiting in the darkness for me to rescue her.

"Angel," she had said.

I walked along the sandy crescent of beach for an hour or more, letting my clothes dry, until I saw a line of taxis waiting in front of a hotel.

I slipped into the back before the driver could get a good look at me.

"Copacabana Palace," I said, thinking I'd have the hotel pay the fare.

We drove through the tropical streets of Rio, and I gingerly touched the fresh cut on my cheekbone. For some reason, it felt right.

———

"You were wrong again, Frank." I stepped inside the room and stared straight at him, somehow knowing just where he would be.

"Wrong about what?" My father's lawyer was stretched out on the bed, a green bottle of mineral water clutched in his age-spotted hand. His face was drawn, the color of ash; his eyes were deeply bloodshot. His usually robust complexion seemed to have been drained of its life, and his flesh hung off the points of his skeleton like his own expensive, rumpled suit. Frank reached for the remote by his side and flicked the television off, leaving a discomforting silence.

"About Angela," I said. "That wasn't her."

I noticed Marcel, too, sitting at the vanity. He wore a tan linen suit and a white shirt. His heavy glasses made shadows over his eyes, but his skin, unlike Frank's, was healthy and pink. In fact, Frank's assistant looked positively refreshed for having flown down here only to run all over the city chasing me through the alien streets.

"What happened to your face?" Frank's usually deep voice was thin, crackly.

I removed the contents of my pockets and placed everything, my wallet, the ring box, on the bedside table, then stepped into the bathroom. "I was mugged." The cut wasn't as bad as I had thought it would be, just a bruise on my left cheekbone and a one-inch line that had already begun to scab over. I slipped out of my wet clothes and into the robe, then stepped back into the room. The red digital clock on the bedside table said it was nine minutes after two. I must have been out for hours. "Sorry to keep you up," I said, "but, you know, Frank, I'm thirty-two years old. I don't exactly need people following me around like this. I have a right to my own —"

"Angel"— he brought himself up to a sitting position, his voice hardening —"you have a right to nothing. You've never had an actual job. You've never paid for a single thing. You've never taken care of yourself. Your father gives you complete autonomy, too much, in my opinion, for what you give back." He sighed bitterly. "He expects nothing from you. The least you could do is let him know where in the world you are." He paused for a moment, inhaling deeply before adding, "And by the way, you're thirty-four."

I sat down on the bed next to him and looked at my hands, at that purple spot of cancer forming over my knuckle.

"Did they get your credit cards?"

I shrugged. "They only took the cash."

"What the hell are you doing here?"

"I wanted to find her."

Frank shook his large, fleshy head. "Your dad is extremely worried about you. He was terrified when he found out you were here. He was ready to send in the fucking marines." He reached a gray finger to my cheek. "This is a dangerous place, which you've obviously learned the hard way." Roughly, he touched my cut, and I flinched, backing away. "We contacted the hotel to make sure you were all right, but he couldn't stand it anymore."

I smiled my iciest smile. It was the same look I had given Angela when I answered the door that first day I met her. "You're his bitch," I said. I knew I shouldn't be saying it, that there would be some horrible retribution for my insolence later, but I couldn't help myself.

Frank smiled back, his oiliest, you-can-say-anything-and-still-not-hurt-me smile.

I had to laugh. "And you're Frank's bitch," I offered to Marcel.

My father's lawyer rubbed his hands over his eyes and looked around as if he had just discovered himself here.

Marcel got up from the chair and grabbed his blazer. "All right if I go?"

Frank made a clicking sound with his tongue and gave Marcel a simultaneous wink.

"Your father asked me," Frank said after Marcel had left, "not to let you out of my sight. But I'm going to go to my room now, too, because I'm exhausted, and then . . . and then we'll all get on the plane first thing in the morning." He heaved himself off the bed, picked up my wallet, and slipped my Visa cards into his hand. He pushed the pieces of gleaming plastic into his pocket. "The plane leaves at nine, so we have to be at the airport by seven. If you know what's good for you, you'll meet me downstairs at six."

———

The Schrödinger book was lying on the dresser where I had left it, so I picked it up now, flipping randomly through its pages and remembering that cat I had buried in the old man's yard. Just to be absurd, I had already started to think of her as Schrödinger's cat. According to the Multiple Worlds Theory, she must be alive in some alternative world, still mewling up at some alternative kitchen window while some alternative version of me stared down at her. Why not? All worlds are possible, right? If there are multiple worlds, I reasoned, why shouldn't I be happy and independent in at least one of them? At the same time, all I could think about was getting back to L.A., slipping back into my routine of staying up all night with *Blade Runner,* a dollop of bourbon in my coffee, my twice-weekly visits to Silowicz, and his endless supply of merciful, memory-dulling meds.

My body was still shot through with adrenaline, probably from being mugged, so I took a bath to try and soothe my nerves, letting my head loll back in the hot water of the luxury tub, listening to those strange, faraway, underwater sounds. Eventually I got out and watched several hours of *Friends* on the hotel television. There was a channel in Rio that played the show over and over, in English with Portuguese subtitles. These characters had become so incredibly old, I thought. A bunch of people in their late thirties acting like idiots in their early twenties, their lives had grown stagnant. But I had stagnated, too, hadn't I? I had fallen into a deep, pointless dream, a reverie that Angela had jerked me out of, even if for one brief moment, before she disappeared, leaving me awake at the wrong hour, the wrong age.

Was I really thirty-four?

I flipped through the Schrödinger book and read more about the Multiple Worlds Theory:

"Faced with a choice on the quantum level, not only the particle itself but the entire universe splits into two versions. In one universe, the particle goes through hole A, in the other it goes through hole B. In each universe there is an observer who sees the particle go through just one hole. And forever afterward the two universes are completely separate and non-interacting."

Forever afterward . . . could that really be true?

If there were multiple cats in multiple worlds, I thought, why shouldn't there be multiple Angelas? Why not even multiple Angels? Perhaps there was another me in another world, an Angel with normal, melanin-rich skin, walking around in the sun, or a world where I didn't need Silowicz's meds, or one where I had even finished writing my stupid screenplay.

There must be some way to get there, I thought, to cross over to one of those other worlds.

My unmedicated mind spun in a million directions, each one an alternative universe all its own.

Then, at around five-thirty a.m., having been able to close my eyes for only a few troubled moments, I got out of bed and dressed in my sour, still damp clothes.

A few minutes later, there was a knock.

On the other side of the door, I discovered Frank's assistant, a serene look on his junior executive face. "Frank's downstairs getting a car," Marcel informed me. "He said to be ready in five minutes."

I considered slipping out the back, finding the rear exit and disappearing, just as Angela had disappeared on me, searching for her in every one of those alternative worlds if I had to.

But I didn't. Instead, I grabbed my stuff and took the elevator downstairs. Besides, I thought, Frank still had my credit cards, and I'd need money in any world.

He was sitting on a pink-and-gold couch in the lobby with his head hanging down, a hand on his drab forehead. He stared at his tasseled loafers, the expensive red-brown leather shining bleakly in the incandescent hotel lobby light.

I took a seat next to him. "Good morning, Frank."

Without looking up, he asked, "Did you sleep well?"

"No."

"Neither did I." His face had grown so old. The lines around his eyes had become cracks; his once-bright irises had gone dull, and his sockets had sunk deep into his skull.

Looking at Frank made me feel old myself.

Thirty-four. How was it possible that I had become thirty-four without even noticing?

At that moment, a man in a red jacket stepped briskly into the lobby. "Sir," he said, aiming his hotel-employee smile at Frank, "your car is waiting."

We stepped out onto the sidewalk. The rising sun had airbrushed a soft, glowing pink across the surface of the sky. This was even more beautiful than the smog-filtered sunrises I had grown accustomed to watching through the miniblinds on San Raphael Crescent.

"Look at that," I couldn't help but say as we got in. "Holy shit, will you look at that, Frank?"

I know that a lot of people have described the sky, the light, the sun rising over an alien horizon, but I felt, I even believed, that I had never seen one this gorgeous before. It must have been the pollution, the impure atmosphere, the permanent haze that hung in filmy sheers over the city, worse, even, than in Los Angeles. Pink, blue, orange, all of these hues harmonized one with the others like the voices of a divine choir. The white flecks of clouds in the sky were like paint strokes left on a canvas by an abstract expressionist, a color-field artist with a sentimental streak. Then it occurred to me that it might have been the work of the same lighting department that had been following me everywhere lately, setting up scenes. The assistant camera operator was in the background, I realized, holding a light meter to the sky. The line producer kept asking if they were ready yet. The whole effect had probably been created by Industrial Light and Magic, and this was all a movie. That's why everything was so beautiful, I thought. That's why all the people I met were stock characters and why the central participants in my life seemed to have been sent down from central casting.

This was a movie, and I was just a character. I could even feel the pages of the script unfolding.

Frank nodded, waving a dismissive hand in the air. "They have no emissions standards down here. All the crap in the air . . ." He never finished his sentence, however, because we took off, moving away from the hotel like the *Millennium Falcon* from the Death Star.

————

An hour later, Frank's assistant was somewhere in the back, flying coach. I had a window seat in first class again, and Frank sat next to me, as if on guard, as if I might try to sneak out of the plane when he wasn't looking. I spent the morning watching the bright light of the sun reflecting off the sparkling clouds. Even through the lenses of my asshole glasses it stung, but for some reason I wanted to watch, for some reason I wanted to see everything as clearly as possible. Eventually, a stewardess asked if I would mind lowering the shade, saying the bright light was bothering the other passengers. I made a personal note of the irony and sat in the darkness of the cabin, letting my consciousness drift and fingering the protruding shape of the velvet box in my pocket.

The engagement ring. I had been so lucky my muggers hadn't found it. Or perhaps when I pissed myself, they had grown disgusted and no longer wanted to touch me. In any event, there it was, and I projected myself into the moment I would give it to her. Angela would gasp, of course, placing an elegant hand over her sensual mouth, and then she would say, "Yes, yes, little prince, oh yes."

Frank opened his briefcase and worked his way through a stack of legal documents, sifting through his pile of papers, contracts, finely printed deals, and proposals. He had become one of Hollywood's most influential entertainment lawyers and had even executive-produced a few movies himself, yet here he was flying all the way to

South America, to Rio de Janeiro, to collect me. I had been study-
ing his face through half-open eyes, watching him work in the
dusty spindle of light that shone down from the airplane ceiling.
But what did I really know about him? What did my father even
know about Frank Heile? I knew he lived in Beverly Hills. I knew
he had a wife named Sara, small-boned and gray-haired and practical, a little sparrow of a woman. I knew that he only drove his
Porsche on weekends and that he was embarrassed to admit it. But
otherwise, he was just Frank, a portrait of evil. I wondered how
many lives he had ruined, how many careers he had destroyed. I remembered how he used to pull me aside when I was a little kid, especially when my mother wasn't around, and threaten me, the grip
of his huge hands on my bony arms.

I slept through the rest of the flight, waking just long enough
to wedge myself against the corner of the seat and adjust the tiny
blanket. It was cold, and a sharp fissure of freezing air kept finding
me, chilling my flesh. I longed for the warm darkness of my apartment in West Hollywood. I dreamed of sitting at my computer and
working on my garbled dialogue and senseless camera directions,
the meaningless utterings, I knew, of an insane dreamer. I even
missed old Silowicz. There was an emptiness inside me when I
woke up that was beyond hunger. "Frank," I said then, "have you
ever lost anyone?" I don't know why I was asking him, but at this
point I was past giving a shit about anything.

He had finished his paperwork and was now reading the *Wall
Street Journal,* tracing his silvery pen down the length of a column.
"Come on, Angel," he said.

"Answer the question."

"Why are you letting this get to you so much?" He didn't even look up from his reading. "She was just some stupid girl."

I glared at him.

"We'll be landing soon."

"What's going to happen?"

"First, we're going to find your car." He sighed. "And then I'm going to take you to your father's house. And then I'm going to go to my office and get some work done."

"What happened to her, Frank?"

He shook his head.

"Is she gone?"

"Take it easy, Angel. Just take it easy and get some rest."

I pressed him. "What really happened?" I knew he knew. For some reason, I knew he just wasn't telling me. He had sent me on a wild goose chase, had led me all the way to Rio to keep me from finding out.

"Angel," he said, "sometimes these women, especially the ones you meet . . . under those circumstances, they just vanish." He was shaking his head. "And you don't ever find them again. And believe me, you don't want to."

I asked him again. "But what happened to her?"

"Angel, listen to me —"

"Frank," I said, "tell me what happened, what really happened." I knew he knew something. I knew Frank was aware of more than he was telling me.

He always did. He was omniscient.

He turned to me, and in the faint light of the plane, his face was black and white, drawn like the face of a villain in a comic book. "Angel," he said, "you don't want this girl, trust me. This is —"

"Don't tell me what I want, Frank. I have never wanted anything in my entire life. I have never asked you for anything, never bothered you or my father for any —"

"Angel," Frank said, and the muscles of his face constricted like a fist, "she's gone, and the worst thing you're imagining, whatever that is, that's what happened, all right?"

———

Observe. Hypothesize. Predict. Experiment. When Angela left the Mask that last night, if anyone had seen her with the man in gray, I reasoned, she would have had to walk through the rear entrance like everyone else. And there was one person who would have seen them, one person I still hadn't spoken to.

Around three-thirty they started coming out: customers dragging their feet through the rear entrance of the Velvet Mask, stepping reluctantly across the parking lot to their Nissans, Hondas, and Jeeps, emerging like light-sensitive moles from the underground. Then the dancers started leaving, too, most of them dressed in their street clothes, lighting cigarettes and waving their quick coworker good-byes to one another like cashiers leaving the late shift at a convenience store. Every now and then, one of them emerged from the club still dressed in a sparkling gown and hanging on the arm of a man, always a white man, almost always in a gray suit. Any one of them could have matched the description of the man Angela had supposedly left with. Any one of them, I realized, could have been the man I had seen in her apartment when I stepped out of the closet.

I had slipped away, of course, had casually told Frank that I needed to go to the bathroom and had disappeared while he waited for Marcel to get the limo. I found the Cadillac where I had parked it and came straight here.

All around me, engines were turning over, headlights blossoming, cars pulling away and going home.

At around four in the morning, he came out, too. The hulking giant in the ridiculous butler costume stood in the pool of inadequate illumination under the high yellow bulb and lit a small joint, smoking it down to the roach in a few powerful drags, then flicked it unceremoniously across the darkness of the lot. It had rained earlier, and I even heard the faint *ffsstttt* of the ember going out when it hit the damp pavement. A blond dancer, the one who had put me in mind of concentration camps the last time I was here, came out behind him. She wore a clinging fluorescent orange pantsuit and six-inch plastic heels. Lester turned to face her, and it looked for all the world like he was talking, but from where I sat inside the Cadillac, I couldn't be sure.

Maybe he was reading her lips. Maybe he was speaking, but in the distorted cadences of the deaf.

Eventually the blonde went back inside, and Lester waddled across the lot toward his extra-long black limo. It wasn't a hearse, exactly, but the kind of vehicle a funeral home uses to transport the family of the deceased. He opened the door, tucked himself into the driver's seat, and started the engine, igniting the headlights and flooding the parking lot with a luminous glare.

I waited a few seconds, then pulled out behind him.

Lester drove onto Sunset and turned right after only a short distance onto La Brea, eventually finding Pico and heading in the direction of Santa Monica. At Lincoln Boulevard he turned onto a side street, then slowed into the front parking lot of a low stucco building, finally coming to a full stop around the side. On the building was a discreet enamel plaque that, like the sign on the side of Lester's car, said Horace & Geary. The building was made of cinder block and stucco, like almost everything else in Los Angeles, and the small, underlit emblem had faded over the years, having become almost illegible. I drove past it and turned into the parking lot of the old piano store next door, taking the Cadillac around the back and stopping behind a Dumpster. I got out and made my way on foot just in time to watch Lester open the rear door. I saw a peel of incandescence issue from inside, which meant, I thought, that it was open, that people were already there. Was that policy? It was four-thirty in the fucking morning. Was someone required to guard the dead through the night? Do funeral homes, like morgues, have a night shift? I crept around the gray building warily, careful, for some reason, to keep my distance. The facade was an ordinary, though slightly more sedate, version of the usual strip mall storefront, but the back looked like something else entirely: It was a virtual factory, a huge metal structure with pipes protruding and projecting from every angle. I didn't quite realize what this meant until I noticed the single smokestack soaring from its rooftop like a spire.

An incinerator, I thought coldly, and I felt a flash of something familiar.

This is where people are cremated.

It was precisely at that moment that I felt the sky opening and heard a distinctive *crack,* which I realized almost instantly was the sound of an enormous gold ring against my fragile albino skull. My body twisted as I dropped to the ground, and what I saw from my sudden new position, looking up, was Lester, a contorted grin disfiguring his Buddha-like face, and his fat fist recoiling. The world went momentarily black and then became bright again as my consciousness slipped away and then came rushing back. I watched shimmering spots of light form in my field of vision and felt a wave of nausea slash through my body, starting in my stomach and pushing its way toward my mouth.

This would spawn another migraine, I knew, a real monster.

I tasted bile at the back of my throat and almost puked right there.

Lester was picking me up by my shirt now, lifting my whole body to his face, saying, "What the *fuck,* just what the *fuck,* the *fuck* do you think you're doing?"

After he dropped me again, I held my hands up and formed a crouching position, a posture I hoped would be sufficiently pitiable.

"Why the *fuck* are you following me, you *fucking* vampire-looking piece of —"

"Don't hit me."

"You're lucky I don't kill you right here, you *fuck.*" Lester had a speech impediment, it seemed, a distinct lisp, and there was something effeminate about the high pitch of his voice that jarred incongruously with his size.

This was why he didn't speak inside the club, I realized. He wasn't deaf, he was embarrassed. "I thought you were deaf."

"I'm not deaf." He cocked his arm back and made a blunt, threatening fist. "I just don't *fucking* talk that much. Is that all-*fucking*-right with you?"

The sun had started to glow over the eastern horizon, and a soft gray-gold had developed in the faraway sky. "I was only looking for Angela — for Jessica Teagarden — for Cassandra," I said, remembering to use all of her names. "Please don't hit me again." The rays of light from the sun were bending toward the planet, curving around to meet us.

"Cassandra is *fucking* gone."

"Where?"

Lester released me, throwing me back on my heels so violently that I almost lost my balance. "You want to know what the *fuck* happened to her?"

"Yes," I said. "That's all I want."

"You really want to *fucking* know?"

I went ahead and told him. "She called me from the dark."

"From the dark?"

"She said my name."

Lester shook his huge head, not understanding.

"My phone rang and it was her. She said my name and then she was cut —"

"If I show you what happened to her, will you stop *fucking* looking for her? Will you leave her the *fuck* alone?"

I nodded.

"Come the *fuck* inside," he said in his crazy voice, "and I'll show you what the *fuck* happened to her." He walked around the corner of the crematorium and through a side door, his head twitching oddly.

I stood up and followed, my hand rubbing the back of my head. There didn't seem to be any blood there, at least, but I could feel a hard knot growing, the size of my knuckle. I wasn't seeing the full aura yet, either, but I knew it would come, I knew at this point it was inevitable. I stepped inside, following Lester's broad back into a gray room containing a metal desk with a tiny plastic Scrabble set on it, midgame. The entire wall above the desk was a control panel. There were dials and knobs, gauges and meters and switches. This whole room was a machine: a set of rails ran from one wall into a gaping opening, and on these rails was a metal box, the mouth of which was just large enough to hold a casket. "It reaches thousands of *fucking* degrees in there," Lester said, a hint of pride in his lispy voice. He slid the door in the wall open and revealed a stainless steel channel. It was lined with ashes. He turned to face me. "And I guess when I put her in there, she still had her *fucking* phone with her. She must have called you." He overpronounced each word. "She must have called you," he said again, speaking slowly and deliberately, "from inside the incinerator . . . right before . . . she burst into flames."

"Frank paid you?"

"Frank?" He could hardly say the word. It came out, *Fthlank.* Lester smiled, revealing the glitter of a single gold tooth. "Who the fuck is Frank?"

I backed away, moving toward the door. Those ashes . . . that was a human being?

Lester was laughing now, chuckling almost good-naturedly, the fat of his body jiggling. He was practically doubling over, flashing his gold tooth, jolly as Santa Claus.

"She called me," I said, "from the dark."

The heavy flesh of Lester's neck twitched, his head correcting for each involuntary movement. "She must have called you right before I turned on the *fucking* flames."

"You're lying." Inside, I was begging for him to tell me he was lying. "You're just saying this to scare me."

"Yeah," Lester said, "Frank paid me to do it." He started to move toward me. "Whoever that is. He paid me to do it to you, too. Said you'd be here."

I reached the door behind me and burst through it. The light was nearing the horizon, and the gray haze was giving way to a dazzling yellow. The Los Angeles sun was arriving, gold beams cascading from the filmy sky. I didn't turn around to look back. I just ran. I found myself seconds later inside my mother's Cadillac. I was hyperventilating, and I had to remind myself to take slow, deep breaths. My entire body was shaking while I fumbled with the keys.

I thought of Angela inside the crematorium, her body bursting into flames.

I had been wrong. She hadn't called from the dark — she had called from the light.

From the light.

And the pain I heard in her voice was the pain of burning.

The light.

Red. Orange. Bright yellow. Burning.

Looking into her face that morning, the morning she stole those hyacinths, I had felt like I was looking into the heart of light.

I had been looking into the future, I thought now.

And when I drove home from Lester's funeral parlor, I was shaking.

And when I arrived at San Raphael Crescent, I was still shaking, thinking that I had loved her, had loved Angela, Jessica, Cassandra, whatever her fucking name was, loved her like I had never loved anyone.

In the apartment, I immediately poured myself a mug of Jack, letting it sting my mouth, letting my tongue go numb first, then the rest of me. I opened the childproof cap of the apricot-colored plastic bottle of Hapistat, still quivering, vibrating like an old man with delirium tremens in complete alcoholic withdrawal, and in full knowledge of the fact that no amount of Inderol or Xanax or Elavil could ever make me stop shaking.

Pure happiness — that's what I needed.

Hapistat.

My ears filled with blood and all I could hear was a rushing sound like heavy waves senselessly attacking a beach, a silence filling the universe, an emptiness far beyond my powers to describe it.

I ate a whole handful of the dry little pills.

Happy, happy Hapistat.

The worst thing, Frank had said.

And this was worse, far worse than anything I could have seen in any nightmare.

I grabbed the bottle of Jack and the little plastic container of meds, got back into the Cadillac, and drove, riding through the city — my city, Los Angeles. I experienced a migraine like never before, my brain going supernova. I welcomed it, pulling over every now and then to puke into the gutter, drinking another swallow of bourbon, taking another tab of Hapistat, or two, repeating this process continually until the sun was fully up, blaring down like the angry eye of God Himself.

Finally, I pulled over to the side of the road in Malibu and closed my eyes, imagining the unimaginable.

———

She stepped out of the back door of the Velvet Mask, having changed into a pair of jeans, an old ImmanuelKantLern T-shirt, and high leather boots. Lester had been waiting under that firefly-yellow bulb. It was late, almost morning, and he was smoking his customary joint, inhaling the whole thing in a few swift hits.

"Save me a toke," she begged.

I imagined that he smiled his little-boy smile and handed her the roach. She took it between her thumb and middle finger and smoked what was left, inhaling expertly, deeply. He always had the best shit, she thought. "Will you *fucking* come with me?" Lester's voice was soft, girlish. He flashed his glittery tooth. There was something about it that persuaded her. Lester had never asked Angela for anything before, and so, she thought tonight, why not? She followed him to the long black limousine he used to drive mourners to the cemetery. He even held the door open for her. She wasn't sure what he wanted but had always been curious about Lester's life. He had asked earlier, as a matter of fact, approaching the stage while she was dancing. She had leaned down, naked, and he had whispered a question in her ear, he wanted to show her something, could she meet with him after they closed?

Why not? she had said, tickling his chin.

Why the *fuck* not?

They pulled out of the Velvet Mask parking lot onto Sunset. "Where are you taking me, Lester?"

He smiled faintly. "I want to show you where the *fuck* I work."

"The funeral parlor?"

"Yeah."

He had a soft mustache, the kind you see on the faces of fourteen-year-old kids. Just to be nice, to show a little affection, she slid across the seat of the limo and leaned against him. "Why do you want me to see your funeral parlor?"

She had placed her bag on the floor by her feet, but she had her cell phone in the pocket of her jeans. It was hard against the pro-truding bone of her hip.

"Because," Lester said, "just because."

"Do you want to be alone with me?" she teased.

He released a bashful breath and looked away, stopping at a light. He smelled like cigarettes and aftershave, and the skin of his neck bulged out around the collar of his shirt.

"How come you never wear anything but this crazy old suit?" she asked playfully.

"I have other clothes," he answered. "It's just that I'm always *fucking* working."

"Why do you work so much, Lester?"

"There's nothing *fucking* else to do." Finally, he turned into an empty parking lot behind an old, underlit building. He stopped the car and said, "Stay here."

Angela waited in her seat while Lester walked the long way around the limo and opened the door for her.

"Oh," she said, getting out, "a gentleman."

"It's inside."

"What is?"

"What I want to *fucking* show you."

She got out and Lester closed the door after her. She followed him to the back door of the funeral home. It was covered with pipes and ducts, a smokestack rising overhead. He opened the door and she stepped in ahead of him. It was just a little room filled with machinery, a panel of knobs and switches above a desk and chair, the minuscule game of Scrabble laid out on the desk. Along the wall ran a conveyor belt, and resting on top of the belt was a metal box. She turned around and Lester was locking the door behind him.

"I'm sorry," he said.

"Sorry for what, sweetheart?"

"It's not *fucking* personal." He went to the metal box and opened the lid.

"Lester, what are you talking about?"

He came toward her, his huge hands moving so quickly she didn't have even a second to react. He lifted her, sweeping her off her feet like a bride at a honeymoon hotel, and carried her toward the box.

"Lester," she said. She wanted to scream, wanted to say something more, but her voice got caught in her throat. "Lester, please," she whispered. *"Please."*

He placed her inside the box, and she clawed at him, leaving a bloody scratch across his face with a sharp, glittery nail.

She started pleading with him, telling him she'd do anything, absolutely anything he wanted if he would only — *stop this.*

Then the lid came down.

She was in the dark. She tried to push it open from the inside but it wouldn't budge. She was still pleading with him. It was so hard to get a breath. She heard something, a whirring sound, a machine coming into service, the grinding of gears, then something jerked, and she felt the box moving, sliding inexorably toward its destination. The air was growing warmer, heating up in the panicked darkness. She had to force herself to think, and that's when she remembered the cell phone in her pocket. She reached in and found it, opening it quickly. The greenish liquid crystal light came on and she saw my name, *Angel,* representing the last number she had dialed. She pushed *send,* waiting for it to ring. She didn't know what she thought she would tell me. She didn't know how I was supposed to save her, but I was.

I was supposed to save her.

The box traveled along the rails, continuing, moving steadily along the conveyer into the heart of the oven as her telephone signal traveled through the air.

"Hello?"

"Angel?"

Click.

Imagine the light, the heart of light, the very center of a hydrogen sun, no reflections, no shielding of your eyes. Angela felt her eyelids melt away, felt her skin bubble and burn and her flesh reveal itself and the cell phone disintegrate along with her connection to me, liquefying in her hands, plastic and metal turning to gas, and her hair was burning, on fire, wouldn't go out. She felt her bones turn to embers like coals in a bonfire. She was still alive, still alive and burning. She kept saying my name, *"Angel,"* saying it over and over as if I could save her, as if saying it could save her. She was ash. Her hands were dust. Her eyes were melted glass. Her bones were coal. Her body was cinder, charcoal, soot. She was black and gray and white, blown into the corners of the metal cremation box, which tipped now, the ashes of her body cooling, and she was poured into an urn, taken away in Lester's arms, held like a bottle and poured out in the weeds behind the parking lot, mingled with the soda cans, cigarette butts, and fast-food wrappers.

Lester kicked at the ground, spreading her body in the weeds so no one would see her remains, saying, *"Fuck, fuck, fuck."*

Ashes to ashes.

But the truth of Angela, the significance, her soul, had merged with the fire, had become the light.

I came to the conclusion that Angela herself was in a superposition.

Particle or wave?

She was Schrödinger's girlfriend, I thought, sitting there in my mother's Cadillac, and I was Schrödinger.

Angela was neither alive nor dead.

And it was up to the observer — it was up to me, Angel Jean-Pierre Veronchek — to determine the outcome.

The light. The *fucking* light.

I had to look into the light.

It had to be decided. Particle or wave? Which would it be?

Alive or dead?

There was only one way to find out. I had to change the out-come, I had to affect the experiment.

I had to open the box.

I had been driving, driving all over the city, the bottle of Jack nestled between my legs, the now-almost-empty bottle of Hapistat in my shirt pocket.

I looked up from where I had parked and saw Zuma Beach, glorious, golden.

I didn't even remember driving here. I swallowed the last of the Hapistat and a few more hard gulps of bourbon, pushed the door of my mother's Cadillac wide, and swung my powdery legs onto the sticky tar of the parking strip, thinking of the words on the medication warning label: *increased sensitivity to the sun.*

I slipped out of the car like a person getting out of bed, step-ping gingerly onto the pebbly road. I removed my sandals, then my clothes down to my boxers.

The soles of my feet comprehended every unsmooth particle, every bump and nodule. I didn't bother to close the door behind me, I simply walked over the grassy embankment that led to the waves. It was one of those zillion-degree afternoons. The sun was a burning eye staring straight at my head, beating into my retinas, even through the lenses of my asshole glasses. The sky, like my brain, had gone supernova, a flaming, atomic yellow. But I didn't give a shit. I was the Little Prince, my white hair sticking straight up. My eyes were already searing when I slipped my sunglasses off and let them drop onto the sand. I didn't know what time it was, but by the light, I thought it might be around two in the afternoon.

What day was this? I asked myself. It must have been a Sunday. What month was it?

July? August?

What year? How old was I?

I didn't know anymore. I didn't give a shit anymore.

The beautiful young men and women of Malibu were lying in the sun, their brown bodies glistening with suntan lotion and alpine-spring-water perspiration. Their children were scampering and cavorting up and down the edge of the water like cartoon mice, running into the waves and laughing, scurrying back, mock afraid. Somewhere out there, I knew, were dolphins — Melanie had pointed them out, hadn't she?— there were happy fucking dolphins swiftly jumping through the waves like these happy human children, wearing permanent smiles on their permanently smiling sea mammal faces. The sand was dry and hot under my feet, burning, burning. A woman nearby looked at me and smiled a sunbeam of a smile. She was radiant, resplendent, gleaming. She was a blossoming flower, a dandelion growing on someone's front yard. I opened my arms and lifted my face to the glow of the sky and thought of Angela, the quick flash she must have felt like this, the warmth of the fire against her skin. I could feel it on my shoulders, my back, the skin of my arms, my face, burning, already burning. Yes. *Orange. Red. Bright yellow. Burning.* Yes, I said to myself, looking into the light. "You're going to need some of this." The glistening woman presented a bottle of sunblock. She had blond hair and wore a yellow one-piece bathing suit. Her skin was permanently damaged, covered in uneven brown spots, destroyed by decades of solar abuse.

Jesus Christ, she was so happy.

Happy, happy, happy.

No, thanks, Mom," I said back to her. "I'm trying to get a tan."

She threw her head back and laughed.

I walked down to the water to get away from the happy, happy woman who reminded me of my mother, letting the acid sand burn my feet, and finally touched the dampness of the ocean water. It didn't seem fair — it was cool, wet, a relief — it seemed wrong that I should feel any solace at all, so I walked back into the scorching sand and let the bottoms of my feet feel just a taste of what Angela must have felt, the burning, quick flaring into light.

I walked back and forth along the edge of the water, watching the waves roll in and the squealing children run up and down and their parents taking them by their little arms and pulling them back to the safety of the beach. So this is the light, I thought. This is the metaphor. This is the all-caps symbol of TRUTH everyone loves so much. I held out my arms and smiled at a little boy. The light danced off his comically red hair, flashed against a wave and shimmered on the sand. It burned like a chemical fire. In the distance, it flared off the smooth metallic edges of the cars driving along the Pacific Coast Highway. The light lay evenly against the lifeless mountains of Malibu Canyon. I thought I could even see the white-peaked San Gabriels glinting in the distance.

The light was general over all of California, I thought, laughing to myself, on all the living and the dead. The light pushed itself into me, through my eyes and into my body and down inside my skin like a billion microscopic needles, and it illuminated everything, laid everything out, my organs bursting into flames, my ideas of what happened to Angela jumping to life like the orange flickers in a brush fire.

"Why is he so white, Daddy?" I heard the little red-haired boy asking. "Why is he so white?"

I turned around and said, "You're pretty white yourself."

There was a man holding the boy's hand, pulling him back toward a towel. "I'm sorry," the man said, a bashful look on his young-father face.

The red-haired boy kept asking, though, directing the question at me. "Why are you so white? What's wrong with you?"

"I don't know," I said. "I was just born this way."

"It's not nice to say things like that to people, Peter. There's nothing wrong with him."

"But he's so white." The little red-haired kid was only five or six years old. I turned around again, still smiling — I was grimacing, is the truth, that aberration on my face — the skin of my body reacting to the bright sun, the heat of it, the infrared rays of destruction, the fire she must have felt. *Increased sensitivity to the sun.* I was burning, just as Angela had burned. I was igniting, I could feel it. I was combusting. I could finally feel something real, something I wasn't supposed to feel. It was pain. It was the agony of reality itself. I was eight years old again, that day by my mother's pool. I was about to rise up like a phoenix.

I was as bright as a sparkler. I was a white-hot camera flash, a roll of film pulled open, completely exposed.

My eyes were stinging, but I forced them to stay open, forced my lids as wide as possible, letting clouds of tears form, cataracts of sunspots and amoebas, floaters, motes, points, and specks of blindness. The migraine that had begun with Lester's blow to my head had gone beyond any kind of pain I had ever experienced — this was a slow-motion seizure, this was wild rapture, epileptic, ecstatic, this was a fugue elevating my consciousness beyond pain into a horrible, soul-twisting rhapsody. I wanted more light to flood in. I didn't care about the burning. I sought it. I hoped for it. I even looked up into the sun and imagined my eyelids melting away, the flesh searing off my bones. Because this was what happened to her. This was Angela's final moment. Her entire body had melted, blistered and blackened, then turned to charcoal, ashes, dust. I wondered if she felt it growing hotter. I wondered if she understood in the last flashing seconds of ignition where she was. I wondered if her bones glowed like coals in a night wind.

What color were her bones?

Blue, I decided, blue like the flame on the stove — fantastically blue like her eyes had been that first moment I had seen her — blue like the spots that had formed on the ceiling of my parents' basement.

Blue, I thought.

Blue, blue, electromagnetic blue.

I thought of Angela and her armful of hyacinths, blue and white, the light that seemed to emanate from her. I was looking into the heart of light again, the silence.

"Angel." I heard my name. It was her, she was calling me.

I lived my life again in every detail of desire, temptation, and surrender.

I saw her. I stepped forward.

Into the light. Into the heart of the light. Into the uncertainty itself.

It was her. She was calling me. Saying my name.

"Angel."

And so I stepped across, into the light, toward Angela.

"Angel," she repeated in a voice no more than a breath, her arms wide to receive me.

I walked through the blinding curtain of illumination and let the photons fall over my body like a photoelectric rain. I saw both particle and wave, as though through a prism, the colors splitting, dividing, the reflection and refraction patterns displayed across the insides of my burning retinas.

I stepped across the quantum divide . . . I opened the box.

WE RAN A TOX SCREEN," A BRIGHT VOICE WAS SAYING, "AND discovered just about everything in there, the entire medicine cabinet, not to mention an alcohol level through the stratosphere." I had a dim recollection of having been inside an ambulance and was presently looking up at the white perforated tiles of a hospital ceiling. My eyes would barely open. "We only gave him a topical anesthetic because," the voice continued, "well, Jesus Christ, this guy won't be feeling anything for weeks."

"Is he coherent?" another voice asked. "Or should I wait?"

"Coherent? I don't know. Why don't we ask him?" A face appeared above me. "Are you ready to talk, Angel?" It was a doctor's face.

"Yes," I whispered with hardly a voice at all. "I think I can talk."

"There's a police detective to see you. Do you feel up to speaking to anyone right now? Or would you like him to come back later?"

"A detective?"

Another face appeared. He had glasses, graying hair. "My name is Detective Dennis," he said. "Would you mind answering a few questions?" It was him. It was the man in gray.

"Questions," I repeated.

"Did you know a woman named Jessica Teagarden?"

My lips were swollen. I could barely move them to speak. "Yes." I was suddenly enveloped by a screaming pain. Every centimeter of my body was burning, on fire. "I knew her."

"Because we found the . . . the ashes of a human being in the parking lot behind the Horace & Geary Funeral Home." He sighed. "And we're afraid that it might be her. Do you have any idea of what might have happened?"

No. I closed my eyes. *No.* This wasn't it. This wasn't right.

WE RAN A TOX SCREEN," A BRIGHT VOICE WAS SAYING, "AND discovered just about everything in there, the entire medicine cabinet, not to mention an alcohol level through the stratosphere." I had a dim recollection of having been inside an ambulance and was presently looking up at the white perforated tiles of a hospital ceiling. My eyes would barely open. "We only gave him a topical anesthetic because," the voice continued, "well, Jesus Christ, this guy won't be feeling anything for weeks."

"Angel?" It was my mother's voice. Her plastic features appeared above me. "Angel . . . what did you do?"

"Mom?"

"Oh, Angel, Angel, my sweet Angel."

No.

WE RAN A TOX SCREEN," A BRIGHT VOICE WAS SAYING, "AND discovered just about everything in there, the entire medicine cabinet, not to mention an alcohol level through the stratosphere."

"Do you think it malfunctioned?"

"Malfunction is an understatement," I heard a voice say. "It became confused, I believe, by the implants. It thought it was human." Tyrell's face appeared above me. "Commerce is our goal here at Tyrell," he said. "More human than human is our motto. Angel is an experiment, nothing more. We began to recognize in him strange obsessions. After all, he is emotionally inexperienced, with only a few years in which to store up the experiences which you and I take for granted. If we gift him with a past, we create a cushion or pillow for his emotions and consequently we can control him better."

"Memories," the doctor said. "You're talking about memories."

"But it was bound to fail."

"Shall I retire it?"

"I don't see any other option."

WE RAN A TOX SCREEN," A BRIGHT VOICE WAS SAYING, "AND discovered just about everything in there, the entire medicine cabinet, not to mention an alcohol level through the stratosphere."

"What happened?" I said. "Where am I?"

"Cut! That was fantastic." Ridley Scott smiled down at me. "Let's do it again, okay? Only this time, Angel, you're even more confused. Everybody back to their positions."

W E RAN A TOX SCREEN," A BRIGHT VOICE WAS SAYING, "AND discovered just about everything in there, the entire medicine cabinet, not to mention an alcohol level through the stratosphere."

I opened my eyes and saw him. He stood over me, his eyes looking past me, looking through me. I thought I heard the fluttering of feathers. He reached over and touched my eyelids, closing them, saying, *"Shhh."*

"Who are you?" I asked, eyes closed, looking up into the comforting darkness. "Tell me who you —"

"Shhh," he said. *"Shhh."*

W<small>E RAN A TOX SCREEN,</small>" <small>A BRIGHT VOICE WAS SAYING,</small> "<small>AND</small> discovered just about everything in there, the entire medicine cabinet, not to mention an alcohol level through the stratosphere." I had a dim recollection of having been inside an ambulance and was presently looking up at the white perforated tiles of a hospital ceiling. My eyes would barely open. "We only gave him a topical anesthetic because," the voice continued, "well, Jesus Christ, this guy won't be feeling anything for weeks."

"What happened?" My voice was whispery despite the extreme light in the room. My eyelids were swollen, too, even my tongue felt bloated. "Where am I?"

A pink moon appeared above me. It was Silowicz, his white

stubble in patches on his craggy skin. "Angel," he said, "why don't you tell *me* what happened?"

"Don't tell my father," I begged. *"Please?"*

Silowicz looked down at me, and the haggard skin of his cheeks drooped. "Angel," he said, as if just saying my name would persuade me.

"Dr. Silowicz . . ."

My psychiatrist glanced over at the young doctor who had also appeared above me, a man with a black, blunt haircut and a face like a movie star, a face so bland you could project anything you wanted onto it.

The doctor hesitated, then started talking. "Angel has a fairly severe sunburn and was already blistering when he was admitted. He's going to be extremely . . . uncomfortable for quite a while, maybe even a couple of weeks." He paused, shifting his gaze. "But at the moment, I'm more concerned with the drugs and alcohol in his system." I could sense in his hesitating voice that he disapproved, not only of me, but of my psychiatrist as well.

"Thank you," Silowicz said curtly. "But I'm personally more concerned with the drugs that are *not* in his system."

The bland young doctor seemed about to respond, then just shrugged and disappeared from view.

"How long have I been here?" I asked.

Dr. Silowicz seemed almost apologetic. "They brought you in yesterday."

"How did you know I was here?"

I could feel my skin crawling beneath the layers of gauze that had been wrapped around my body. There was a sliminess forming there that could have been the blisters themselves or the topical anesthesia, I wasn't sure.

Dr. Silowicz looked down at me, and his eyes were bright, like the liquid eyes of a soap opera actor. "Frank sent someone to look for you, an investigator. He had been trailing you before, apparently, and when you disappeared from the airport, Frank called him. He called an ambulance when he caught up with you on the beach, and the EMT guy must have found the bottle of medication in your hand . . . the Hapistat. The prescription had my name and reference number on it, I guess, so . . ."

"Increased sensitivity to the sun," I repeated.

Then everything went dark, like the iris closing at the end of a Warner Brothers cartoon.

———

"Angel" — My father stood over me, his bald head gleaming in the antiseptic light — "what are you doing to me?"

Fucking Silowicz, was all I thought. He had told my father even when I had specifically asked him not to.

"To *you?*"

I should sue, I thought. It was a flagrant breach of doctor-patient confidentiality.

"Why would you burn yourself like this?"

"I needed to see the light," I said. "I needed to look inside the light."

"You're not making any sense, Angel." It was Melanie. I could see little Gabriel on her hip.

The iris closed.

It opened. Angela appeared above me, her eyes like twin blue suns.

"Angela," I said. "I stepped across. I opened the box."

"Who's Angela?"

"I stepped across," I insisted.

"That's okay, honey," the pretty nurse with soft blue eyes sang. "You don't have to step across anything. You stay right where you are."

The iris closed, then opened.

It was Frank who appeared above me this time. "You're going to heal, Angel," he said. "You're going to heal, and then we're going to take you home."

———

I had the feeling it was dark outside. How long had he been in this room? Three days? A week? My shoulders, neck, and back were covered in a layer of gauze, and I felt an unpleasant greasiness beneath it, but I didn't dare move for fear of creating a new ripple of pain.

With every breath, I perceived a new sensitivity, a distinct tingling.

"I think I'm starting to freak out," I said to no one.

I pictured my skin falling away from my body like the flesh of a boiled chicken.

The pink moon appeared. "You sound agitated, Angel," Dr. Silowicz said. "Do you want me to call the doctor?"

Then he vanished. He had taken a chair somewhere to my left, over by the window, and I could hear his disembodied, sandpapery voice.

Agitated? I was fucking hysterical.

"Just talk to me."

Oh God, I was thinking, *oh God, oh God, oh God.*

My skin was prickling, and millions of tiny spiders were running across my skin.

I could hear Silowicz leaning back in the chair, the metal legs screeching across the linoleum.

I let my eyes close and felt a scratchiness beneath the lids. Could I have burned the inside of my eyelids? Was that even possible?

"Dr. Silowicz," I took the opportunity to say, "you can notify my mother. You can tell Mom I'm here. I'd like to see her. Just not my father, all right?"

"Your father was already here," Silowicz said. "Don't you remember?"

"Oh yeah." I did remember. "I was going to sue you about that."

I lay in bed, attended by a diligent nurse, hardly speaking to anyone, entering a kind of flickering half dream that never descended into a full-on sleep and never rose to complete wakefulness. My skin was trying to get away from me, I believed. I had the feeling that if I got out of bed quickly enough, I might slip free of my own body, that I could leave myself lying there and escape from the hospital through the window.

The iris closed, opened, closed, opened again.

I saw Dr. Silowicz, Melanie, my father, even Frank.

The girl who I had thought was Angela was only a blue-eyed nurse.

At one point, the room had been filled with flowers and balloons, and then they were gone.

I imagined worlds.

I imagined one world in which Angela had been killed, cremated, turned to ash. I imagined another in which she was alive. They were equally viable, I thought. Particle or wave. I lay in bed and listened to the inhuman hospital noises and imagined a world in which I had never moved into my West Hollywood apartment, and another one where *Blade Runner* still played endlessly on my TV. I imagined a world in which I had normal skin, a world in which I could walk in the sun, my eyes open, absorbing the light. I dreamed without sleeping. I imagined worlds multiplying. I envisioned infinitesimal photons turning from particle to wave, wave to particle, dividing and redividing, worlds mounting one on top of the other, worlds blossoming into being like the petals of a hyacinth blossom, worlds splitting like atoms inside a hydrogen bomb, the universe growing heavier with boundless exponential expansion. Is it only random, I wondered, this world, the one I was in? Had I really chosen it, created it myself? Had I really stepped across? There were infinite worlds, worlds where every possibility was realized. It was scientific, indisputable. There was a world in which the oceans were made of sand, where hyacinths rained from the sky. There was a world in which my mother hadn't succumbed to all that surgery and her face had grown dignified instead of plasticized. There was a world in which my father had never come to this country, and another one in which I had never been born. There was a world where I was sane.

Versions and versions of worlds.

Worlds without end.

My skin itched insanely, and I dreamed of these other worlds. I visited so many, my imagination traveling across the expanding universe like Gulliver, a giant stepping over mountains, sloshing through seas, sidestepping cities. There was a world in which Angela still lived, I came to believe, a world in which she had not been absorbed by Lester's red, orange, bright yellow, burning light.

My imagination itself grew heavy. I think it may even have collapsed.

As if thinking for a moment, as if considering whether he should even mention this, Dr. Silowicz said, "Angel, I wanted to ask you about . . . about your mother."

"Describe in single words," Holden says in the first dialogue scene of *Blade Runner*, "only the good things that come to mind . . . about your mother."

"My mother?" Leon answers. "Let me tell you about my mother."

"What do you mean?" I was sitting in a hard chair of molded yellow plastic. I lowered my voice. "What about her?" Behind me was a window facing a rolling green meadow. Linden trees shuddered in a warm breeze — they didn't want Silowicz asking questions about her, either.

"What's the last thing you remember?" His voice had become almost a hiss, as though the room itself had fallen into shadows. But it was, as ever, unmercifully bright — the white walls, the white lights, the polished white floors — all gleaming like the set of a game show. Halogen, fluorescent, tungsten, incandescent, they were using every bulb they had, it seemed, burning through an entire power plant. I had been brought here straight from the hospital. After my skin had healed, they had delivered me to Saint Michael's Psychiatric. I had been residing here for what seemed like years, but Dr. Silowicz told me it had been only a couple of weeks.

"The headaches, I guess."

"Can you describe them for me, these headaches your mother was having . . . everything you remember?"

"She was getting them every day," I answered. I remembered this: My mother had tried everything for the migraines, every drug, all the treatments, so when they started coming every morning, she didn't bother to go to the doctor, thinking nothing could help anyway. "The headaches," I said, remembering poor Monique, her hand flying to her forehead, the ripple of pain flashing across her brittle, plastic face. "She couldn't do anything about them."

"Why was that, Angel?"

I shrugged. "Nothing worked."

"And then what happened? Do you remember what happened next?"

What came next. I shook my head. But that was a lie. Because I did . . . I did remember. "Dr. Evanson came next," I offered.

"That's right," Silowicz said in his crackly, hissing voice. "Your mother, she went to see the neurologist."

Eventually my mother was forced to visit a migraine specialist, a tall, panicky woman with a squeaky voice and fluttery hands. "Dr. Evanson," I said again. By the time my mother had been diagnosed with a tumor growing in the right frontal lobe of her brain, there was virtually nothing that could be done. They had removed what they could, shaving her Farrah Fawcett hair and cutting into her fragile French-Swiss skull. Then Mom had been forced to undergo radiation, chemotherapy, the usual treatments . . .

I thought for a moment longer. I remembered a medical environment like this one, only finer.

"Am I glowing?" I asked.

"What do you mean, Angel?"

"Am I glowing?" my mother would ask from her wheelchair. She was bald, and when her hair started to grow back in, it was gray, the gray hair of an old gray woman. She looked like a famous movie actress in a dramatic role, I thought, an Academy Award nominee in her final Oscar bid. Her entire being had been stripped of its glamour but was somehow made even more glamorous in the process.

"How is she?" I asked Silowicz right now. "Is she all right?"

"Angel," he said again, as though trying to make me hush.

"I wanted to be an electromagnetic scientist," I said. "I wanted to be a screenwriter."

"You still can be those things." Silowicz leaned forward in his chair. "You still can be anything you want."

"You can be anything," my mother said from the bed, "anything, my little prince."

"This is a mistake," I said, looking around. "This is all wrong."

I was crying, of course, warm tears falling down my cheeks. But it was a familiar feeling, crying in a hospital. "I wanted to be a lighting director," I said absurdly. "I wanted to be a long-distance runner." These memories of my mother . . . it was like I had just discovered them there in my mind, as though Silowicz himself had reached into my brain and inserted them with some kind of invasive psychiatric device.

"These are all things you can still pursue," he said evenly. "You're still a young man, and you're so lucky that you have your father and . . . and Melanie to help you."

"I'm not that young," I said, "and I don't feel so lucky." Then something occurred to me, something terrible. "Please tell me," I whispered. "Dr. Silowicz, you'd tell me, wouldn't you? Am I a replicant? Are these memories real?"

I didn't need to see the scene. It was there, playing on the movie screen beneath my eyelids.

Rick Deckard leans forward and asks, "How can it not know what it is?"

Tyrell clasps his hands and says, "Commerce is our goal here at Tyrell. More human than human is our motto."

Deckard doesn't look up. "Memories," he says. "You're talking about memories."

"You stopped taking your medication."

"I take tons of it." I was crying even harder. "I take everything you give me." I pictured the bottles littering my kitchen counter, the amber shells containing those powdery prisons, each pill a sentence to reality. Every time I swallowed one, I was left flopping on the surface of the world, like a gasping fish that had been dragged up onto a dock.

"But not the right ones, Angel. Not the important ones." He meant Reality, of course, and it was true. I hadn't been taking them.

"I take it now," I said. "I don't have any choice." They brought it to me every day, as a matter of fact, twice a day.

"What else, Angel?" he prodded me softly. "What else do you recall?"

These weren't real memories, I knew, they were implants, but I remembered trying to study on a vinyl couch in the hospice lobby, listening to the building's soft noises, the machinery keeping people alive — burping, pumping, gasping, farting — the hallways flooded with sterile fluorescence. Every now and then I would walk down a long corridor of medical light to my mother's room, passing the night nurses, an old nodding orderly, a winking security guard, a somnambulant janitor who buffed the floor tiles with a whirring machine. I would peek around the door. Her room was private, of course, with furniture that belonged more in a luxury hotel, and filled with flowers, and I would see her there, her mouth open, a stack of satin pillows behind her shaved, delicate head. Sometimes, if she was awake, she'd call me over, saying, "Angel, Angel, my sweet Angel."

"Is there anything I can get you, Mom? Some water?"

She would take my hand and gaze at me.

"Are you feeling all right?"

"I'm on drugs," I remember her saying. "I feel wonderful. I've never felt better in my life."

I could see every vein in her glasslike face. I could see straight through her eyes into her butchered brain.

"Try not to be alone all the time," she said one night. And then her face shattered like a mirror. "Oh, Angel, such a good boy you were."

I had a lot of migraines there, too, and if they had an empty bed somewhere, the nurses would let me lie down. The truth is, I never felt so at home.

These artificial memories drifted in front of my eyes like motes of light on a bright day in a dusty room.

Silowicz encouraged me, pushed me along, asking just the right questions to jar them loose, saying just the right things to make me remember. He had inserted these memories, I assumed, and wanted to make sure they had taken root, and now they blossomed like those hyacinths in the old man's garden.

———

When my mother fell sick, I was in college. I used to sit at the back of all my classes, trying to hide in a patch of shadow in the brightly lit lecture halls. If anyone even glanced in my direction, I averted my eyes, careful to avoid contact, living in mortal fear of speaking aloud. One class in particular was called Concepts in Modern Physics. It was extremely popular, with almost every seat occupied at the beginning of the semester. I remained in the back, my head down, scribbling my notes onto my colored sheets of paper. I made an attempt to record every word the professor said, and later, in the dim light of my mother's room, I would scour those handwritten sentences for meaning.

The professor's name was Dr. Natalie Lem, a petite woman with limp brown hair, long in the back, and soft bangs that she perpetually brushed out of her own evasive eyes. She wore jeans and a beige linen jacket, a crisp pink shirt, the same clothes every day. Her voice was soft, the voice of a person speaking in a dimly lit room. She carried a heavy tote bag filled with notebooks — notebooks illuminated with thoughts, I was certain, of endless depth and dimension. Inside that bag, I believed, were the very secrets of the universe. And in her lectures she explained them, unveiling the mysteries I had been waiting a lifetime to understand. She defined the properties and behavior of light, the particle/wave duality, the discovery that if you look deeply into the very heart of matter itself, into reality, you discover uncertainty, *unreality* . . . you discover your own imagination staring back at you, a mischievous smile on its scientific lips.

One night I was going over my notes from Dr. Lem's class — the topic was Heisenberg's uncertainty principle — and I came across something significant. During the lecture, I hadn't thought it contained any particular meaning, but there in my mother's room, it leapt out at me, frighteningly crucial. "Many physicists at the time," Professor Lem had said, "felt that the debate that resulted in Heisenberg's theory was the same kind of blather that had led medieval clerics to question if an angel can dance on the head of a pin."

In class, I had simply written it down, but now I stared at it.

Why had she chosen to use that particular phrase? It couldn't have been coincidental. Professor Lem had used my name — *Angel* — for a very specific purpose. She must have known I was sitting in the back of the lecture hall and wanted to send me a message.

. . . if an angel can dance on the head of a pin.

What did she mean?

I went back over my notes more carefully this time, looking for deeper significance in every phrase. There were clues everywhere, bits and pieces of meaning that, added together, revealed a covert system of communication.

I simply hadn't decoded it yet.

In class, I sat a few rows closer, braving the intruding eyes of other students so I'd be sure not to miss a single word.

I decided to follow her, bringing my Leica along one day and waiting in the corridor until Professor Lem stepped out. She walked down the hallway alone, the tote bag weighing down her shoulder. Surreptitiously, I took my first picture. I had forgotten to turn off the flash, so it surprised a few nearby students.

"Sorry," I murmured.

Luckily, she didn't turn around.

I followed her into the parking lot, all the way to her car, and watched her drive away.

That night, I scoured the course catalog, and the next afternoon, I waited for her to emerge from a physics lab and followed her in my own car. She visited the mall, going from store to store, and I tried to locate a pattern in the shops she chose — Book Star, Banana Republic, Patagonia. I found it especially interesting when she bought a large 7 UP at the food court and sat at a table all by herself, sipping it over a *National Geographic*.

I remembered reading an article about albinos all over the world in a *National Geographic* once.

Obviously, this was another message. She was aware that I was observing her.

I kept going over my notes. There in the hospice waiting room, down the hall from my mother, I found layers of meaning, veils of significance, signs and secrets. Professor Lem was sending me clues, I was certain. I had come to the conclusion that she was in love with me but was unable to say anything about it — publicly, anyway. The university would fire her if they found out; an affair between a professor and student would result in my expulsion and her dismissal at the very least, if not her outright criminal prosecution. She had to be more than circumspect: Our relationship had to be completely covert. I looked for patterns in her lectures, circling every fourth word, for instance, and piecing them together to form new sentences, searching for symbolic significance in particular passages in the accompanying texts. This is where I first learned about the uncertainty principle, not coincidentally, and I believed Professor Lem was asking me to make a choice of my own.

The outcome depends on the observer, she had said in her lecture.

And I had been observing.

I had been observing for some time, and she knew it. I followed her every day, taking photographs as she went about the business of her life. I even followed her home one afternoon, to a small boxlike house in the Valley.

She was the cat, and I was the scientist, and this — this little house — this was the box.

I drove back to my mother's hospice that evening and I was shaking. Professor Lem was asking me to enter her house, I thought, to follow her inside. I was shaking with the knowledge of what she wanted me to do, that everything would be revealed.

I sat awake all night, there in the luxurious medical room with my mother, staring at my notes.

"Angel," she said, "little prince . . ."

"What is it, Mom?"

She would wake up bewildered sometimes, panicking to know where she was . . . where *I* was . . .

"Angel?"

"I'm right here." I grabbed her hand.

"Oh, sweetheart," she said.

"How are you, Mom? Is there anything I can get you? Some ice water?"

"I bought the most beautiful things," she said. "Margaret and I went to Fred Segal, and they have the most beautiful —"

I wanted to tell her about Professor Lem. "I fell in love, Mom."

"— dresses, and they have the most exquisite set of luggage, with pony hair and apricot-colored handles, tortoiseshell, I think —"

"I fell in love with a girl," I said.

"Would you like to go to your grandmother's?" she was saying. "To Switzerland?"

"Mom?"

"We could stay for as long as you want. Zurich is so beautiful this time of year. There's no snow at all."

"Go back to sleep," I said.

"We could go shopping. You could help me find a necklace, Angel, my Angel, my sweet, sweet Angel . . ."

———

"Do you remember the rest?" Dr. Silowicz asked. This was another day entirely. He was sitting across from me in his plastic chair, legs crossed, still whispering.

"The rest of what?"

"You do remember, don't you, Angel?" He cleared his throat. "You just don't want to."

I looked down at my hands. "I remember."

"The funeral?" he said softly.

"The funeral," I repeated.

The funeral. The casket. The ceremony.

The cremation.

They burned her — I remembered that. The ashes.

Red. Orange. Bright yellow.

Burning.

They burned my mother's body, then shipped her ashes back to Switzerland to rest on a shelf in the family mausoleum.

"No," I said. "I don't remember. Not really."

These memories, I thought, they couldn't be real. These were implants. They had to be.

I lifted my head so I could see my psychiatrist across the white room. He wasn't looking at me; his eyes were directed somewhere beyond. I wanted to scream like I had that day when I was just a kid, standing there in the kitchen, covered in Annabelle's butter, my mother's hummingbird hands fluttering all around me.

But I remembered: Monique was dead, cremated. She was

ashes. I thought of her face, of my face, the face we had shared. I thought of my mother's skin, the way it had been pulled so tightly across her bones by the plastic surgeon. I remembered her funeral, remembered the parade of half-assed celebrities. I remembered the obituary my father had shown me in *Variety*, a "socialite," it had called her, "wife of a well-known director/producer," "a staple of the Hollywood scene . . ." When my mother died, it was like she had turned to wax. Her skin, even when it was alive, had developed a taut, gummy sheen from all those operations, and in death her flesh seemed as though it had been cured like expensive leather over her fine, pointy bones. Her eyes were half open, just as they had often been in sleep. I remember staring into her face and watching the migraine aura form in front of my eyes. It was just daybreak, and in the mild confusion that accompanied the change of shift, no one came to check on her.

But it didn't matter. I just wanted to let her sleep. I just wanted the pain to be gone.

No more headaches.

It's funny, but when I was a kid, staying in all those hotels, when Mom had a migraine, I would call housekeeping and ask if they could please be extra quiet in the hallways.

I felt that way then. Every noise was a potential disturbance.

Please, everyone, I wanted to say, please be quiet.

Stop the buffer. Silence the intercom. Lower the blinds. Draw the curtains over the windows. Dim the lights.

Don't disturb her now. Don't make a noise.

Don't even breathe.

Death to a quantum physicist means entropy, inertia, means

the ultimate result of bodies coming to rest and remaining at rest. There will come a time in the universe when every atom will be equally distant from every other atom, and this will be the end of things, the very last moment of the universe as we imagine it. The long, slow pull back toward infinite density will begin, and another universe will get its chance.

I sat in the hospice with my mother and lost my eyesight that day, an amoeba of watery gray forming in my line of vision, and I haven't seen clearly since.

———

Chicken noodle soup and a bologna sandwich. A glass of orange juice. Green Jell-O for dessert. I sat by the window and watched the clouds moving like cataracts across the giant iris of a sky. Every night, in the entertainment lounge, they played another movie. I would sit at a safe distance from the rest of the patients and watch. I remembered more, of course. I remembered that when my mother died, I turned to watch the sun rising beyond the window blinds. I remembered all of this, these images and sensations just there, placed there, as though sitting on a shelf in my memory. I remembered seeing a white glow emanating from the parking lot outside. I remembered slipping out of the room and into my car, driving in the early morning traffic to the small, boxlike house in the Valley. I remembered waiting on the street, watching the door while the newspaper delivery boy dropped a copy of the *Los Angeles Times* in front of it and pedaled away. I remembered how a few minutes later, a slender female arm reached out and pulled the newspaper inside.

It was another message, I believed. Professor Lem, she was beckoning me.

Open the box, she was saying.

Look inside.

I got out of the car and stepped across the dry lawn. I went to the door and placed my hand on the knob. It turned easily, opening into a sparse living room. A radio was on somewhere, the scratchy sound of the news announcer reciting the morning's disasters. I smelled coffee. There was a blue love seat. There was a white rattan rocking chair. There was a matching kitchen table with a glass top, also made of white rattan, and two aluminum folding chairs. Everything was brand-new. Everything appeared to have been bought yesterday. The walls were white, entirely absent of pictures.

Slowly, I stepped around the corner and peered into the kitchen. Professor Lem was sitting on a high stool near the counter. Coffee was dripping into a pot like medication dripping into my mother's veins. She hovered over the newspaper, absently licking a finger as she turned each page.

I was opening my mouth to speak when she turned her face toward me.

We didn't move, neither one of us moved, for one long, unendurable moment.

I felt my whiteness so sharply. I felt the stark pinkness of my eyes, the aluminum blue of my lips. I was so suddenly *me.*

"You're a student," she said finally, and her voice was even and clear.

I don't even know if I moved.

"You're in my Concepts class."

"Yes," I said.

"Did you . . . did you follow me?"

I didn't know how to respond. I was waiting for something, for some important revelation. But I was beginning to realize that it was not forthcoming, that all of this had been a mistake.

I was overwhelmed by self-consciousness.

My name is Angel Jean-Pierre Veronchek, I wanted to say. *I am an albino, son of the famous movie producer Milos Veronchek, son of the recently deceased Monique Veronchek, former French movie actress and runway model. I will die of skin cancer one day. One day I will be crucified by the light.*

"Would you like something?" Professor Lem asked. "Would you like to sit down?" She came toward me, a look of worry in her intelligent, feline eyes. "Would you like a cup of coffee?"

I was shaking. I remember shaking, my whole body, my whole soul, my whole being, trembling. "In your lecture," I managed to get out, "you said . . . you said, 'Angel.'"

"Angel," she repeated.

"You said my name."

"Your name is Angel?"

I lifted my pink eyes to see her.

"Would you like a cup of coffee, Angel?" She was leading me into the living room, guiding me to the couch.

I sat with my hands on my legs and looked up at her. "I am the observer," I said. "This morning I observed my mother's death."

"It's okay," Professor Lem said gently, her voice soothing, "it's going to be all right, Angel. Can you wait here? I'm going to get you a cup of coffee, and then I'll be right back."

"I am the observer," I said again, listening to her dial the phone, those three numbers.

———

At night, in the clinic, I lay in bed, overcome by a strange combination of memory and forgetfulness, my past and present blurring together like the hues of a poorly painted watercolor. Sometimes I would rise and walk to the window and listen to the rustle of the trees outside.

One night, an orderly walked by, saying, "What are you doing up now? Aren't you supposed to be asleep?"

"I'm Angel," I tried to tell him.

He smiled, not understanding. "Of course you're an angel," he said, leading me back to my bed. "And I'm Jimmy Stewart."

———

"You've made such excellent progress." Silowicz clasped his hands together. This was a few months later, enough time to let the antipsychotics take hold, enough time for Reality, the drug, and reality itself, to take over again. I had spent time at Saint Michael's before, of course, had spent two whole years here after my mother died, after the incident with Professor Lem, two years that I had folded like clean sheets and placed on a shelf.

My mind, though far from normal, was operating in that permanent present tense again.

"I know you don't like compliments, Angel," he added, "but . . ."

"It has only been with your help." I offered as sincere a smile as I could manage and hoped it was at least mildly convincing.

"I'm only guiding you," Silowicz said. "You're doing all the work."

I looked at my shoes. At some point, someone — Melanie, I think — had brought me these Nikes. They had coils inside the heels. They were like bouncing machines on my feet. I was actually worried that I would be ejected into the ceiling. Over the course of the past several sessions, I had been forced to confront the traumatic fact of my mother's death and had been convinced that I was just an ordinary human albino and not a *Blade Runner* replicant. It was even funny now.

"I think you're finally ready for us to talk about the rest," Silowicz said now.

"The rest of what?" I was still looking down at my spring-loaded sneakers, waiting for my feet to jump up on their own.

"Of what happened."

I looked up. "Something happened?"

Silowicz cleared his phlegmy throat. *"Angel,"* he said disapprovingly.

I waited. I knew what he was getting at.

"She contacted us."

"Who?"

"Miss Teagarden," Silowicz said. "She contacted Frank."

I could feel the blood coursing through my colorless veins.

"You frightened her," Silowicz said, a sympathetic tone lodged in his voice. "Apparently, you —"

"What did I do?"

"She said you nearly killed her."

"Killed her?"

"You went swimming one night, and you . . . and you tried to drown her."

The pool, I remembered the pool.

But I had rescued her, hadn't I?— scooping her body into my arms. She had been coughing, choking. No, I thought. She had *pretended* to drown, and I had saved her. It had all been make-believe, a game. "That's not what happened," I told Silowicz, shaking my head. "That's not the way it —"

"She said you became jealous, that she was teasing you, and you —"

"It doesn't make any sense."

He went on, describing events that had supposedly happened between the night Angela took me night swimming on that down-town rooftop and the morning she disappeared, describing things I hadn't been able to bring myself to remember:

At first she had thought I was just a lonely eccentric, and she had even been attracted to me. She really had come over to apolo-gize for the noise. She really had grown to like me. But then I had become possessive, even scary, and had begun to follow her around Los Angeles. I broke into her apartment. I went through her trash, sought out and questioned her old neighbors.

"No," I told Silowicz, "that was all *after* she disappeared. I was *looking* for her."

"Angel," he said gravely, "that was *before* . . . that was all be-fore."

"But Angela is dead, anyway," I told Silowicz. "Lester killed her."

Silowicz shook his head, making an apology out of his old, broken face — smiling eyes, a frowning mouth. "She had contacted Frank. She begged him to get you to leave her alone. You had stopped taking your proper medication, and you weren't seeing things as they truly were." He paused, allowing almost too much time before using the strangest expression: "You scared the daylights out of her."

The daylights.

What Dr. Silowicz was saying made terrifying sense.

Everything here at Saint Michael's Psychiatric Center made terrifying, scientific sense.

I looked at my spring-loaded sneakers. "Why didn't you tell me?"

"We didn't want to upset you," Silowicz answered. "Your father, especially, he didn't want to —"

"Like waking a sleepwalker."

"Right." My psychiatrist smiled benignly. "An excellent metaphor, Angel, as always . . . like waking a sleepwalker."

"What about the note?"

"You wrote that note, Angel." Silowicz touched his fingers together and leaned forward in his plastic chair. "You wrote quite a lot of things." He leaned down to his old brown leather briefcase, which was resting beside his old brown leather feet, and pulled out a manuscript. I recognized it immediately, the most recent draft of *Los Angeles,* printed on electromagnetic blue paper. "It's all here," Silowicz said, handing it to me.

I flipped open to the first page.

"FADE IN," it said. "EXT. SUNRISE OVER THE CITY."

Silowicz exhaled. "It's the story of an albino son of a famous movie producer who falls in love with the girl who moves in down the hall," he said. "In the first scene, she brings him a pot of lamb stew."

I scanned the type.

INT. HALLWAY — AFTERNOON

A BLACK GIRL in her late twenties, relatively tall, with long straightened hair colored an unnatural reddish blond, she wears jeans, a Guns N' Roses T-shirt. Her feet are bare, her toenails painte d a glittery green metallic. Her eyes are blue.

I turned the pages, reading ahead.

Angel opens the envelope. A stack of HUNDRED-DOLLAR BILLS falls in slow motion onto the floor.

CU on note as Angel reads:

When you're gone I disappear.

When I see you I am resurrected

Dr. Silowicz sighed. "That money was an advance on one of your credit cards, Angel. That's why Frank hired that private investigator to follow you. You had been spending large sums of cash and he wanted to know where it was all going."

"The man in gray," I said.

Silowicz nodded. "That's what you call him in the screenplay, though you seemed to think he had a much more menacing purpose. He followed you to that topless bar."

I shook my head. "What do you mean?"

"There was a dancer. I never spoke to her directly, but the name she used at the club was Cassandra. According to Frank, you met her through an escort service . . . she came to your apartment and you found out she worked there, and you started . . . well, you stalked her, too."

"Wait a minute," I said. "She was a different —"

"She was a completely different young woman, Angel." Silowicz nodded. "She wasn't even the same person at all. But it seems you were stalking her, too."

I looked into Silowicz's stubbly, gray face and pictured that waitress I had questioned at the Mask. This was so long ago now, and the memory was already like old videotape, but I recalled the way she had been so friendly the first time, so evasive the next. I remembered her furtive glances to the silhouetted figure in the yellow window.

"A different actress in the same role," I whispered.

"An interesting way to look at it." Silowicz paused, then added, "And that man, the one who worked there —"

"Lester?"

"Lester," Silowicz nodded. "It was horrible, what he said . . . the incinerator, the cremation. But he knew you had been bothering the dancers, and . . . well, he hoped it might scare you away."

"I saw her."

"What's that?"

"In Rio. That must have been her, but I didn't . . . didn't recognize her." I touched my face. Tears. I was crying again.

Fuck.

Finding these memories through the haze of my psyche was like looking for a single tear in a hail of rain.

"So none of these things really happened?"

"It all happened," Silowicz said, "just not the way you apparently remember. I get the impression that you wrote some of these scenes ahead of time, then acted them out, and that some of them were sort of . . . adapted after the fact." He sighed. "And there are some beautifully rendered moments." He moved his head slightly back and forth in appreciation. "When she goes next door for the hyacinths? Gorgeous, Angel. Really." Then he winked. "Though I think I recognize a little T. S. Eliot in there."

As Dr. Silowicz said these things, some of these memories came back. I remembered going to a cash machine and taking fistfuls of money to the Mask. I remembered sitting down at my computer and typing out dialogue, lighting directions, scene descriptions, printing out the pages on that electromagnetic blue paper. I even remembered placing that note on the doorstep of Jessica's old duplex and then pretending to find it again a few days later. I had been going through the motions of a scripted drama, obviously, a plot I had worked out with screenwriting software.

That's why I kept thinking there was a film crew around every corner. Because it *was* a film.

"I stepped across," I said under my breath. I had found a world, I realized, in which all that had happened was only fiction.

"What's that?"

"Nothing." I looked up. "Nothing." All of this had once been real, absolutely real — but I stepped into another world.

Silowicz smiled beneficently. "All human beings create their own realities, to some degree. Yours just happened to be more vivid than most." The way he said that was almost proud. "You had everyone so worried." Silowicz shook his head. "And that poor kid —"

"What kid?"

"Victor Whitehead. His mother is threatening to sue over what you did to him."

I tried to think back. I remembered his bedroom, trying to get Victor to recall something about Angela. "What did I do?" I started flipping through the screenplay.

"You forced him to stare into a lightbulb," Silowicz answered. "There could have been permanent damage to his retinas if you had made him do it for much longer. But even more significantly, the little guy was traumatized."

"Her name, Angela, why did she tell me —"

"She never told you her name was Angela. That was just another part of your script." He breathed heavily through his nostrils. "We checked your phone records and saw that you had been contacting . . . well, you were using an escort service . . ." I could see a flicker of embarrassment in his eyes when Dr. Silowicz said, "Frank did some asking around, and apparently you insisted that all the escorts call themselves by that name."

I fell silent.

Softly, he cleared his throat. "I think a way to look at it is . . . is that you split apart, in a manner of speaking, into a light and dark, male and female, the two sides of your nature. In order to reconnect your two halves, you created this . . . Angela character, an image

you projected onto these women" — he sighed — "most unfortunately onto your neighbor, Jessica Teagarden."

I remembered all those different-colored eyes.

I realized now it was because they were the eyes of different
women.

"You were trying to get back together, I guess, trying to reinte-
grate all of those opposing impulses, like the polar opposites of two
magnets."

I didn't have an answer for this. I didn't know what to say.
"That's why I didn't recognize her in Rio."

Silowicz nodded. "I believe at that point, you were starting to
differentiate. You must have recognized Cassandra for who she
truly was and not as this projected Angela character."

"A character," I repeated.

"They're all characters in your story," Silowicz said. "Even me."

"But she's alive, right? Jessica Teagarden, she's alive?"

"Yes, Angel," Silowicz answered drily. "Jessica Teagarden is
alive and well."

"How does it end?" I asked.

"You wrote it yourself — don't you remember?"

"No."

He put his hands on his knees and started to rise from his chair.
"Why don't you read it, then?"

In the original theatrical release of *Blade Runner,* Rick Deckard es-
capes from Los Angeles with Rachael. She is a replicant, of course,
created by the Tyrell Corporation, but hasn't been given an expira-

tion date. The two of them are seen flying in a hover car over verdant mountains, escaping to some perfect world of undivided natural light. The scene is set to a melancholy yet triumphal score.

That is one ending, anyway.

In the director's cut, which is the version I had permanently lodged in the DVD player of my San Raphael Crescent cave, there is a different ending entirely: Deckard discovers Rachael waiting for him in his apartment. He could kill her, or *retire* her, in the parlance of the movie, but of course he doesn't. Instead, he takes her by the hand into the elevator. The final shot is a freeze-frame, and it is unclear to the viewer if Rick and Rachael will even make it out of the building alive, unclear who is human or even what human is.

Some have even suggested that Deckard was a replicant, too. Recently, in fact, Ridley Scott admitted that he was.

I sat in my little white room at Saint Michael's Psychiatric and read my whole screenplay straight through to the end.

The last line of *Los Angeles* describes Angela inside Lester's cremator, fumbling for her cell phone.

She hears my voice answering, "Hello?"

"*Angel?*" she says, as the flames engulf her.

I put down the blue draft of the screenplay I had written and felt the credits rolling on my own science-fiction movie.

Picture a contemplative shot of my white face apprehending a dazzling southern California sun from the window of Saint Michael's Psychiatric. Picture an ever-widening helicopter shot of the Greater Los Angeles area, the other lives it implies, the other stories unfolding. . . . Picture the screen going black, the lights coming back on, everyone in the theater getting up to leave . . .

IN THE MORNING THE LOS ANGELES SUN ROLLS OVER THE DUSTY San Gabriel Mountains and snores through a gray-brown smog that drapes the city like a dirty sheet. When the smog lifts and the sun crawls out, hungover, its eyes swollen, its hair a mess, it takes a few moments for its daily ablutions, then puts on its gaudiest, most audacious costume — it becomes Louis the XVI, Amen-Ra, and Vegas Elvis all rolled into one. It wears brass buckles, gold rings, and a glittering necklace hung with pendants of BMWs, Mercedes, and Porsches.

If you turn your eyes to the Los Angeles sun on the freeway, it flashes a gold-toothed smile and twists its frosted hair with a silvery pink fingernail. Call me later, it mouths. It has to run. It doesn't have time to talk. Its people are waiting. The commercial directors, television show producers, and studio cinematographers, they're all out at this early hour, waiting for it to arrive like a white limo at a movie premiere, their eyes squinting, their weather-worn faces crinkly and lined, and the L.A. sun has gotten up just for them.

Throughout the afternoon, it rises, glorious, arrogant, demanding its juice, its trailer, its retinue of assistants and grips.

But when the day ends, the Los Angeles sun flashes its satin cape and beams for all the attention it has received throughout the day. *Good night,* it says like a lounge singer leaving the stage, giving us one last flamboyant bow, its voice velvety and its eyes misty with sentiment. *Good night.*

Good night, sweet ladies, good night.

Meanwhile, the L.A. dark, sheathed in blue denim and black leather, has been waiting out in the parking lot, smoking a filterless Camel. It leans back against the hood of a convertible and watches the starry sky, seeing but not seeing, like a *noir* detective. It doesn't give a shit. It looks straight through you. If you try to approach it, it just shakes its head and looks the other way.

Don't bother me, it says. *In fact, fuck off.* It doesn't want your attention. It doesn't need you and it never did. Who is it waiting for? Someone else. Someone more interesting than you.

And then it disappears with your girlfriend.

WHEN I STEPPED INTO MY NEW BEDROOM AT MY FATHER'S house, I found that my entire belongings, everything I owned — books, compact discs, clothes, even my stacks of colored paper — all of it had been removed from my apartment in West Hollywood and brought here. "We're going to spend time together," my father said, "you and me and Melanie and Gabriel." He coughed one of his rumbling coughs, an old man's cough, and led me into a bedroom. "You're going to stay with us, and of course you can come and go as you please, day and night, and not worry about anything." Then he added what was supposed to be a humorous afterthought. "But you can't leave the country."

Dr. Silowicz had dropped me off at the door, and my father had greeted me, wrapping an arm around my shoulders, and guided me into the house.

I looked around.

The room was significantly larger than my entire San Raphael Crescent apartment had been, a long parallelogram-shaped space with a king-size bed placed precisely in the middle. The floor was a mosaic of concrete, tile, see-through glass, and flat beige carpeting. Along the opposite wall were built-in aluminum-and-wire bookcases, newly installed. On the shelves were all of my books, placed in perfect alphabetical order. On the lower shelves were my stacks of colored paper, arranged in the same spectrum of hues they had been in before. There were other books, too, books from the old house that I thought had been thrown out or given away years ago. I walked to the shelves and placed my fingers on the spines of the *Great Books*. I wondered if Dad knew how much they meant to me or if it had just been an accident. On the bedside table were the digital wave machine and an odd collection of random items, including a candle, a handful of coins, even the Leica, all arranged haphazardly to create the illusion that someone had really lived here.

There was also a boomerang-shaped desk with a brand-new, flat-screen computer facing the wall-to-ceiling window — which, in turn, faced the glassy water of the beach and the emerald Pacific beyond.

"And watch this," my father said, barely able to contain his exuberance. He picked up a remote control from the bedside table and pointed it toward the window. From the ceiling descended a sheet of amber Mylar, bathing the room in a soft orange glow. "And now . . ." He pressed another button and a white blackout shade was lowered, too, reducing the room's natural light to unqualified darkness. He pushed still another button and a cool luminescence filled the air, the diffuse glow of recessed ceiling fixtures. "We had them put in all over the house, in every room." He threw the cardboard-thin remote toward me. "And this thing works everywhere you go." I fumbled to catch it. "You just carry it around with you and lower the shades," my father said. "You never have to worry about that bad light hurting your eyes again."

"Isn't it great?" Melanie enthused.

My father turned. "Just wait till you see the bathroom."

I followed him in. Tiled in beige, white, and brown, it was perfectly round and contained a whirlpool tub and freestanding shower. There were three metal sinks and a slanted skylight letting in the sun from above.

Dad noticed me glance up at it. "You can close that, too." He indicated an electronic panel on the wall. He turned the lights on and off, covered the skylight, and showed me how I could adjust the temperature of the water in Celsius or Fahrenheit. "I tried to think of everything," he said, "but if there's something I forgot, you just do it. Don't bother asking. Just tell someone on the staff, and they'll take care of it right away. There's no reason —" He was about to say something else, I guess, but cut himself off. "Well, there's just no reason." I noticed that all of my medication had been brought here, too, and the little amber bottles had been neatly arranged on a glass shelf above one of the sinks, including the bottle of Reality, which rose by a half inch above the rest.

We stepped back into the bedroom, Melanie following behind us. My father walked to the little suite and sat on the modernist couch. He rubbed his brown head with his brown hands and took a heavy breath. It struck me that in his striped sweater he looked like Picasso. I wanted to ask him what he thought he was doing, why he thought he could simply move my things here without asking. But all I could think to say was, "You look like Picasso."

Dad laughed. "That's what Melanie told me. It's this stupid sweater."

"It's cool," Melanie offered.

"Cool?" He nodded his head to the chair across from him, indicating that I should sit. "I don't know what cool is anymore. I have to hire people to tell me what cool is."

I sat down. Even from here I could hear his breathing, the air moving heavily in and out of his hairy, old-man nostrils.

"Angel, I know what you're thinking," he said. "I know you are angry. So I'm asking a favor. I'll give you all the privacy you need, whatever you want. Just stay here. *Please.* I want you to stay here until you get it all together, until you get it all figured out." He cleared his throat. "I was not a good father to you. I made stupid mistakes. I was too busy, self-absorbed. I let your mother raise you almost completely on her own, and I know you loved her and she was a good mother . . ." He reconsidered. "Well, no, damn it, she was not a good mother." Then his face seemed to twist through the middle. "Ah . . . shit, I don't know what she was. But I want to change things. I want to see you. I want you to be a part of my new family, to get to know Melanie, to help with Gabriel. He's adopted, but he's still your brother, your little brother, something you should have had all those years ago."

I started playing with the remote control, sending the blackout shades up and down, up and down.

"Angel," my father snapped, "I'm talking to you."

Later that night, I turned on the electronic wave machine — it had been brought from West Hollywood with the rest of my things — and wrapped myself in its comforting aural blur. But eventually I remembered there were actual waves outside, the entire Pacific Ocean, so I raised the blinds and slid the window open. I slept with the sound of the rain and the surf loud in my ears, a sound that seemed to cover everything, to smother my troubled thoughts, to surround my anxious dreams in a merciful white noise and soften the discord of my subconscious like a blanket wrapped around a pistol.

In the morning I woke to the light, the wet reflection of the rising sun on the water shining down over the house from the east. The sky had been washed clean. The digital clock announced like a beacon that it was six-fifteen. I reached for the remote control and lowered the shades, first the Mylar, then the blackout. It was virtually lightless in the room now, and I could have returned to sleep, to the world of dreams . . .

But I decided to get up. I stepped into the bathroom, where I found a new robe hanging on a hook; it was made of waffled cotton, cream-colored, the kind they give you in an expensive spa. Then I walked across the alternating flat-pile carpet and marble floor, through the long hallway, and over the artificial stream, and finally arrived in the kitchen, where Melanie sat at the stainless steel island thumbing through an issue of *Architectural Digest* that featured this very house.

"Good morning," she said. Her smile was affectionate, yielding, perhaps even genuine.

The light was soft in here, only a reflection off the western waves. "Hi." I went to the coffeemaker and found it full of fragrant kona. I poured myself a cup, then took a few sips, noting its strange flavor without my customary dollop of bourbon. "Where's Gabriel?" I said finally.

"He's with Theresa." She meant the nanny.

"Dad?"

"At work." Melanie was accustomed to this, I thought, a house like this, cars, servants, money. I realized that I had grown up wealthy, too. I was accustomed to this, too. Alone on San Raphael Crescent, I had grown unaccustomed to, had almost forgotten, what it was like. I sat down next to her at the counter and examined my cup. It was white, cylindrical, another example of the overall structure's perfect geometry.

"The house is beautiful," I acknowledged, nodding toward the magazine. I knew Melanie had overseen its design and construction, its layout and decor.

She smiled a thank-you. "Were you up late?" She and my father didn't sleep together anymore, if they ever had. He was too old, he said, coughed too much, got up too often to pee.

"Not so late."

"You must be tired."

I shrugged. "I'm fine."

"It was your father's idea about the shades." Her voice became slightly apologetic now, plaintive. "He wants you to stay. He wants you to be comfortable, Angel, so you'll stay with us for as long as you want."

I took another sip of coffee, said, "I'm not going anywhere," and took my cup and the *Los Angeles Times* into my room. I climbed into bed and read the entire thing, peering through the words and sentences and paragraphs for anything that might get my attention. In the news were the usual worries, the international subterfuges, the wars and rumors of wars, the attacks on freedom, embargoes on totalitarianism. In local news there were accidents and carjackings, convenience store holdups and slow-speed chases. The world, as always, was coming to an end; serial killers were on the loose; madmen ruled entire countries, especially ours; CEOs were petty criminals. It was the same old world, nothing had changed, nothing had changed in years. I even looked at the ads, the large type announcing sales on everything from automobiles to tropical vacations, the minuscule copy at the bottom explaining why the above offer wasn't really true.

Nothing was true, I thought. There was no such thing as the truth.

Even Angela hadn't been true.

Eventually I stepped into the shower, standing awkwardly in the middle of the large, open cylinder. I let the warm water gush over me while I jerked off, conjuring mental images of Angela — on stage at the Velvet Mask, in bed with me in West Hollywood, coming into the living room with that armful of blue and white hyacinths, that terrible, gorgeous light stinging my eyes.

I knew she wasn't real, but I still thought of her. She still lived in my imagination.

My mind cleared of the pressing need for sexual release, I sought emotional release, too, sobbing pathetically there in the architecturally perfect shower.

How could I miss someone so terribly if she wasn't even real? What was wrong with me?

As always, I remembered her fingers, those long glittery nails on my chest, and I wondered who's they really were. Cassandra's? Jessica's? Some escort's?

Exhausted, I slipped into the waffled robe, then went down to find Melanie on the sundeck. She had changed into a black one-piece bathing suit.

She smiled serenely, her hair pulled back, and peered up at me through a pair of dark Gucci lenses.

———

That day passed. And then others. Weeks, months. Nights, I borrowed one of my father's cars and drove through the city. I was still searching, I suppose, but now I didn't know what for. I watched the taillights of automobiles create a red halo over the blackened streets. I watched the hills darken, bright points of white and yellow flickering through the heavy branches and the dense overgrowth like stars in a fallen firmament.

The Los Angeles night descends like a curtain over a stage. I have spent years observing its velvet draperies, its translucent filters of blue, brown, and black. From Sunset Boulevard, the famous Hollywood sign glows atop Mount Lee, the letters gleaming like beacons to the millions who come here every year to gawk or to become famous themselves. On warmer nights, torches are lit, and L.A. burns. Great billboards of smoking cowboys and gleaming wedges of California cheese flare up like beacons in the darkness. Gorgeous supermodels hover over intersections, their teeth beaming their toothpaste-white perfection. Two-story-tall rock stars glare down insolently from building rooftops. Of course, nothing is brighter than the billboards advertising movies — my father's, in particular. In this one, Will Smith grins churlishly in a policeman's uniform. Here, Cameron Diaz offers a karate kick in a wedding dress. A gray-haired but still bright-eyed Jack Nicholson glowers mischievously at the waiting traffic.

If you are high enough in the hills, you can see underlit pools radiating a cool blue like gems set randomly across a gown.

Televisions cast eerie blue illumination from bedroom windows.

For no reason at all, some houses are decorated for Christmas, which is months away.

At home, from my bedroom window at my father's house, the darkness was general over Zuma Beach. Only a few lights were visible from the houses hidden among the cliffs. The crests of waves caught the faint light of the moon. Sometimes, when the sky was concealed in fog, there was only the sound of the churning ocean, so persistent that I often wondered why it didn't put the whole of California to sleep.

———

"I think I might like to get a job," I told Melanie one morning.

"Like what?" She had moved an umbrella over the hot-tub portion of the pool so I could sit with her and now lowered herself a centimeter at a time into the steaming water.

"I don't know," I said. "Maybe in a bookstore, maybe a library."

"Why not work for your father?"

"Doing what?" I put my legs in the warm water, too.

"A million things, are you kidding? Production, development —"

"No." I shook my head and kicked my feet. "I'd always be the boss's kid."

"Yeah." She leaned back, wetting her hair, and when she came out, her head was steaming. "That's why I quit. I had become the boss's wife." Melanie had worked in production for my father. She had even developed a couple of relatively successful movies on her own. "People weren't treating me the way they had before. They weren't taking me seriously." She shrugged. "Or they were taking me too seriously. Or something."

"Something during the day." I pictured an office, a desk, a sheaf of colored papers, a computer screen.

"You could be a reader for the studio," she suggested. "No one would care if you're the boss's kid. No one would even know."

"A reader?"

"All you have to do is read screenplays and write a brief synopsis, then pass it along. You don't even have to talk to anyone. You could even do it here."

"I was thinking I'd like to be around other people, at least a little bit." This idea had come from Dr. Silowicz, actually. He had suggested I get out into the world more, find something that was all my own.

Melanie pulled herself out of the water and sat across from me on the black marble. Her skin had gone bright pink against her bathing suit. "What about your screenplay?"

"What about it?"

"Are you finished?"

I laughed.

She looked over at Gabriel, who smashed his body against the gray mesh webbing of his pen and held a red ball in his fist, muttering to himself in his secret, incomprehensible language.

"I wonder what he'll want to do with his life," she asked.

"It all depends," I said, "on how he's raised, on what he sees his parents doing."

We spoke as if he were normal, as if Gabriel's problem, autism, retardation, whatever it was, would eventually be overcome. This is the faith our mothers have in us, I thought. My mother had that kind of faith in me once, too.

"Do you think it's hereditary?"

For a moment I thought she meant his condition. Then I asked, "You mean what you do in life?"

She nodded.

I shook my head. "Look at me. I'm a disaster." I thought for a moment longer, watching a puffy cloud roll over the sea's distant horizon. Then I chuckled. "Maybe it *is* hereditary. I'm a disaster, and my father makes disaster movies."

"I don't know very much about his biological parents."

"I'm surprised you know anything at all."

"Sometimes they seal the information," Melanie went on, "but now, you know, they can release it in case there's a medical problem." A servant had placed a stack of those waffled, cream-colored towels by the pool's edge. Melanie reached for one. "I don't know anything about Gabriel's biological father at all, I don't think anyone does, but I requested his medical information in case there was something that may have influenced . . ." She threw a glance over to her little boy.

"Did you meet her?"

"We saw her the day he was born," Melanie said. "It wasn't on purpose. We were there, you know, in the hospital. The whole thing had been prearranged. They had to move her because there was some unanticipated internal situation, bleeding or something, nothing to do with Gabriel, thank goodness, but they wheeled her past me in the hallway."

"Does he look like her?"

"I didn't get a very good look at her face." She shook her head slightly. "She was black."

I laughed, looking at this little kid, his dark skin, my brother. For some reason, I had always imagined that his mother was white and his father was black — my own racist scripting, I guess.

Melanie got up, wrapping herself in a towel, and walked over to him. She leaned over the playpen and kissed his face a dozen times, saying, "My baby, my baby, my baby."

"Was that weird?" This question suddenly occurred to me. "Seeing Gabriel's mother wheel past you like that?"

"It wasn't supposed to happen." She leaned down and took him into her arms. "Frank seemed more shaken up about it than anyone else."

"Frank was there?"

"Yeah, you know . . . he arranged the whole thing. Your father wasn't around, as usual. As usual, he was on his way."

"Frank was in the hospital with you?" I don't know why, but

this irritated me, the idea of Frank insinuating himself so deeply into every aspect of our private lives. I wondered if he was going to threaten Gabriel the way he had threatened me and planned to make sure he didn't.

Melanie put Gabriel down and came back to the hot tub. "Frank set up everything." She shrugged. "Frank arranges everything for Milos. You know that."

"Did Frank arrange the adoption?"

"Of course." Melanie laughed. "He even pays the phone bill."

"Too much Frank." I splashed my feet.

"He takes care of your dad." Melanie frowned, weighing Frank's and my father's affection for one another. "Your dad takes care of him."

"Symbiosis," I said. "Frank is like one of those eels that eat the dead flesh out of a shark's mouth."

"Whatever it is," Melanie said, "he seemed kind of weirded out."

"What do you mean, *weirded out?*"

"When he saw her, Gabriel's birth mother, Frank" — Melanie bit her lip — "I don't know. He seemed upset."

"Why?"

"He had met her already, I think, when she was pregnant. He knew her somehow."

My face started to burn. "What did she look like?"

"I told you, I didn't really get a good look at her face."

"What about her hair?"

Melanie looked at me, a little surprised. "Yeah. Her hair was really strange. It was blond, really unnatural, like it had been dyed a million times."

I looked at Gabriel and saw everything, it was all there in his eyes. They were her eyes.

Angela's eyes.

"Do you remember her name?"

"Angel, what's wrong?"

"Do you remember it?"

"No, I —"

"Do you have it written on a piece of paper? A document? A form or something?"

"It's in her medical file," she said fearfully. "I have a copy upstairs."

I couldn't stop staring at Gabriel now, because I was staring at Angela. "Where?" I asked. "Exactly where is it?" I pulled my foot out of the water and stood up.

"In a drawer, in the closet." Melanie got out, too.

"Which closet?" I started walking into the house.

Melanie lifted Gabriel and followed, holding him against her hip. They were behind me, but I could tell from the soft whimpering noises he was making inside his throat that he was about to cry.

"Hold on, Angel," Melanie said, "and I'll show you."

I was bounding up the glass-and-wire stairs toward Melanie's room. I walked down the hall, slipped through her door, found her closet, and began opening the built-in drawers, flinging their contents, underwear, socks, costume jewelry, onto the floor.

Finally, Melanie caught up with me. "It's the second one from the bottom," she said, "on the far left. All you had to do was ask."

"I did ask." I went to that drawer and slid it open. There were neat stacks of papers and envelopes inside it.

"It should be somewhere near the top. A blue folder."

Gabriel was crying, a high-pitched, open moan.

I found a cornflower-blue folder with a private hospital logo on it. There were a series of official documents inside, the kind of papers you keep in a drawer forever but never find any reason to use, the kind of documents you put away for safekeeping, with information that will never be relevant to anyone.

But it was relevant now.

Gabriel was crying full-out, almost screaming.

I flipped through the pages, scanning the typed-in words until I found the ones I was looking for.

Biological Mother: Jessica Teagarden.

There followed her blood type, medical history, social security number, everything I would need to find her.

"Angel, what's wrong? What is it?"

Have you ever seen magnesium burning?

Have you ever stared into the heart of a bright white sun?

Gabriel was screaming, and a string of spit connected his mouth to Melanie's shoulder.

"Everything," I said. "My whole life."

———

"Where is he?" I asked. "Where the hell is Frank?"

"Mr. Heile is upstairs." Flustered, the receptionist started to rise. "But I have to —"

I bounded up a set of thickly carpeted steps, holding Jessica Teagarden's crumpled medical files in my angry pink fist. I walked past bewildered young Hollywood lawyers and paralegals, past men and women in distinctive eyewear and dark, expensive suits, all of whom turned their handsome faces to follow me down the hushed corridor, racing like a fire consuming the building. Outside, it was a modern structure, a typical Wilshire Boulevard glass-and-granite office building, but the interior of Heile Associates was an explosion of pinks, blues, and golds, with heavy antique furniture upholstered in multicolored jacquard sateens. Frank's offices were like the chambers of a secret museum, I thought, with minor Impressionist pieces on the wood-paneled walls and ornate oriental carpets covering the marble floors. I passed his stately old secretary and pushed my way through an enormous brass-and-wooden door that could only be Frank's.

"I found out," I said, practically crashing into the room.

There was a gigantic desk, elaborately carved, with a red leather swivel chair. Frank was in it, of course, surrounded by his onion-skin papers in multiple pastel hues. His ancient briefcase lay open at his feet, and the detritus of a thousand legal documents cluttered every surface.

"Angel," he said, "what are you —"

I had the adoption papers in my hand. I held them up so he could see, brandishing them like the evidence in a courtroom drama.

His secretary, a grand woman with one squinting eye, came in behind me.

"It's all right, Felicia." Frank waved her away, using my father's characteristic gesture.

"I want a fucking explanation," I yelled. "I need to know what happened, Frank, what really —"

His hands asked me to lower the volume.

"I need to know where she is," I said. "I need to know the truth."

He smiled. "No more bullshit?"

I couldn't even respond.

Slowly, he got up from behind the desk and went to the dark leather couch along the wall, sitting down.

"Okay." His green eyes fixed on me. "Jessica Teagarden is Gabriel's birth mother," he began. "I paid . . . paid an enormous amount of money to help her, all of her medical expenses, the delivery." He inhaled. "But then she found out . . . well, she already knew who your father was . . . and who you were . . . who you are, Angel, and she . . . she decided she wanted something more than what I had given her." His eyes narrowed. His face said he was leveling with me. "She moved into the place next door to you, thinking she would . . ." He waved his hands in the air like a conductor in front of a silent orchestra. "She wanted to insinuate herself into your life," he said. "She wanted to —"

"Get close to her son," I said, completing the thought.

He shook his head. "I wish it were that easy." He brought a hand to his mouth and wiped the corners of his lips. "She wanted to blackmail me."

"Blackmail *you?*" This made no sense at all. "For what?"

"Angel, you have to understand. Your father doesn't —" He hesitated.

"Doesn't what?"

"He doesn't *know.*" He got up from the couch and started pacing back and forth in front of the window, eyeing the traffic outside.

"I don't get why Dad would give a shit about Gabriel's birth mother." I shook my head. "And why didn't she just go through legal channels? Couldn't she have hired a lawyer herself? Couldn't she have —"

He sighed. "She doesn't operate that way, Angel. She's a fucking —"

"But why *you?*" There had to be more to this, I thought. "What is this really about?"

Frank threw his eyes around the room. "Can't you just let it go?" Once again, he sank heavily onto the leather couch. He rubbed his cheeks with the backs of his age-spotted hands.

"I'm not letting anything go. Sorry."

He sighed. "I told her . . . things. I don't know why. I don't know what it was about her, but I guess I just wanted to tell somebody . . . I needed to tell someone . . . things I had been carrying around for years. There was . . . something about Jessica that made me tell her . . ."

"What?" I shook my head. "What did you tell her?"

Frank offered me the strangest look.

The afternoon was crystal bright through the window. I glanced out at the street. It was still early, and sunlight fell in yellow sheets over the mounting Santa Monica–bound traffic.

"When I was younger," Frank began, "I drank. In the mornings I would wake up and have vodka with my breakfast cereal. Sounds funny, right? Your father remembers what I was like in those days. The problem was, it never interfered with my functioning. If it had, I'm sure I would have stopped a lot sooner. What ultimately made me quit, though, were the blackouts. I'd wake up in hotel rooms, not knowing how I got there. I'd find myself with women I didn't even remember meeting." He shook his head. "It all sounds hysterical, doesn't it?" He thought for a moment. "You asked me why I don't drive. That's because my license was revoked, years ago."

"What are you telling me, Frank?"

"I'm telling you what I told Jessica." He sighed. "Just listen. There was a particular woman, a woman not my wife, with whom I had a . . . relationship." He looked up at me. "I loved her more than anything . . . more than anyone. I would have done anything for her." He touched his hands to his eyes, pressing down on the lids. "But she decided to break it off, probably because of the drinking, but there were other reasons, too. She told me one morning that it was over. You have to understand that I had spent years with her, Angel — years. Anyway, I had already been drinking, of course, but that day I really let everything go." Softly, he cleared his throat. "The next day —" Frank's voice broke. Jesus Christ, he was actually revealing an emotion.

"What?" I asked softly. "What happened the next day?"

"The next day, I woke up in my car in a parking lot somewhere, and the woman . . . and she was in the hospital." Frank made the smallest sound, something between a laugh and a cry. "I had . . . done things to her. I broke her nose, shattered her cheekbone, snapped her wrist. I had done some pretty terrible things already in my life at that point but never anything like that." He looked directly at me.

My whole body drained of its heat. I could hear my own insides, the liquid squish of organs. "The monster," I said. The monster that came into our house at night when I was a little kid. Those violent, shadowy images . . . I had imagined a horrible animal thrashing at my mother's throat, slashing her apart. "That was you."

"I won't tell you I'm sorry, Angel. I know it wouldn't mean anything."

"Why didn't she —" I didn't even know what I was asking. "Why wouldn't she —"

"Go to the police? Tell your father? Have me thrown in jail? Because she loved me. Can you believe that?" He smiled ironically. "A person loving *me?* It also would have meant revealing the affair to your father, to the world. Your mother" — Frank breathed in, then out — "such a private person." His voice became small. "Like you, Angel."

"And that's what you told Jessica?"

He nodded. "And now you know, too."

"How did you know her?" I asked.

"Jessica Teagarden was an actress." Frank sighed. "I met her several years ago when she first came to Hollywood. She was just someone I was sleeping with. She moved in next door to you and tried to . . . tried to get you to fall in love with her. It worked, I guess. But there's a bit of a monster in you, too, Angel, and she found that out."

That was why she knew about the lamb stew, I realized, and about night swimming. That was why she had known so much about me. Frank had told her. I had thought it was instinct. I had believed Angela and I possessed some kind of magical, preternatural link. But now I knew that it had all been constructed. Even the way she had used the name Angela — it had all been calculated to create a false connection, as though we really had something in common. *What were the chances?* She had asked that very question the day we met. The chances were nonexistent. Nothing had been left to chance. I turned to look at the glare flashing off the wind-shields of the cars on Wilshire Boulevard and put the final pieces together. "He's yours, isn't he?" I pictured him, my little brother, a handful of tofu oozing from his fingers, a string of drool dangling from his chin. This was Frank's son, his flesh and blood. I almost puked to think of it.

Frank became quiet. I could hear him breathing for a full thirty seconds. Then he said, "She was using you, Angel. She was just a girl I slept with and told too much to . . . I thought I could kill two birds. Melanie and your father had been trying" — he shook his head sadly — "they had been trying . . ."

The light in the room came from recessed bulbs that buzzed faintly in the ceiling. I looked up, for one quick moment letting my eyes flicker against the electric light, as if I could find some truth there like Victor, and then looked back at Frank. "What did you do to her?" I thought I could see the skeleton beneath his skin, the death's head staring back at me.

"Do to her?"

"Before she disappeared," I said now, "she called me, she called me from the dark."

Momentarily, he brought his eyes up to meet mine. "We were in the car, and she was threatening . . . threatening to tell you if I didn't give her what she wanted. She had her cell phone and she di-aled your number, and when you answered, she said your name. That's when I grabbed the phone . . . I took it out of her hand. She was about to tell you the truth, and I couldn't have that." He closed his eyes. "I couldn't live with that."

———

I remembered, remembered her saying that she adored me, that I was her *Angel to Love*. Whatever she had done, I told myself, it didn't matter. Whoever she had been would be washed away. My love, my faith in her, I thought as I boarded the plane, was like the light. It would illuminate her. It would wash away the shadows. It would change her back.

As the plane took off, I fingered the stack of photographs I had taken of Gabriel, the little boy who had been the cause of all of this. It had been all she had wanted, just to see him again, to get close to him. She'd made a mistake, that was all. Frank had convinced her to give up her own son, and afterward she only wanted to be near him.

I held the velvet box in my hand. My palm curled around it.

I pictured light. I pictured a misted sky and multicolored clouds reflecting in the pristine and shining metal of a car. I pictured the muted sun burning beneath a blanket of white and gray, the yellow of a billion tons of flaming hydrogen blistering through a cover of vapor, pictured my white hands on the light-absorbing black steering wheel of a beautiful new car, the recent lines that had formed at the edges of Angela's sun-damaged face, and her hair, now in a tight black afro cut close to her perfectly shaped scalp, and her eyes, gorgeous, almond-shaped, long-lashed, and her long, delicate fingers and perfectly manicured nails, painted green, metallic seafoam. I pictured the photons of energy moving through space toward earth, toward us, reflecting and refracting off the curves of the car's metal, flashing off the wet road ahead of us.

I sat on the plane and thought of the light, as always, of what it was truly doing, how it was making its way toward us, particle and wave.

I imagined that Angela had folded her legs beneath her and put a disc in the stereo. It was ImmanuelKantLern, of course. The music was dark, solemn, but not so unsmiling as their earlier work, with even a few acoustic touches. And in this daydream, Angela sang along, already familiar, somehow, with the lyrics, and on her finger was a darkly reflective sapphire, catching a momentary fire.

———

Jesus Christ, it was cold. The last time I had experienced weather like this was at the Vancouver School, staring out at that icy Canadian meadow. But now I was somewhere on Madison Avenue, New York City, experiencing a wind that blew through my bones and chilled my flesh like fear itself. Stupidly, I had gotten out of the taxi too soon. Waiting in traffic had been making me impatient, and since I had noticed that we were already on the right street, I went ahead and paid the driver, then stepped out onto the sidewalk, not realizing that I still had a million blocks to go. I should mention that albinos who live in Los Angeles do not think to bring an overcoat when they visit New York City.

Albinos who live in Los Angeles do not own overcoats.

I walked through the slickly shadowed Manhattan streets with my hands jammed in my pockets and my teeth chattering and noticed that almost no one looked at me except to glance up quickly and then get the hell out of the way. I had never seen more purposeful human beings in my life. These people moved down the sidewalk like the citizens of Tokyo scurrying away from Godzilla, weaving and sidestepping and sweeping past my shoulders in what appeared to be only a barely controlled panic. It was just past six in the evening, and the sun already was completely down. An East Coast bleakness pervaded the atmosphere, a cold northern gloom that was more visceral than visual.

I wondered for a moment what it would be like to live here, thinking of the anonymous streets, the anxious urbanites too caught up in their own neuroses to notice the ultrawhite man in their midst.

But the thought, like these people, passed quickly. I could never leave my Los Angeles.

After several shivering blocks, and after having to double back twice, I finally located the right building. It featured a marble-floored lobby with brass fixtures and a uniformed doorman standing at military attention.

I told him who I was here to see.

"Your name, sir?"

"Angel."

"One moment, please." He picked up the phone and pressed a single number. I couldn't help but picture Angela on the other end of the line, those eyes, the tapered fingers. "An Angel is here to see you," he said into the phone, tapping his fingers on the surface of his counter. Then he looked up at me and sighed. "Angel who?"

"Angel Veronchek," I offered. "From Los Angeles."

He spoke into the phone again. "Says he's from L.A. . . . Veronchek . . ." The doorman waited a few slight seconds, then gently placed the phone back in its cradle, shaking his head. He made his eyes go hard. "Wait at the diner across the street. She'll meet you in five minutes."

"Across the street?"

"Straight across," the doorman said, pointing toward the entrance. "It's called the Cosmos. You can't miss it."

"Okay."

Out on the frozen sidewalk again, I looked across the street at the Cosmos Diner, a fluorescent jumble of lights and darks behind a glistening window. I made my way across Madison and stepped inside, asking the waiter for a booth by the window. I wanted to see her when she emerged from her building. I wanted to watch her walk toward me. I wanted to see Angela as soon as possible.

The waiter led me to the table, and I ordered a coffee and a glass of water. There were pills I had to take — Reality, of course — and I thought I might as well do it now. I focused on the street, the quick-passing, confident striders, these aliens in their black leather jackets and black-rimmed glasses.

"Angel."

I looked up.

"What are you doing here?" Jessica — her name was *Jessica* — must have come across the street without my noticing. I must have watched her without even realizing it was her. That was probably because her hair was so different now. It was bright red, like the red hair of an Irish person, and as straight as a movie star's. Her makeup was elegant, her lips a faint shade of glistening beige. She wore a blond leather coat with a shearling collar.

"I won't —" I started. I had actually come with the conscious intention of apologizing, of setting things right. "I'm better now. I promise I won't do anything . . ."

But suddenly I realized there was another intention, too, one I hadn't even admitted to myself.

Jessica smiled thinly. "That's nice to know."

I looked around the diner at all the strange people. "You moved to New York."

"I got engaged, Angel. I met someone."

"He lives here?"

As though talking to a child, she said, "This is where *I* live now."

"Oh, but I thought —" I stopped myself.

"What is it?"

"I wanted to . . ." I could hardly speak. "I wanted to say that I was . . . wanted to say how sorry . . ." I couldn't stop staring at her face, at her eyes — they were so blue. Blue, blue, electromagnetic blue. I tried to separate in my memory the girl who had come to my door that night with the lamb stew from all the others, the girl from the Mask, Cassandra, all those escorts . . . I had more distinct memories of them now, at least of some of them, but they still blurred together in my mind, still spoke in a single voice.

There must have been something in my face, because hers softened with that look of understanding, the same one I had seen that first day I met her. It was nice to know that some things hadn't been scripted, that some things had been brought over from the other universe. "It's okay, Angel," she said and slid into the booth, facing me.

"And I was hoping to find out what happened," I went on. "Why you —" But I couldn't finish.

This was all wrong. This wasn't the way I had imagined it at all. I had imagined a tearful reunion. I had imagined an embrace, the events of the past dissolving like sugar in hot tea. I wanted to go back. I wanted to wake up in the hospital. *We ran a tox screen,* I wanted to hear, *and found just about everything* . . . But I was still here, still in the Cosmos Diner on Madison Avenue in New York City. Jessica still wore her shearling coat, obviously prepared to leave at any second.

"What happened." It was a statement. She was expressing her own stupefaction, as if I were supposed to know, as if everyone in the entire world knew.

She shook her head and smiled. "You're so fucking crazy, you know that, Angel?"

"I didn't mean to hurt anyone. I wasn't . . . myself." I think I started hyperventilating again. A blind spot was forming on my field of vision, a blur of shine that had situated itself right in front of Jessica's face.

I tried to see her eyes, to apprehend that shade of blue again, but they were occluded.

"Your family," she said, "those people, your doctor . . . they just lie to you, Angel. They think they're protecting you, but they're not."

I reached into my pocket and pulled out the photographs, pictures I had taken of Gabriel. "I thought you . . ." I couldn't even get it out. I could hardly even see her now. Another migraine was forming. It was the same sensation I'd had after Lester hit me at the crematorium. It was the same feeling I'd had that day on the highway, driving toward Orange Blossom Boulevard. It was the same feeling I'd had that day on the beach when I stepped into the light.

Red. Orange. Bright yellow. Burning.

She picked up the pictures and sifted through them. "I can't," she said. Jessica's auburn hair shimmered in the warm incandescence of the diner. She looked through the window at her building across the street. "My fiancé is going to be home soon, anyway." She pushed the photos back toward me. "And he doesn't know."

I reached into my side pocket and pulled out the velvet box. I opened it and pushed it toward her. "I got this for you," I said. "I was in Rio, and I —"

"Rio?"

I shrugged. "It's a long story."

She leaned forward, eyeing the glistening sapphire. "What do you want?"

I shook my head. "I want . . . I only wanted . . ."

She got up abruptly. "Do you want to *marry* me?"

"I don't —" I stammered. "I just —"

"You practically killed me," she said. "Don't you remember that? You tried to drown me."

"I'm sorry," I answered. "I just don't remember it that way. From my point of view, it didn't happen that way."

"Your point of view?" She made an incredulous face. "Listen," she said. "Why don't you take your ring and go back to Los Angeles where you belong?"

"You weren't like this," I managed to choke out, "in the other world."

"The other —"

329

"You loved me."

"— world? Christ," she said, "you're fucking delusional, you know that?"

"You don't even want the pictures?"

I looked up at the lamp hanging above our booth, staring, for some reason, straight into the bulb, as if I might find some answer there. This is the world, I realized, that I had crossed over to. This was the actual world, and in this world, Angela lived but didn't love me.

I let that light burn my eyes for a few more painful seconds, and then I closed them, and when I opened them again, she was gone.

———

There is only one kind of object that can exhibit the properties of both particles and waves, and that is the string. It's simple, really. When looked at from the front, a string looks and acts like a particle. From the side it looks and acts like a wave. I know you've heard of it, too. String Theory is apparently prevailing as the great Unified Field Theory that physicists have been searching for for so long. It is opening up entire branches of science. There was even an article about it in the science section of the *New York Times,* which I read on the plane on the way back to L.A. I won't pretend I understand it, and I suspect that Professor Lem may even have gotten around to explaining String Theory in her lectures after I left her class. But the theory includes a way of describing both the particle properties and the wave properties of light without having to resort to complex, multidimensional geometries. Or even multiple worlds.

It doesn't matter. I was losing interest in physics at that point, anyway.

———

I came home from New York, and my father made grilled cheese sandwiches with tons of butter, which we ate at the vast stainless steel island in the middle of his kitchen, and conspicuously did not mention that I had been gone at all. "I'm not supposed to eat butter." He laughed. "But I don't care. It's the only thing I can enjoy anymore." He winked at Melanie. Dad hadn't bothered to cut any of the sandwiches in two, just plopped them down on the counter.

A member of the staff, a pretty girl with long black hair, rushed around behind him, trying to keep things clean. He finally told her to get the hell out, so now it was just us, the Veroncheks, bizarre family that we were. Dad pushed a large bowl of fruit over toward me with a greedy smile. He had always loved fruit, had always behaved as though it were some terrific treat, a throwback, I suppose, to his underprivileged childhood.

I tried to remember if my father had ever made me anything to eat before, and he must've read my thoughts, because he said, "Your mother was always around, overprotecting you. She wouldn't let me take you anywhere. She always said it was your skin, that you were too delicate, somehow I'd —"

"It's all right, Dad."

"And then everything happened with the doctor, and then Canada, that Vancouver place. The whole thing with the divorce and your mother's illness, and then, well, the thing in college . . . it just sent you over the edge."

At some point the nanny brought Gabriel in, and now Melanie turned her attention to him.

"And what would you like, buster?" she said. "Are you hungry?"

The little boy ran to the refrigerator. He had become so skinny, I noticed, like a piece of string himself.

"Where are you going?" Melanie asked.

"Does he maybe want me to make him a sandwich, too?" My father was hopeful.

"Jesus, not one of those," Melanie said with a sniff. She reached inside the glass refrigerator and found a plastic bowl. She pulled off the lid and handed Gabriel a white, rubbery cube.

"Is that what you want?" Dad got off his stool and leaned down to look at him. *"Tofu?"*

Gabriel looked up like a spaniel, his head cocked to one side. His little face contorted. He twisted his mouth and tried to force out a word.

"What is it, sweetheart? Say what you want."

The little boy continued to stare at my father. He was about to speak, I thought, but only revealed a mouthful of gooey white mush.

Dad shook his head and placed a hand on Gabriel's chin, gently closing his jaw.

I couldn't help but laugh.

Melanie found a high chair, and I helped pick the kid up and put him in it, threading his scrawny limbs through the leg holes. She arranged a small plate of tofu and broccoli. His eyes grew wide, from hunger, I guess, and from excitement to be eating. Melanie poured herself a glass of juice and sat directly in front of him. She wasn't as beautiful as my mother had been, not even remotely as glamorous, but she was warm, natural, her body composed of a hundred circles, with brown hair and olive skin and soft brown eyes and a face that had never been altered. Melanie had practical hands that were always moving, touching, caressing, grooming. She had grown up wealthy, my father once told me, so none of his money meant anything to her. She must have married him for love, he had said, because look at him, it wasn't for looks. I hadn't believed it, of course. Standing there in their gigantic kitchen, I still didn't. Money and power had to have somehow figured into Melanie's decision to marry my father, but I could see at that moment that she loved this little boy, and maybe, I thought, that was enough.

Right now both she and my father came around on either side of Gabriel and kissed his cheeks, making foolish, overly loud smooching sounds. Gabriel's face broke into a mushy, slobbery smile, and his eyes closed rapturously. He held a piece of broccoli in one hand and a cube of tofu in the other, both of which oozed between his fingers, green and white.

My father looked up at me. "He loves this," he said in his faint accent. "He's like on drugs."

———

In Los Angeles, the light finds its way into you. It tears at your oculus with its photoelectric teeth. You try to close your eyes against it, but you still see it, a throbbing ball of incandescence, a splash of lava under your eyelids.

Red. Orange. Bright yellow. Burning.

It dances across your field of vision; it swims over the waxy leaves of the succulents like a school of glittering fish; it licks your skin like a cat with an ultraviolet tongue and warms the streets of the city like a lamp in a tanning salon.

This is the light, the Los Angeles light. Gleaming radiantly off the chrome of the BMW ahead of you, it shines like a painful metaphor for the truth. It traces an outline around the features of the beautiful people and radiates an aura of intensity around their golden, faultless bodies. Daylight in Los Angeles is flashing chrome and metal, radios too loud in every car, tanned arms lifting cigarettes to lipsticked mouths. It is BMWs, Mercedes, Jaguars, Porsches; it is resplendent hair, reflective sunglasses, shining jewels dangling from perspiring ears; white-asphalt-and-blue skies, a fantastic, extreme-close-up sun, crisp white shirts, gorgeous faces in flamboyant cars.

Imagine what it must have been like for the filmmakers of the teens and twenties, for Charlie Chaplin, D. W. Griffith, and John Ford, for those first cinematographers who came out here and stood on the sandy plateau to appreciate the uniform light, what it must have been like to apprehend those long, golden sunrises and glorious sunsets. Day after day like this, hour after hour of immaculate light and hard, filmable shadows. They set up their cameras and shot, exposing roll after roll, exposing themselves, their bodies, their skin, and their souls, exposing the rest of the world, too, movie by movie, scene by scene.

But then the cars came, and the industries filled the Valley with factories, smokestacks, and assembly plants, and the city grew more and more alluring, and the light of Los Angeles became more and more gorgeous because the film technology finally advanced enough to capture its spectrum of tones and hues, its pinks and blues and golds and yellows, its Technicolor subtleties. We waited for the sun to come to us, we invited it in, even seduced it when necessary, trying to capture it inside our little black boxes, happy just to possess it for those few moments, to record it, to make use of it for our public fictions and our private dreams, and when it left for the night, we stood there smiling — burnt, blistered, scorched, dying of skin cancer, but intoxicated, in love.

Every morning I woke up earlier and earlier, until finally I found myself coming downstairs around six a.m. to help with Gabriel. It got to the point where I was even feeding him myself, sitting at the kitchen table with my mug of black coffee and spooning breakfast goo into his hungry, inarticulate mouth. Even though he should have been talking in complete sentences by now, and feeding himself, all my little brother wanted was to eat and murmur incoherently. There was something else about him, too — there is something about small children, I guess, his smell, his soft cheeks, the drool permanently glossing his chin — something that made me forget. I marveled at Gabriel's fine, wiry hair, his brown skin and red lips.

After breakfast I would take him into the living room and lie on the floor, me in my waffled bathrobe, Gabriel in his pajamas. My father always left the house by six-thirty, so it was only me and Gabriel and Melanie by then. I'd lie on the rug and curl my body around his, letting his dark limbs squirm against my chalky chest. With his daily therapy, he was trying to learn to talk. Every afternoon a specialist came over and sat with him, a young man with a receding hairline and wire-rimmed glasses who laid out a series of

simple images on the table — a cat, a house, a baby, a car. My little brother stared into space, babbled, and twisted his hands.

It's important to mention this, too:

One day not long after I returned from New York, Frank got
up from his ornate desk in his Beverly Hills home office, walked
down through his kitchen into his four-car garage, removed the
plastic tube from the bag that he had bought years ago at a hard-
ware store, and connected it to the exhaust pipe of his Porsche —
the red Porsche he had been so embarrassed to tell me about, because he wasn't even allowed to drive it. He curled the tube around
to the passenger side window, sat in the driver's seat, and engaged
the ignition. I'm not sure how long these things take, but I imagine
he sat there for a while before losing consciousness, thinking over
the complex events of his life. He had devoted himself to my family. He had been so dedicated to my father, to my mother — and
to me, too, I guess. Other than his wife, he had no family of his
own. He left several notes. There was one for my father, of course,
which explained in detail the remaining legal issues regarding their
upcoming feature film, including completed drafts of contracts
and casting recommendations. There was a letter for Gabriel,
which was not supposed to be opened until his twenty-first birthday and which was entrusted to me for safekeeping.

And there was also a letter for me, in which he said he was sorry
about everything I had gone through, that he knew I'd had a tough
time of it. He said that he thought I should know about him and
my mother, that it was only fair. He said he hoped it wouldn't hurt
me, but he thought I should be aware of how much he loved her

and that at one point in time, at least, she had loved him. When he lost Monique, he wrote, his real life had ended. These past several years had only been to fulfill his remaining obligations. He hoped he had done so, he wrote, and that I would forgive him someday. He understood completely, however, if I couldn't. These were his letter's last words: *I may not have been a very good person, Angel, but I wasn't a monster.*

Every evening I would stay up after dinner and talk to my father, refusing even a glass of wine. He would drink his expensive bourbon and smoke his black-market Cuban, puffing away until it was too cold to remain outside, and then he would amble off to sleep. I'd go to my room and watch DVDs. I tried watching Dad's movies sometimes, out of politeness if nothing else, but I could never connect — the explosions, the sentimental romances, the melodramatic heroes launching into their hopeless missions. In my father's movies people are always themselves, the characters so flawlessly delineated, their goals so perfectly clear. I'd always wanted that, to be purely myself, with a certain, unwavering mission, like a character in a movie. But I am perpetually filled with uncertainty, a deviation from the character I set out to be. Particle or wave.

Most nights, I'd let the disc run down and I would lie in the television's cerulean glow, still dreaming the movie's dream. Sometimes I'd open the window and listen to the loud Malibu surf, my arms spread wide, my eyes wide, too, staring at the ceiling, but asleep, letting Dr. Silowicz's psychotropic medication work its forgetful alchemy.

And I slept, dreamlessly, relentlessly, mindlessly, the sleep of a person attempting to recover from a long illness. I was sleeping like that, I remember, lying in bed one morning, when I felt something tugging at my hand. I opened my eyes and saw Gabriel. A little boy now, Jesus Christ, he was so tall, and he wanted to play, saying, "Angel," he said, speaking as clearly as if he had been speaking all his life, saying, "Angel, it's time . . . it's time to wake up."

Acknowledgments

The following people deserve my gratitude: Asya Muchnick, my infinitely talented and patient editor, who worked even harder on this book than I did and who knows far more about it than I ever will (with a special tribute to Sabrina, who probably suffered some prenatal nightmares because of me); Zainab Zakari, Michael Pietsch, Heather Rizzo, Marlena Bittner, Pamela Marshall, and everyone else at Little, Brown, all of whom have been so kind and respectful and *lenient,* especially about deadlines; Paul Sidey, my UK publisher; Jonas Axelsson, my Swedish publisher; all my other international publishers whom I haven't met but who, hopefully, will take me to dinner when I visit their countries one day; Mary Ann Naples, my supportive and thoughtful literary agent, who never reminds me that it isn't her job to listen to me whine (it's her job to listen to Josephine whine), her partner Debra Goldstein, and everyone else at The Creative Culture, Inc.; Matthew Snyder at CAA; Ellen Pall, an early reader who tolerated my nonsense; Karin Slaughter, my friend in the trenches; my colleagues at BBDO NY, especially my friend Mike Gambino; my friends in L.A., Lance and Claire O'Conner, Sandra Christou, and Steve Peckingham; as always, E-ma and Grand-dad, Dad, Jul, and Val, Cal, Brett, and Liv; my wife, Brigette, about whom I will always be a little crazy — okay, a *lot;* the real city of Los Angeles, as well as my imaginary City of Angels and all the Angels and Angelas who live there.

Finally, this book is dedicated with love and admiration to Anne Love Smith, whom I have tried all my life to be like. Thanks, Mom.

Peter Moore Smith is the author of *Raveling*, which was nominated for an Edgar Award. He has had stories selected for the Pushcart Prize and *Best Mystery Stories* collections. He lives in New York City.